John St. Loe Strachey

From grave to gay

Being essays and studies concerned with certain subjects of serious interest

John St. Loe Strachey

From grave to gay
Being essays and studies concerned with certain subjects of serious interest

ISBN/EAN: 9783337204501

Printed in Europe, USA, Canada, Australia, Japan

Cover: Foto ©Andreas Hilbeck / pixelio.de

More available books at **www.hansebooks.com**

FROM GRAVE TO GAY

BEING

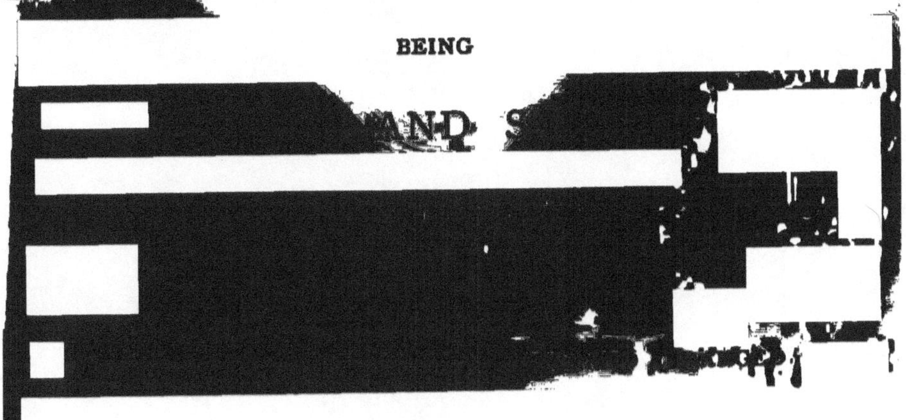

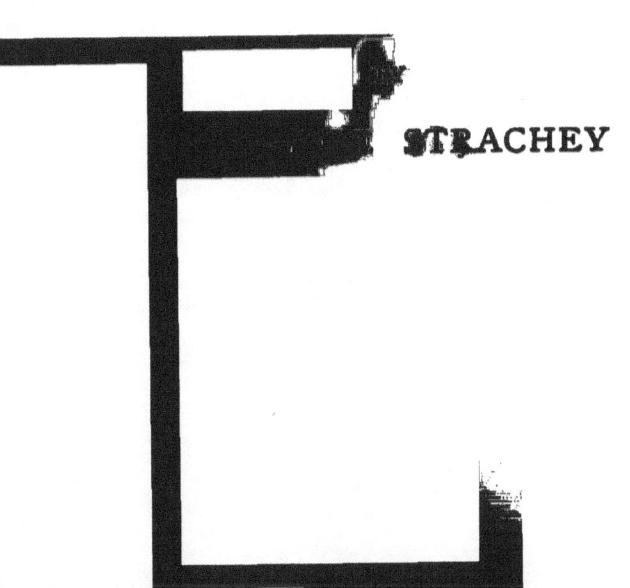

DEDICATION

My dear Father,

'Wild as they are, accept them.' So said our ancestor William Strachey in the verses which follow the dedication of his Virginian Travels to Francis Bacon. I will borrow his words in asking you to accept my Essays. That they are not rougher and wilder is due to you. With what infinite kindness and patience did you labour with me when I began to write. How well I recall how we two have sat in the Great Parlour at Sutton—the very place where John Locke once sat and talked of a Free Port with his friend John Strachey—and hammered sense and simplicity out of a chaos of long sentences, and of periods which stopped not with the meaning, but 'only because the writer was out of breath.' Such memories are indeed for us an itinerary, for, wherever we were when I was a boy, you helped me to find the way to say what I wanted. Whether we were 'seated in hearing' of our Somerset-shire rooks or of the great torrent that thunders through Promontogno, or in the Villa of the little Tower by the Mediterranean, it was all the same. Your readiness to help was invincible. I dare say I did not profit as much as I ought, but at least I carried away one literary maxim which I hope never to forget. You made me realise that the essential thing in writing is to be intelligible, and that it is perfectly useless to write what cannot be clearly and immediately understood. That, after all, is the golden rule of letters. But though the teaching of this simple secret demands an acknowledgment, it is not the real reason why I dedicate this book to you. That reason lies in the hearts of your children, and will be clear to all who know you. To say more would be to say more than enough. I therefore only ask you again to take my book.

Your affectionate Son,

J. St. Loe Strachey.

INTRODUCTION

THE Introduction has died a natural death in many, nay, in most forms of literature. It is, however, still considered imperative when essays and other occasional papers are collected and republished. The reason seems to be that something is required to justify the act of saving from oblivion anything not first published between Boards. Especially and beyond other men is the Journalist expected to show his passport and give an account of his motives and intentions when he tries to enter the land of books. He is 'suspect' in literature, and must allege some excuse for not being content with that station in life to which it has pleased Providence to call him. The position, in fact, is like that of a humble labourer a hundred years ago who wished to leave the village and see the world. No one, perhaps, could legally prevent him, but he was expected before he took such a step at the very least to explain his reasons to the Squire.

I cannot, of course, claim to be allowed to break the custom, and so must give my apology for this volume in an Introduction. But, though I am only a Journalist, I expect that my real reason for coming before the public with a book of previously printed matter is very much like that of regular authors. I want to try my luck like the rest, and to see whether I cannot get a certain number of readers to agree with me on the topics I have chosen. I shall be specially pleased if I can do so in the essays I have called 'The Puritans,' for there I have tried to show that the Puritans were not the harsh, dull sectaries they are so often described, but, in their truest and worthiest representatives, men inspired with the love of beauty in literature and art, and, above all, men of the noblest and widest patriotism. This is, of course, no new discovery, but only a partly obscured fact. If, however, I can help to make it more fully visible, and to induce men to realise that the Puritan element is one which is absolutely essential to the national well-being, I shall have done what I have tried to do. And here I may mention that, though the greater portion of these Puritan studies have appeared in the 'Spectator,' they have been remodelled, re-arranged, and in many places rewritten. The rest of the studies in the present volume have been somewhat less altered, but even in their case there is not one which has not undergone a process of revision.

When I have stated these facts, thanked my chiefs on the 'Spectator' for their kindness in allowing me to reprint from their pages, and have said again that I reprint these essays in the hope that somebody may care to read them, and, if they read, may be made to think or to smile, I have said all I have to say. I will only add a word of excuse addressed to any critics who may object to this or that essay, or batch of essays, being included, and reprove me accordingly. That there will be such critics I cannot doubt, for I have been a reviewer myself. Let me ask the man who scolds me for including too much to remember what I have excluded. When he realises that I have spared him two essays on the Referendum, one on the Canadian Constitution, and another on the duties of the Privy Council, he will surely feel towards me far more of gratitude than of indignation.

CONTENTS

STUDIES IN SERIOUSNESS

PAGE

THE SUPERSTITIONS OF SCIENCE . . 3
THE POET'S FUNCTION AS INTERPRETER . . . 10
TASTING LIFE 18
THE DREAD OF THOUGHT 25
THE HORROR OF ASTRONOMY . . . 32
A DAMAGED EASTERN SAGE 37
AMERICAN OPTIMISM 42
THE MAGIC OF WORDS 49
A STUDY IN CONVERSATION 55

LITERARY STUDIES

A STUDY OF LOUIS STEVENSON 73
    Robert Louis Stevenson and his Work—Mr. Stevenson's
    Poetry—Mr. Stevenson as an Essayist—'The Wrecker'
    —Mr. Stevenson's last Romance—Mr. Louis Stevenson
    on Art.
EDGAR ALLAN POE 115
THE MELODY OF PROSE 121
WILLIAM BARNES 131
HERMAN MELVILLE 139

THE PURITANS

PAGE

CROMWELL 147
A PURITAN GONE ROTTEN 167
A PURITAN TURNED SOUR 173
MILTON'S PROSE 182
A PURITAN COURTSHIP 190
ABRAHAM LINCOLN, THE LAST OF THE PURITANS . . 198
A PURITAN MICAWBER 209
PURITAN POLITICS 215

   The Puritans and the Rise of Modern Democracy—Constitution-making under the Puritans.

HUMOURS OF THE FRAY

STUDIES IN OFFICIAL DIGNITY 233

   Straw Hats and Judicial Dignity—Cycles and Episcopal Dignity.

EVERY BOY IN HIS HUMOUR 246

   The Ideal Boy and the Real—Jack's Friends—Wicked Boys—Children's Manners—Home for the Holidays.

THE SOCIETY BOARDER 276
INANE JOCULARITIES 283
'A PERFECT LADY' 290
WHERE SHALL WE GO? 296
ARE OUR MANNERS DEGENERATING? 302
BOWER-BIRD HUSBANDS 308
THE BRITISH GENTLEMAN 314
CLERGYMEN'S WIVES 320
THE INTERROGATIVE BORE 328

STUDIES IN SERIOUSNESS

WE have no quarrel with the men of science, for they do a great deal to make life easier, pleasanter, and more interesting. We cannot, however, help observing that they are among the most superstitious of mankind. Their faith in chimæras, their readiness to be run away with by words, their tendency to take the part for the whole, and to worship blindly and perversely at their own little shrine is often perfectly astounding. Not only are they sure that what they know not is not knowledge [1]; but they hold that science when applied to life is producing an absolute revolution in the world and altering man's position in the universe. Only let science have a little more time to apply its discoveries, and the earth will be a completely different place. That is the attitude of many of the natural philosophers of the present day.

M. Berthelot, the great French chemist, and his brother men of science lately indulged in an orgy of this kind of talk. At a great International Congress of Applied Chemistry held in Paris M. Berthelot

---

[1] Of course, when we say 'they' we only mean the conventionally minded men of science, and not the greater minds who learn humility, not cocksureness, from the sight of that vast ocean by whose shore they pick up their pebbles.

told his delighted hearers that modern science had, during the last seventy-five years, produced changes so marked that 'a new man was being created in a new earth.' All the ordinary social and political phenomena to which we are accustomed, he implied, are of no account. They are mere walls of Jericho ready to fall down before the blasts of the trumpet of applied chemistry. When meat and wheat are produced by a chemical process 'the international conditions of the world will be changed.' So ran M. Berthelot's song of triumph, or rather prophecy of the golden age of science, when, in the words of Mr. Graves's charming rendering of the Pollio, 'everything needful will grow everywhere : '—

> Then, relieved from the annual labours of sowing,
> Of ploughing and stacking, of reaping and hoeing,
> Ev'ry son of the soil, whether stupid or clever,
> Will be free to do nothing for ever and ever :
> As for weavers and dyers, they'll find, the poor fellows,
> Their whole occupation is gone, like Othello's.
> For the rams in the field, if you ask them politely,
> Will furnish all colours and patterns, like Whiteley :
> And the frolicking lamb, as the grasses he chews,
> Assume the most gorgeous of Liberty's hues.

Now, with all due deference to M. Berthelot, we are obliged to declare that this dream of a beneficent 'Aluminium age,' in which mankind shall sit enthroned like a god with a sceptre marked 'Chemical Process' in one hand and an orb in the other inscribed with the blessed words 'Electric Motor,' is pure superstition. Man may carry chemical process as far as he likes ; he may produce mutton chops direct from ' selected fodder grasses ;' he may make his intestines shine like a lamp, and photograph his brain thinking or his stomach digesting ; but this will not make him a new man in a new world. If M. Berthelot could only shake off the cant of science for a moment, could forget to 'wink and shut his apprehensions up from common sense of what men were and are,' if he were not, in fact, among those 'who would not know what men must be,' he would see that all these things are in truth nothing but curious toys or else mere pieces of machinery—appliances for doing faster and more copiously what man has done slowly and sparsely before. You may produce wildernesses of machinery and pile process upon process, but the mind of man remains untouched and unchanged.

It is not the perfecting of the arts of life or any revolution in the trades of the butcher, the baker, and the smith that will make a new man in a new earth. The great changes in the world, the revolutions that really count, that shake the globe, and do indeed leave a new man in a new earth, come when the spirit is touched, not when this or that ingenious triumph is achieved over matter. One word that is capable of touching the heart and moving the conscience of mankind is more potent, more prevailing, than the discovery of any trick, however strange and subtle, for harnessing the lightning or bringing bread from earth and stones.

Does M. Berthelot suppose that if our Lord, instead of preaching the Sermon on the Mount, had explained to his hearers the use of steam and electricity or the means of discovering a dozen new metals He would have made thereby new men in a new world? The Roman world would have rolled its triumphant tide as before, and nothing would have been changed except the superficies. The iron engines would have panted down the Appian Way and the Imperial City would have doubled her luxury and her population, but her heart would have remained as stony and her citizens 'the atheists and Epicures' they were before. The Sermon on the Mount did not make new men and a new world by chemical process. Its discoveries were of a very different kind. 'Blessed are the meek, for they shall inherit the earth.' 'Blessed are the pure in heart, for they shall see God.' 'Love your enemies, bless them that curse you, do good to them that hate you, and pray for them which despitefully use you and persecute you.' 'Judge not, that ye be not judged.' These were the new-found truths that touched the heart and quickened the conscience, and made in time an utterly new race of men in a new world. The sense of pity and ruth and of a mercy infinite and unstrained, the overwhelming of the wild justice of revenge in the higher justice of forgiveness, the doctrine of love invincible, unearned, and unbought had come into the earth and changed it for ever.

The Christian world is indeed a new world. The world, since steam and electricity, is simply the world of the eighteenth century *plus* a certain number of extra facilities which it would now seem hard to lose, but which, when they had them not, men did without quite cheerfully. Sydney Smith once enumerated all the improvements he had lived to see, and then added, with his keen irony, that he was ashamed to think how perfectly happy and contented he used to be before any of them were invented. That is the bare truth ; all the mere superficial improvements matter little or nothing. What matter are the things of the spirit. When we can touch the spirit, but not till then, let us talk of making a new man in a new world.

Anyone who chooses to think for a moment can see proof of what we are saying, even if he combats our assertion that our Lord's words changed the universe. Suppose for a moment that the wildest dreams of science come true—that the air becomes as easily navigable as the sea, and is cut by thousands of aerial keels; that new discoveries in hygiene make men live a hundred and fifty years; that disease is almost banished; and that a thousand facilities are added to the conduct of life by the gift of science. Now, can anyone seriously declare that under such conditions man and the world would be in reality very much changed, that he would think more deeply than Socrates, or live more nobly than St. Francis of Assisi or John Wesley, or that he would be less liable to passion and error than the man of to-day? Would the Röntgen rays, even when finally developed, fulfil 'the splendid purpose in his eyes,' or beef by chemical process take the deceit from his heart and the lie from his lips? A thousand times 'No.' They might make us live longer and multiply more freely, but nothing more.

Now, consider what would happen if by any chance those who are now trying to investigate the phenomena of the soul and its operations should be able to show mankind beyond doubt that they had negatived the materialistic explanation of the universe, had proved to demonstration the continued existence of the spirit after death, and had made the world beyond the grave, and the possibility of communicating therewith, a matter of certainty, not of conjecture. No doubt that may be a wild hypothesis, and we do not state it because we think it likely to happen, but merely by way of assumption. Still, supposing these spiritual discoveries were made positive facts, can anyone doubt for an instant that the effects on man would be infinitely greater than those which could be produced by any conceivable material improvement or by any of the gifts of applied chemistry? The certain knowledge of another world would indeed make a new man and a new world. Flying-machines would no more alter the world than did steam. The day after their invention they would be sneered at as 'improved balloons,' while the 'process' chops and steaks would be criticised as nothing but 'our old friend Parrish's chemical food made in a solid form and cut into lengths.' Who can pretend that, if an after-life were to become as demonstrable as the movement of the planets, mankind would ever be the same?

But in truth we need not labour the point. We doubt not that those who see deepest into the mysteries of Nature, the true men of science, will feel just as we feel in regard to the preposterous claim put forward by M. Berthelot on behalf of applied science. They will feel with us that his attitude is nothing but superstitious —the parody of faith, the rendering of religious veneration to that which is unworthy of such an offering. As Mr. Stevenson has pointed out, the passionate production of improved steam-engines does not really tend to increase human happiness or greatness. Even if we take far lower ground than we have yet chosen, those—*i.e.* the lawgiver and the statesman—who can tell us

> What makes a nation happy, keeps it so,
> What ruins kingdoms and lays cities flat—

do far more for mankind than the inventor. Better a wholesome polity with oil lamps than ' a pocket edition of hell ' with a nobler installation of electric-light than was ever yet dreamed of by the ' Wizard of Menlo Park.' Whatever way we look at it, this worship of applied science is pure superstition. Applied science has done much to reduce friction and increase population, and may do more, but she cannot overstep the limits set her. To talk of science making new men in a new world is utterly absurd. Not till she finds out the cause and meaning of life will she be capable of any such claim. If and when she has done that, but not till then, M. Berthelot may claim what he claims for her without superstition.

THE POET'S FUNCTION AS INTERPRETER

PEOPLE are apt to talk as if the poet had no function in the modern world, or at any rate as if his only function were to amuse and entertain, and as if the State, in its higher and political aspect, had no need of him. The poet, we are told in effect, is an anachronism in an age like the present—a mere survival from more primitive times. Those who argue thus are badly instructed, and are reasoning from the imperfect premises afforded by the early and middle Victorian epoch. For a moment the world was exclusively occupied with industrial and other utilitarian objects, and naturally enough the poet seemed out of place. He proved nothing, he made nothing, and he discovered nothing—or at any rate nothing in the regions of science and invention. But this overshadowing of the poet's function in the State was not real, but merely accidental and temporary. Though people thought so for the moment, machinery is not everything ; nor is it the least true to say that the song of the singer is never something done, something actual. Tennyson put this with splendid insight when, in his plea for the poet, he reminded the world that

> The song that nerves a nation's heart
> Is in itself a deed.

While the possible need for a Tyrtæus exists, and that need can never be wholly banished, the poet must always have a real use. But there are other functions no less real, and hardly less important, which a poet may perform in the modern State. He may act as interpreter to the nation, and show it, as only he can, the true relations and the true meaning of the different parts which make up the whole. The great difficulty of every nation is its inability to realise and understand itself. Could it do this truly, a nation could hardly take the wrong road and bring itself to ruin and confusion. But few nations have this faculty, and therefore they need so sorely an interpreter, one who by his clearer vision shall show them what they are and whither they tend.

And for the mass of mankind only the poet can do this. The ordinary man, whether rich or poor, educated or uneducated, apprehends very little and very vaguely save through his senses and his emotions. Maps and figures, dissertations and statistics, fall like water off a duck's back when you talk to him of the British Empire, of the magnitude of our rule in India, and of the problem of its dark races ; of the growth of the English-speaking people in Canada and in Australia ; and of how our fate, as a nation, is inextricably bound up with the lordship of the sea. He hears, but he does not mark. But the poet, if he has the gift of the interpreter—and without that gift in some shape or form he is hardly a poet— whether he works in prose or verse can bring home the secrets of empire and the call of destiny to the hearts of the people. Of course he cannot touch all, but when he does touch he kindles. He lays the live coal on men's minds ; and those who are capable of being roused have henceforth a new and different feeling and understanding of what he tells.

Mr. Kipling's fascinating poem, 'The Native Born,' is a reminder to us of how large a share he possesses of this interpreting power. His work is of extraordinary value in making the nation realise itself, especially as regards the Empire and the oneness of our kin. One of the great difficulties of the mere politician, who knows himself but cannot interpret, is to get the people of this country to understand that when the Englishmen born over-sea assert themselves, and express their glory in and love for the new land, they are not somehow injuring or slighting the old home. When Englishmen hear of and but·partly understand the ideas of young Australia, young Canada, or young South Africa, as the case may be, they sadly or bitterly declare that there is no love of England left in the Colonies, and that the men of the new lands think only of themselves, and dislike, or are indifferent to, the mother-country.

The way in which the pride and exultation of the 'native born' is conveyed makes that pride and exultation misunderstood. When we hear people talk a language which we do not know we are always apt to think that they are full of anger and contempt, and that we are the objects of this anger and contempt. Now the uninspired social analyst or the statistical politician might have preached and analysed for years and yet not have got the nation to understand the true spirit of the 'native born,' and how in reality it neither slights the old land nor injures the unity of the Empire. His efforts to prove that the passionate feeling of the 'native born' should be encouraged, not suppressed, fall, for the most part, on empty ears.   He may convince a few philosophers, but the great world heeds him not.   But if, and when, the true poet comes, he can interpret for the mass of men and make clear and of good omen what before seemed dark and lowering.

Take the poem by Mr. Kipling to which we have just alluded. The poet does not reason with us, or argue, or bring proofs ; instead he enables us to enter into the spirit of the ' native born,' and by a flash of that lightning which he brings straight from heaven he makes us understand how the men of Australia, and Canada, and Africa feel towards the land in which they were born.   Thus interpreted, their pride ceases to sound harsh to our ears, and we realise that the ' native born ' may love their deep-blue hills, their ice-bound lakes and snow-wreathed forests, their rolling uplands, or their palms and canes, and yet not neglect their duty to the mother-land or to the Empire and the race. Surely a man who can do this has done something, and something of vast importance for the whole English kin. He has dropped the tiny drop of solvent acid into the bowl, and made what was before a turbid mixture a clear and lucent liquor.   But we must not write of the poem and not remind our readers of its quality by a quotation.   To show its power of interpretation, take the first three verses :

> We've drunk to the Queen, God bless her !
>   We've drunk to our mother's land,
> We've drunk to our English brother
>   (But he does not understand) ;
> We've drunk to the wide creation,
>   And the Cross swings low to the dawn—
> Last toast, and of obligation—
>   A health to the Native-born !

They change their skies above them,
　　But not their hearts that roam !
We learned from our wistful mothers
　　To call old England 'home ; '
We read of the English skylark,
　　Of the spring in the English lanes,
But we screamed with the painted lories
　　As we rode on the dusty plains !

They passed with their old-world legends—
　　Their tales of wrong and dearth—
Our fathers held by purchase,
　　But we by the right of birth ;
Our heart's where they rocked our cradle,
　　Our love where we spent our toil,
And our faith and our hope and our honour
　　We pledge to our native soil !

The verses, and those that follow, are a positive initiation. As we read them our hearts beat and cheeks glow, and as by fire we realise the feeling of the ' native born '—how he loves his own land, and yet gives his homage to ' the dread high altars ' of the race. Let no one suppose when we speak thus of this particular poem that we imagine it is going suddenly to become a household word in England, Scotland, and Ireland, or that the world will immediately grasp its meaning. That is given to few poems. But, without doing this, the poem, we believe, will have its effect on public opinion. Before it becomes popular in the ordinary sense it will work its way into the minds, first, of the more imaginative politicians and journalists and men of letters. Then through them and by various channels it will filter down and affect the mass of the people.

What will happen will be not unlike that which

happened in regard to the feeling of the nation towards the privates of the British Army.   Mr. Kipling, in his capacity of interpreter, and by means of his 'Barrack-room Ballads,' made the nation appreciate and understand its soldiers infinitely better than they had ever done before.   Indeed, it is not too much to say that by means of this process of interpretation he changed the attitude of the nation.   But though many thousands of people read how

It's Tommy this an' Tommy that, an' 'chuck him out, the brute ; '
But it's 'saviour of his country' when the guns begin to shoot,

the change was for the most part wrought indirectly. When you let fly into a whole heap of billiard balls all are moved and affected, though only one or two feel the impact direct.   It is enough if the poet touches those who can influence the rest.

Another example of Mr. Kipling's power of interpretation as a poet is to be seen in his sea-poems. 'The Bolivar,' 'The Clampherdown,' and 'The Flag of England' are of incalculable value in making Englishmen realise that they have been and are still the lords of the sea, and what that priceless heritage means.   You may talk to Robinson, the bill-broker, till you are black in the face about the command of the sea, and its political, commercial, and moral importance.   He agrees, no doubt, and seems quite intelligent, but in reality marks you not.   If, however, you can get him to listen to what the four winds made answer when they were asked what and where is the flag of England, who knows but you may have lighted a flame of inspiration which will remain with him and make him realise the grandeur and high destiny of this realm of England?

Take, again, the way in which Mr. Kipling has interpreted the native East for Englishmen, and made them understand, as but few of them understood before, the gulf that stretches between the East and West, and realise that East and West, though each has its destiny, can never be one. Yet another example of Mr. Kipling's power of interpretation is to be found in the marvellous poem which he wrote on the American spirit, taking the Chicago riots as his 'peg.' The poet, as we point out in another essay in this volume, was not quite as careful as he ought to have been to avoid wounding the feelings of our American kinsfolk, but for insight and exposition it was a work of rare genius. It interpreted a certain side of the American character to perfection. And to do this at that moment was a most useful work, for over here men were bewildered and distracted by what was happening in the West.

We have spoken above only of Mr. Kipling, but it must not be supposed that we regard him as the only poet who acts as interpreter to the nation. We chose him because he does so to such practical effect. All true poets are, as we have said, interpreters, each in his own sphere. If they are not, they are mere embroiderers of melodious words. Mr. Watson, for example, has shown true inspiration in interpreting for us the great poets and the great movements of literature. His verses on Wordsworth, on Shelley, on Matthew Arnold, and on Burns are examples of what we mean. In those noble poems he brought many of us far nearer these mighty singers than we had ever yet approached, while in his 'Father of the Forest' he interprets for his country-men the splendid pageant of their past, and, as the lightning calls hill and vale out of the darkness, calls up for an instant the mighty dead of England.

No, as long as States are made and unmade, and men in their communities grope and wander, asking for the light, so long will the world need the poet's help. While there is anything to interpret and make clear to men who will act on what comes to them through their emotions, but will remain cold to the mere teachings of reason, the poet and his art will survive. When we are all so coldly reasonable that we cannot be stirred by 'Chevy Chase,' then, but not till then, will the poet's occupation be gone. Meantime let us remember that we lost America because we did not understand the feelings of the ' native born,' and thank heaven we have a poet-interpreter to help to save us from another such treason to our race as that to which George III. and Lord North incited.

TASTING LIFE

THERE is at the present moment a large and growing class of people who not only consider that they have a right to taste life as a man tastes claret or cigars, out of curiosity, or the desire to find what tickles his palate most pleasantly, but who believe that they are doing something which is almost meritorious *per se* in subjecting themselves to every possible form of sensation, mental and physical.

For example, M. Fénéon, a French War Office clerk, a year or two ago when put on his trial for complicity in an Anarchist plot, produced as a defence which he evidently thought would justify his conduct before the world the plea that he was only tasting Anarchy as he was wont to taste other forms of life. He was, he said, a Symbolist and an Impressionist, and he merely went into Anarchy out of curiosity. In fact, he had made sensation-seeking, and the tasting of life in all its forms, his hobby. But the study of Anarchy and the society of Anarchists offered a completely fresh vintage. What, then, was more reasonable than that he should 'sample' the new liquor? The explanation of his conduct was really too clear to need elaboration. It was, of course, altogether unnecessary to point out that he had no sympathy with Anarchists. Though M. Fénéon did not use the phrase, it was evident that he expected the public to recognise that the desire to taste life was quite enough motive to make a man take up Anarchy for a season. Unfortunately for M. Fénéon, he took his sip of Anarchy at an inconvenient moment, and found himself undergoing an experience with which he would doubtless have preferred to dispense—a trial before the Assize Court.

It is not often that the advocates of tasting life rather than of living it get so direct and plain a reminder of the anti-moral and anti-social character of their acts. As a rule, their tastes of the evil side of existence are so judiciously taken that they avoid, or appear to avoid, any unpleasant consequences. But though it is seldom that the life-taster can be brought to book, it would be difficult to imagine a more entirely immoral attitude towards life than that which he adopts.

The fact that a man lives with a set of profligates, gamblers, and drunkards, not because he has any inclination towards their vices, but merely because he wants to judge of that sort of life at first hand, affords him no excuse. It is no defence for a man who has made love to his neighbour's wife to say that he had not the least desire to break the seventh commandment, but merely wanted to gain the experience of life involved in an intrigue. The explanation makes the offence twice as bad by taking away the excuse of passion. This is easily seen in a yet plainer case. The man who joins a body of brigands and helps them to commit murders out of his desire to try what it feels like to be a brigand is a worse man than the poor half-starved wretch who takes to the road because he might other-wise die of hunger.

But perhaps it will be said that we are exaggerating, or, at any rate, confusing the issue. Provided that a man himself does nothing criminal or immoral, there is, it will be argued, nothing wrong in gaining as much experience of life as possible—in tasting, that is, all forms of existence. As long as a man does not join in the evil deeds of a particular society, there is no harm in his mixing with it and getting to know about it at first hand and from personal contact. The private individual cannot hope to prevent people 'going the pace,' and therefore he does no harm in playing the part of the intelligent observer at close quarters. Nay, he may even allow a body of profligates to think he is sharing their life, if that is the only passport to associating with them, provided, of course, that he in fact keeps his own hands clean. In other words, Fénéon was perfectly justified in studying Anarchy at first hand so long as he abstained from committing outrages or helping other people to commit them.

A man does not prevent bad things from happening by shutting his eyes to them, and therefore he has a right to gratify his curiosity by putting himself into the position of this or that class and learning all that is to be known about it. By doing so, indeed, he makes himself a more complete man. He has dared to look on life as a whole, and to understand all its phases. In spite of the specious air of reason about this plea for tasting life so long as you ultimately spit out the naughty stuff and do not swallow it, it is altogether un-sound. It is founded upon an utterly immoral view of human society. What right has a man to take this detached view of life, to consider that existence is a sort of café where the men and women sit at little tables, and that he has a right to saunter round, finding out what is being said or done by this or that group, and then passing on to examine the next? That sort of attitude towards life may build up a cynically wise type of mind—Goethe developed his intelligence on these lines—but it will not make a good man.

It is a man's duty to live his own life worthily, and not to be continually pawing the lives of his neighbours. Depend upon it, the man who is always tasting other lives instead of living his own will make a bad business of life. The life-taster's way of looking at the world is in its essence vicious and insane. Life is far more like a camp than a café, and the soldier's business is to see that he discharges his duties properly and makes himself efficient in his particular arm—not to try first what cavalry service is like, then to go through the experiences of the gunner, next to sample the engineer's work, then to try the army service corps, and not to rest till he has also seen how things look from the point of view of the camp-follower. Wordsworth put the true way of looking at life with admirable force and passion in 'The Happy Warrior.' The Happy Warrior looks at life in a sense exactly opposite to that of Ulysses— the man ever anxious to see men and cities and to gain more experiences. He is the man who is not distracted by a hundred feverish fancies, but shows a simplicity and singleness of aim—who

> Plays, in the many games of life, that one
> Where what he most doth value must be won.

The whole poem would have to be cited to illustrate
fully what we mean, but a few more lines may be
quoted :—

> It is the generous Spirit, who, when brought
> Among the tasks of real life, hath wrought
> Upon the plan that pleased his boyish thought ;
> Whose high endeavours are an inward light
> That makes the path before him always bright :
> Who, with a natural instinct to discern
> What knowledge can perform, is diligent to learn ;
> Abides by the resolve, and stops not there,
> But makes his moral being his prime care.

The different results obtained by the two ways of
looking at life are inferentially well brought out by
Wordsworth. He tells us what happens to the man
who looks at life from the standpoint of the Happy
Warrior when he is called upon to face

> Some awful moment to which Heaven has joined
> Great issues, good or bad for human kind.

He then

> Is happy as a lover, and attired
> With sudden brightness, like a man inspired.

How different is the effect of being called upon to face
great issues on the man who adopts the Goethe attitude
towards life. They leave him cold, observant, uninspired.
When Germany awoke to shake off the Napoleonic
tyranny, Goethe had little or no share in the movement. His tasting of life had left him unable to
express or even to feel the best things which the good
citizen is capable of feeling—to feel, that is, the only
true happiness of life. Remember what is the best that

one who showed an adoration for Goethe's genius that was almost excessive could say of Goethe's final mood towards life :—

> And he was happy, if to know
> Causes of things, and far below
> His feet to see the lurid flow
> Of trouble and insane distress,
> And headlong fate, be happiness.

At the highest this is what the life-taster attains to, while he who takes the other view of life is happy, and even transfigured and inspired. 'Spirits,' says Shakespeare, 'are not finely touched but to fine issues.' But the fine issues do not touch the life-taster : his senses have been dulled by his continual desire for new sensations.

The truer attitude towards life—the attitude which we have described as that of the Happy Warrior—the attitude which is the antithesis of the life-taster's, is well illustrated in the beautiful passage in which Milton does homage to the chivalry of the old Romances. He speaks of every free and gentle spirit being born a knight and needing not the gold spur nor the laying on of the sword to make him undertake a knight's service. Take it in its highest expression, the knightly way of looking at the world comes very near to what we mean. The knight's ideal was not to learn skill in the game of life, to know causes of things, or to watch the human animalculus scurrying round his drop of water and preying on his fellows. It was to be 'a very perfect, gentle knight,' to make in fact 'his moral being his prime care'—to live well and do well rather than to know well.

But we must not speak too absolutely. Here, as elsewhere in moral and social questions, the problem is largely one of degree. Though it can never be right to treat life as if it were something meant to be taken in sips, and to [regard life-tasting as an end, it would be absurd to rule out of life the gaining of innocent experiences. Within proper limits, a man has a right to expand his mind by gaining experience. As long as those experiences are not obtained by giving an indirect or an implicit sanction to what is wrong, as long as a man does not make his main aim the tasting of life, he has of course a perfect right to accumulate knowledge of all kinds. The gaining of innocent experiences may indeed be made a most useful discipline.

Goethe was right to force upon himself the experiences to be gained by climbing the spire of Strassburg Cathedral. He disliked going on to the spire. It was a useful victory for his will to oblige himself to become accustomed to standing on the edge of a sheer precipice of masonry. By all means let men learn all they can learn innocently, and let them use experience as a mental discipline ; but do not let them imagine that the attitude of the mere life-taster is a fitting one from which to contemplate life. It is one that the good citizen can never occupy.

THE DREAD OF THOUGHT

AND, friend, when dost thee think?' was the reply made by the Quaker lady to whom Southey had explained, with no little satisfaction, how he spent his day. He told her how he studied Portuguese grammar while he was shaving, how he read Spanish for an hour before breakfast, how, after breakfast, he wrote or studied till dinner, and so on, and so on—how, in a word, every corner of the twenty-four hours was exactly filled by writing, reading, eating, talking, taking exercise, and sleeping ; ·and she replied with the very pertinent question we have just given. That there are very few men, and not many women—women are, on the whole, more given to meditation than men—who could give a satisfactory answer to the question will, we believe, be admitted at once.

The idea of thinking for thinking's sake is, to most men, positively repellent. They have an intense objection—an objection which, too, they believe to be, on the whole, a laudable one—to time passed not in eating, sleeping, working, talking, reading, writing, or taking exercise or playing at games. Time not occupied by any of these occupations is held to be lost time, and loss of time, like every other loss, is something to be avoided.

The departure of the summer calls forth complaints in a hundred suburban trains. 'As long as there is light,' says the City man who lives an hour out of London, 'I find the journey quite a pleasant rest—a quiet time, in which to enjoy one's evening paper, or any novel one may be reading. Now, however, that the days are getting too dark to read comfortably after five I hardly know how to bear the journey back. Unless one happens to meet a friend, that hour of enforced idleness is positive torture. There is nothing to do, and sometimes the temptation to destroy one's eyesight by reading by the carriage-lamp becomes irresistible. Living out of town may be paradise in summer, but in winter it is purgatory.'

The feeling is a very common one, no doubt, and, most people would add, a very natural one ; but to this we should emphatically demur. Why is it natural for a man to dread being thrown back upon his own thoughts ? Why should he find meditation so unnatural, and reading so natural ? After all, we were not born with copies of the evening papers in our hands, and the process of thinking is not one which has to be acquired. We believe that the dread of thought in a great measure comes from lack of habit. All children pass a good deal of time in thinking ; but men, in the press of business and of pleasure, forget how to think, and grow to regard reading as the only possible way of passing the time quietly,

There is a story of a man who gave up hunting because he found the waiting about at the covert-side, with nothing to do, quite unbearable. If he could have had a book to read till the hounds got away he would have been happy, and would, he said, have enjoyed the run. As it was, the pleasure of hunting was outweighed by the pain of doing nothing. We venture to think, however, that a very little patience and a very little practice would soon make most men give up their dread of thinking, and would make an hour spent without books or talk a pleasure instead of a pain. No doubt this is not true of all men. There are certain persons cursed with a constitutional melancholy so deep that it is impossible for them to think cheerfully. Thinking with them means a black procession of waking night-mares, which take possession of the mind the moment it ceases to be distracted by something external. They cannot force themselves to think of what they will, but seem compelled to let their thoughts wander through the waste places and deserts of despair.

Special circumstances, again, may give a man a right to dread his thoughts. Those under a cloud of sorrow or disappointment, those worried by some adverse turn in their affairs—a family quarrel or a bad speculation— or those engaged in some scheme trembling in the balance of failure or success do wisely in avoiding their own thoughts. They cannot, unless they are cast in a specially heroic mould, avoid thinking of their 'grand concern,' as Governor Pitt styled the great diamond which dominated his existence, and therefore they had better not think at all, but should divert their minds in every way they can. These, however, are the abnormal cases. The ordinary man at ordinary times has no real reason for dreading his thoughts. It is merely want of habit that makes him dislike thinking. Let him make the plunge, and select something definite to think about, and ten to one he will find following a train of thought a very agreeable exercise.

Letting the mind veer backwards and forwards like a weathercock, at the suggestion of this or that external circumstance, is, of course, dull and worrying ; but the man who knows how to think does not do that. He thinks, as he reads, with a definite purpose. One cannot, of course, propose lines of thought in the abstract for unknown persons, but one may indicate one or two of the ways in which a man may learn to get pleasure from thinking. To begin with, he may follow the example of the wise man who said : ' When I have nothing else to do, I sort my thoughts and label them.' That was an excellent plan. There are few men whose thoughts would not be improved by being put through the process to which we subject a drawer full of papers —which have lacked for some time that rare combination of leisure and inclination which is necessary for tidying· Most of us, again, have confused thoughts and intuitions, that this or that thing connected with ourselves or our families might be better done than it is done.

Let the man, then, who complains of his intolerable hour on the South-Western, or the London and Brighton, or the Great Eastern, absorb himself in a definite scheme of meditation upon something which has already clamoured to be thought out, and he will find the time passes quickly enough. He must not wait till the thought comes to him. He must, by a conscious and deliberate exercise of will, set his mind to his subject. In plain words, he must say to himself : ' Now, I will regularly think out whether it is a good plan ' to do this that, or the other. For those who have artistic, literary, scientific, or historical tastes, the problem of what to think about is specially easy. A thousand delightful vistas of thought are open before them, and in these shady avenues they may wander with infinite delight. They must, no doubt, go through the somewhat laborious preliminary of definitely choosing a subject, and determining to think about it ; but this done, their path is easy and pleasant.

What, for instance, could be more delightful than to speculate why the arts of sculpture and painting are given to some nations and withheld from others, or why the ancient world, so exquisitely sensitive to the beauty of the human form, had but a feeble appreciation of the beauty of landscape ; or to wonder what would have happened to the East if Clive's pistol had not missed fire when he put it to his temple ; or, to follow out the thought—would it be possible, given some means of overcoming the physical difficulty of boring so deep, to pierce the earth, and what would happen to the law of gravity when the centre was reached ? And when such speculations as these tire, what can be more entertaining than the luxury of a little castle-building in the airy highlands of Spain ? Wondering what one would do if one had a million is not a game that need, in the nature of things, be confined to girls and boys.

It is all nonsense to say that the domestic mutton tastes worse because one has been picturing a perfect short dinner served in the little dining-room in a palace in Park Lane, to which Dorchester House would look like a superior parsonage. On the contrary, the excursion into the realms of the unreal is not unlikely to give one an appetite. And even for those who do not want more luxuries than they have there are plenty of day-dreams possible. Few people have built an ideal house and laid out an ideal garden and park. Let those, then, who have not, lay down their visionary plans, and rear for themselves chimneys that never smoke, and trees that never grow where they ought not, but exactly where they should.

We have not dealt here with the more serious side of the value of thinking. That is so often pressed upon men's minds by religious teachers of all kinds that it would seem out of place to restate it here. It is hardly necessary to say that all men need to 'swing' the moral compass from time to time, and to take their bearings in the sea of life. The advice is as true as it is conventional. Upon the use of thinking for such purposes we shall not, then, dwell. We may, however, point out that, as a means of strengthening and invigorating the mind in a secular and worldly sense, the habit of thinking is of the greatest possible value. The minds of those who dread thinking as if it were a penance become like the bodies of those fed solely on spoon-meat—soft, and unable to stand the slightest strain. Reading, as one ordinarily reads, is like swallowing pap; thinking, like eating solid food.

The man who trains his mental powers by meditation and by following out lines of thought obtains an intellectual instrument a hundred times more powerful than he who is content never to think seriously and consecutively. The things one merely reads about never stick. Those on which one thinks become permanent acquisitions. Hence the man who is not afraid of thinking, and who does not dread 'that cursed hour in the dark,' is at a distinct advantage on every ground. He passes the time without being bored, and he strengthens his mind. To say this may, no doubt, sound slightly priggish, but it is none the less true. The man who can enjoy and make use of his own thoughts has a heritage which can never be alienated. Even blindness for him loses some of its terrors.

THE HORROR OF ASTRONOMY

MOST people are shy of confessing even to themselves that they have experienced in regard to any intellectual conception the real sense of horror—the sense which benumbs and oppresses the intellect with a dull ache. If, however, the civilised portion of the human race could be put to the question, we believe that the majority would be found to experience this feeling in regard to the facts and deductions of astronomy. Every human being knows what it is to feel at times a sudden nameless horror—a shivering fit of the soul as well defined as an ague of the body. The mental agitation and distress caused by doubts, forebodings, and difficulties connected with religion, or with the sense of misconduct, is something very different. The sensation we mean is neither a matter of melancholy, of religious opinion, nor of remorse. It is, instead, if we may be allowed the expression, a physical experience of the intellect.

For some reason or other this formless sense of horror is evoked more strongly by the science of astronomy than by any other. That it is not due to fear, in the ordinary sense of the word, is quite obvious. Astronomy may have disclosed certain risks run by mankind, but they are nothing when compared with those that are made known by plenty of other sciences. The notion that we may some day be rammed by a comet can perhaps be rendered alarming ; but, as a rule, the alarms of astronomy concern a distant age, when the sun shall have cooled, or when a new force of attraction shall have arisen to lead the errant earth into a dangerous and untravelled path. Again, many of the astronomical facts which most easily conjure up this sense of awe and terror have little or no relation to our planet. What is so heart-shaking as the thought of a star that has foundered and gone out in the mid-firmament of heaven ? We may be reasoned into regarding it as commonplace, but at first it is terrific and awe-inspiring in no ordinary degree. Yet even if, when the lost star cooled or burst into a million meteorites, or was cannoned into space by the impact of some other world, it contained ten thousand million of inhabitants, no ground exists for any special regret. If subject to death, they would have been dead by now. The catastrophe of the heavens which overtook them only shortened their lives. It is clear that it is not merely pity for the possible inhabitants that causes the sensation.

Again, the sensation is called up equally acutely by thought of the vastness and the solitude of space, by the height and fury of the flames that are leaping from the sun, and by the thought that the whole Solar System, and all the million systems that are its neighbours, are hurrying from some unknown and unknowable starting-point to some equally unknown and unknowable goal. What we would fain discover is the reason why these thoughts stun and intimidate the soul.

We believe that one explanation is to be found in the unfamiliarity of the facts of astronomy. They appal because we cannot easily make them fit in with our general conception of existence. Whether consciously or unconsciously, the human brain maps out its conceptions in a kind of order, and gives each its relative importance. It happens, however, that though most men learn the elementary facts of astronomy, they give them very little attention. These facts are not, as a rule, retained in active memory and worked upon automatically by the mind. Hence, when any new discovery or fresh point of view in regard to astronomy is presented to the mind it produces, as it were, a disturbing element. It does not fit in or square with ordinary human thought. The mind resists its reception just as it resists an experience which is believed to be supernatural.

A man who sees a ghostly manifestation and believes it to be a hoax is naturally enough not inspired by any sense of horror or awe. Another, however, who for some reason thinks the manifestation supernatural, at once feels a sensation akin to that which we are trying to analyse. He is face to face with a fact which will not fit in with his ordinary intellectual conceptions, and so is disturbed and bewildered—and disturbed and bewildered so acutely as to experience an actual sense of pain. That this is the cause of the sense of mental disturbance produced in many people by astronomy is also shown by the fact that those who study astronomy and make themselves familiar with the science of the heavens do not feel it. They have mapped out their mental conceptions on the proper scale, and the march of the Solar System through space is to them a phenomenon as little disturbing as the fall of an apple to the ground. Familiarity and the power of properly adjusting their mental outlook have made them insensible to the horror of the stars. After all, there is nothing essentially more awe-inspiring in the facts of astronomy than in the tendency of water to run down-hill.

That it is the consciousness of something unfamiliar, of something that has not been mentally assimilated, which primarily produces sensations which at first sight seem so inexplicable is also shown in the fact that many people experience as great a horror at the discoveries of the microscope as of the telescope. There is something intellectually horrible in the thought of the infinite multiplication of life in a drop of dirty water. If each drop contains a universe of its own, how appalling is the sum-total of vitality in the pond!

The student of microscopic investigation gets his ideas on these matters into order, but the ordinary man suddenly confronted with them is easily horrified. The infinities inside our world become as awesome as the infinities of space. Yet, in reality, both series of facts and deductions have only got to be properly known and understood to lose all their horror. In the case of astronomy, however, we cannot help thinking that the horror is to a certain extent intensified by the thought of the insignificance of man as compared with the world of the stars. There must, we should imagine, be something oppressive even to the astronomer in the vastness of his field of study and the pettiness of man. Tennyson's thought—

What is it all but a trouble of ants in the gleam of a million
   million of suns ?

must sometimes give even the Astronomer-Royal a
momentary scorn for his kind. No doubt reason will
soon bring him a corrective by asking what littleness
or bigness has got to do with it ; but this philosophic
balance must, one would think, be at times upset by
keeping the eyes and thoughts always on vastness.
For the mass of mankind, in some form or other, a
certain horror will at any rate cling to the stars—or,
rather, to the mental conceptions which attach to them.
Matters so momentous, yet so aloof from our ordinary
thought, are sure to perplex and disturb.

A DAMAGED EASTERN SAGE

CHARLES LAMB called Coleridge a slightly damaged archangel. It would have been truer had he called him a slightly damaged Guru or Eastern sage and mystic. A Guru is a man who feels within himself the desire to become, and the belief that he can become, conversant with the inner mystery of things—can put aside the seemings and shadows of the world, can gain a knowledge and perception of the oneness of the universe, and so can hold communion with God. But to gain that knowledge and hold that communion he must, as far as may be, shake off the trammels of the flesh, and conquer not only desire, but the senses of pleasure and of pain. To give his soul its rights, and to endow himself with the full heritage of the spirit, he adopts the ascetic life in its severest form. Naked and alone, with little thought for the day, and wholly without thought for the morrow, he wanders or stays still, as chance directs, until he has achieved his emancipation. Then, and when ' the world is as ashes ' to him, and the victory won, he enjoys the sense of a cosmic consciousness, and can help others to follow the path which led him to those thrilling heights of thought and feeling.

Those who read the book of Coleridge's spiritual outpourings, ' Anima Poetæ,' and bear in mind the aim and nature of the Guru, will realise vividly what we mean when we say that Coleridge was in truth a damaged Eastern sage and mystic. The poet's grandson, Mr. Ernest Hartley Coleridge, in his preface, puts with rare insight and sympathy, though with a different thought in view, Coleridge's mental attitude. 'The invisible pageantry of thought and passion which for ever floated into his spiritual ken, the perpetual hope, the half belief, that the veil of the senses would be rent in twain, and that he, and not another, would be the first to lay bare the mysteries of being and to solve the problem of the ages—of these was the breath of his soul.'

This is exactly the frame of mind which marks the Guru. Coleridge has expressed this feeling in his own words in many of the passages from his private note-books, out of which 'Anima Poetæ' is compiled. Here is a passage which shows the yearning of his soul to enter upon the inner knowledge and grasp the secret of the universe, and his belief that this yearning was in no sense impossible of fulfilment. 'Rest! motion! O ye strange locks of intricate simplicity, who shall find the key? He shall throw wide open the portals of the palace of sensuous or symbolical truth, and the Holy of Holies will be found in the adyta. Rest = enjoyment and death. Motion = enjoyment and life. O the depth of the proverb, " Extremes meet ! " I will at least make the attempt to explain to myself the origin of moral evil from the streamy nature of association, which thinking curbs and rudders. Do not the bad passions in dreams throw light and show of proof upon this hypothesis ? If I can but explain those passions I shall gain light, I am sure.   A clue ! a clue ! a Hecatomb *à la* Pythagoras, if it unlabyrinth me.'

But this is no wayward imagining, no accident or access of poetic fever.   All through these most personal and private musings on paper are shot with what, for want of a better definition, we must call the emotions and aspiration of the Guru. 'Good heavens !' he writes, 'that there should be anything and not nothing.' Again, he is for ever dwelling upon 'oneness,' upon the mystery that underlies the proverb ' Extremes meet,' and on the communion with God which is guaranteed by His omniscience. 'That deep intuition of our oneness,' he exclaims, and in the next note he draws a passionate comfort from the thought '"Thou knowest." Oh ! what a thought ! Never to be friendless : never to be unintelligible.' Take, too, his outburst, 'If my researches are shadowy, what in the name of reason are you ? or do you resign all pretence to reason, and consider yourself —nay, even that is a contradiction—as a passive 0 among nothings?' How often, when some Western has interrogated the brooding East, has some such answer and reproof as this been returned ? How marked, too, is the Guru element in the following passages :—

We might as well attempt to conceive more than three dimensions of space as to imagine more than three kinds of living existence—God, man, and beast. And even of these the last (division) is obscure, and scarce endures a fixed contemplation without passing into an unripe or degenerated humanity.

Did you deduce your own being? Even this is less absurd than the conceit of deducing the Divine Being. Never would you have had the notion had you not had the idea—rather, had not the idea worked in you like the memory of a name which we cannot recollect, and yet feel that we have, and which reveals its existence in the mind only by a restless anticipation, and proves its *à priori* actuality by the almost explosive instantaneity with which it is welcomed and recognised on its re-emersion out of the cloud, or its re-ascent from the horizon of consciousness.

So far from deeming it, in a religious point of view, criminal to spread doubts of God, immortality and virtue (that 3—1) in the minds of individuals, I seem to see in it a duty—lest men, by taking the *words* for granted, never attain the feeling or the true *faith*. They only forbear, that is, even to suspect that the idea is erroneous or the communicators deceivers, but do not *believe* the idea itself. Whereas to *doubt* has more of faith, nay, even to disbelieve, than that blank negation of all such thoughts and feelings which is the lot of the herd of church-and-meeting-trotters.

How like an Eastern sage, too, was Coleridge's habit of illustration and parable, his love for aphorism and apophthegm, and his apparent belief that words might somehow convey more than the mere meaning which they could be demonstrated to express !

But if it is easy to show that Coleridge had in reality the mind of a Guru, it is, alas ! no less easy to show that he was a ruined—a more than slightly damaged—Eastern sage. The long distraction and disorder of his life proves that. His life was not that of a Guru, but of a man tormented by the world and, though not in the most fleshly sense, ruined by the flesh. Whether in reality he might have attained to the secret to which he believed he had come so near we dare not presume to say. But at least it is clear that he would have done better had he absented himself from the earthly felicities of hearth and home—felicities for which he was so ill-designed—and from the clash of the world, and had tried to lead the life of the Eastern sage. Had he learned to subdue the passions, and desires, and affections, how much more calmly and clearly would he have seen and reasoned. His misfortunes, both as a man and sage, seem, indeed, to point to the truth that there are still uses for the ascetic mode of life.

But though we may hold that Coleridge and those formed like him would be better were they deliberately to free themselves from the trammels of the world, we by no means hold that the ascetic life—the life that is of positive and direct asceticism—can ever be in the truest sense the higher life. He may do well who gives his soul full play by the methods of the Guru, but he does better who lives in the world and shares its burdens and its cares—who belongs to that band whose one bond is that all have been 'unspotted from the world,' who lives the common life and yet keeps his eyes undimmed. To live the higher life in the world, not the ascetic life outside it, is the ideal. And was not this after all the lesson taught in Syria nigh two thousand years ago ? Christ was not a Guru, and did not live among the Essenes ; but ate and drank as other men, and lived the life of a Galilean. Coleridge was, no doubt, a damaged. Guru ; and might have been an undamaged one had he lived the life of the Guru ; but, though we say this, let no one suppose that we put forward the Eastern sage and mystic as the ideal of spiritual life.

AMERICAN OPTIMISM

THE Englishman over the water in New England, considered as a man, and in isolation, seems to differ very little from the Englishman in Great Britain. We are all subjects of King Shakespeare, and all guided by much the same rules of conduct and ways of looking at life. What is honourable to one is honourable to the other, and both condemn the same acts as dishonourable. When, however, we come to compare the general spirit of the English-speaking man in the New World with that of the English-speaking man at home we note a real difference—a distinct divergence. The ruling passion of the two peoples is seen to be different, and the American spirit stands out as something separate and apart.

What are the characteristics which mark off the American spirit? To begin with, there is a tolerance of things unseemly and unmeet, inconvenient and even wrong *per se*, which is not to be found here.

This tolerance is observable everywhere in America and in everything, from badly paved streets to courts of Justice so inefficient that even the best citizens have to organise lynching parties. Burke said, ' I must bear with inconveniences till they fester into crimes.' The American carries out this principle far too thoroughly.

The festering point with him is put so high that it is almost impossible to get him to admit that toleration is no longer possible. Things which would make other nations mad with rage, and in an instant, he endures for years almost without a groan. The American does not like corrupt and inefficient municipalities, has no preference for seeing city property flung away piece-meal, and would prefer properly paved streets ; but, when he does not get them, instead of making a fuss and insisting on a change, he quietly submits, in the pious hope that things will get properly fixed some day.

To understand the cause of this tolerance is to understand the American. It is the tolerance, not of weariness, or cynicism, or lack of interest, but of optimism. The American cannot find it in his heart to be energetically angry over public inconveniences, because he is so profoundly impressed with the belief that things will come right in the end. In the true American there is not an atom of pessimism anywhere. You may talk to him till doomsday, but you shall never convince him that there is any real risk of things going permanently wrong. He will admit any amount of superficial wrongs, but at the back of his mind is the conviction that things are bound to worry through—a conviction which has come to have all the force and influence of an instinct. This colossal hopefulness, this essential and ineradicable optimism, makes it seem foolish to bother about little things. The Englishman is forced not to tolerate social or political wrongs because he has always the feeling that it is conceivable the social fabric may collapse and the nation go to ruin.

With him the feeling is: 'I must look alive and use every effort, or we shall very likely go on to the rocks.' The American, on the other hand, feels: 'I am shooting clear ahead into calm water, and nothing can stop me reaching it. What does it matter, then, if I am kept back for a minute or two by this or that eddy or back-wash?'

The origin of this optimism is not far to seek. What wonder that the men who threw off the burdensome connection with the old world, and, as they thought, ended for ever the ancient tale of wrong and misery, believed that they were the heirs of all the ages, and could not miss making something nobler and better out of human society than had ever been made before. The great West, with all its promises of material prosperity, was just opening out before them—'a banner bright unfurled before them suddenly.' What wonder that the men who had so splendid a physical as well as so magnificent a moral horizon should have become filled with infinite hope! The nation fed on its great future till it became, drunk with hope. Hopefulness was in the air. Hopefulness became the habit of the whole people. But infinite hopefulness as to the future is bound to produce a certain amount of carelessness as to the present.

If you are certain that everything will in the end be for the best, and that nothing can prevent the realisation of a future splendid, prosperous, and worthy, it is not in human nature to worry about details. You can get into a fuss and take vigorous action if you feel yourself sliding down-hill. You cannot, as long as you believe you are going steadily up-hill to your goal, bother very greatly as to little irregularities, which at the most only slightly reduce your pace. This invincible optimism, though it has had a bad result in making the American people careless and indifferent in face of grave evils, and tolerant of things which are really intolerable, has also its good side. It gives the nation an extraordinary recuperative power. Mr. Rudyard Kipling, writing of the Chicago rioters, in some verses first published in the *St. James's Gazette*, spoke in condemnation of the spirit of the American—

> That leaves him careless 'mid his dead,
> The scandal of the elder earth.

But he did not forget to note the other characteristic of the American, and how at once

> He turns his keen, untroubled face,
> Home to the instant need of things.

One may regret that the American does not take his scandals a little more to heart; but one cannot help admiring the way in which he acts on the principle that it is useless to cry over spilt milk.

This optimism, however, does more than merely produce a careless tolerance and an untroubled resolve to make the best of things. It gives a sort of sunniness to the national character which is very attractive, but which you miss in the Englishman in England. Take them as a whole, the Americans are the kindliest race on the face of the earth. In spite of their eagerness, their push, their desire to be in the front rank at all times and all seasons, the true American seldom fails in kindness. He wants badly to prevent anyone getting ahead of him mentally, physically, and morally, but if his competitor falls in the struggle he will make untold sacrifices to help him up. The rule in American business is pure cut-throat competition carried to its logical conclusion. You are expected to push and press every point as far as it can possibly be pushed and pressed, and no one is expected to consider whether, in making a commercial *coup*, you will not ruin Brown, Jones, or Robinson. The moment, however, that Brown, Jones, or Robinson actually goes under he is treated with the utmost generosity and consideration. The hand which struck him down is instantly stretched forth to help him, and as much care and trouble are used to put him on his feet once again as were originally employed to knock him off them.

In social intercourse this kindliness and sunniness is specially attractive. The American will take infinite pains to make the merest stranger happy. He is courteous and pleasant-spoken, not, like the Frenchman, from convention, but from the sense of pleasure which his instinctive optimism teaches him to diffuse. His optimism has even proved strong enough to break down the shyness which naturally belongs to the English race. One sees, no doubt, survivals of it in the American ; but in most cases the sense that all is for the best in the best possible of worlds has mastered it altogether. Even the fundamental melancholy of the Teuton has given way, or rather has been transmuted, and reappears not as a diluted melancholy, but in the form of dry humour—an All's-for-the-best sort of Melancholy. That is the genesis of American humour. This quality is the predominant partner in the American character—is the quality

> That checks him foolish—hot and fond ;
> That chuckles through his deepest ire ;
> That gilds the slough of his despond,
> And dims the goal of his desire.

This note of gladness in the American character was very cleverly caught by Mr. Frederick Myers when he compared the American girl with her English sister :—

> But ah, the life, the smile untaught,
> The floating presence feathery fair,
> The eyes and aspect that have caught
> The brightness of Columbian air.

So he writes of the American. The meaning is made clearer in the stanza which deals with the English-woman :—

> Through English eyes more calmly soft
> Looks from grey deeps the appealing charm ;
> Reddens on English cheeks more oft
> The rose of innocent alarm ;
> Our Old World heart more gravely feels,
> Has learnt more force, more self-control ;
> For us through sterner music peals
> The full accord of soul and soul.

The sense of a bright new world and the thought of all its possibilities have caused the golden flower of joy to grow somewhere in every American heart. Customs and conventions may conceal it, but search only long enough and you will find it, even in the heart of a New England farmer. The American cannot be a pessimist, do what he will. He may curse and rave and bully and fight and swear he is the worst-used man in creation ; but at heart he is solaced by the ever-present thought that he is the heir of the ages, and that fate looks to him to bring in the golden age. How well has Mr. Stevenson illustrated this aspect of the case in the character of Pinkerton in 'The Wrecker'! 'If we fail, what is there left? We are under bond to build up the type.'

With Pinkerton this optimism is a religion which inspires him at every turn. We may see faults in the American spirit; but it is difficult to doubt that it will greatly help to accomplish the vast work before the American people—the work of licking into shape that awful continent, and making that terrible mixture of populations 'right English.' Nothing but invincible optimism could avail for a task so colossal. Mr. Rudyard Kipling, in the poem we have already quoted—a poem full of genius, but much too strongly worded for fairness or good taste—sees this truth. The Spirit of America speaks thus of the American :—

> Enslaved, illogical, elate,
>   He greets th' embarrassed Gods, nor fears
> To shake the iron hand of Fate,
>   Or toss with Destiny for beers.
>
> Lo ! Imperturbable he rules
>   Unkempt, disreputable, vast—
> And in the teeth of all the schools
>   I—I shall save him at the last !

So be it, and so it shall be. The Americans will be saved through the optimism which for the time disfigures them. Through them, and therefore through that optimism, the English tongue and the English ideals o honour, truth, freedom, and courage shall possess the earth. Meantime let the Americans look to it that their future does not too greatly overshadow their present. By putting their furnished lodgings in decent order they will not in the least impair the certainty of one day possessing a palace.

THE MAGIC OF WORDS

'WITH words we govern men,' said Lord Beaconsfield. There is doubtless a good deal of truth in this assertion of the power of words and the vast importance of those short, sharp phrases which, as Bacon said, fly about the world like darts. It would, however, be very easy to exaggerate their effect. It must never be forgotten that the potent phrases, the words which seem to govern men, are not intrinsically potent, do not carry their own strength with them. They are only important when they translate, and put swiftly, the common thoughts of men. Unless they hit the psychological moment, and fall as seed on prepared ground, they are worthless. The philosopher or the man of letters in his study may frame the most mordant sentences and compress an infinity of scorn or love into three words, but it will all be of no avail unless the people are touched.

Words and phrases seem of the utmost moment—seem, indeed, as if they were the leaders of men and the controllers of their destinies, but in reality they are only the concentration of the general thought. A cistern is slowly overflowing, and the water is being dissipated by trickling down the sides. Some one comes and drives in a tube, and the water shoots out in a clear, strong stream, all the unmarked oozings and runnings being collected together. We note the power of the jet of water, and may even see it turning a wheel, but we do not ascribe the power to the tube, but to the water which it collects. So the power is not in the phrase, but in the popular feeling behind it. The tube without the water is nothing—but so, no doubt, is the water without the tube.

It is this fact—that potent phrases are a kind of trickery—which makes South's description of them so happy. In his famous sermon on 'The Fatal Imposture and Force of Words,' he speaks of them as 'verbal magic,' and so in truth they are. They have the magical faculty of seeming other than they are. The phrases which exert the greatest influence follow while they seem to lead. But the verbal magic does not stop here. It is true that a phrase cannot catch hold of the world unless it expresses something which the world is feeling. When once, however, it has come into exist-ence and has 'caught on,' it begins to exercise a sort of reactive power. It is like the image in the story of Frankenstein, and masters its makers. The phrase gains strength as it goes, and holds subject the minds from which it sprang.

Take the phrase that Spain was 'our natural enemy.' That arose when men feared that the fleets of Spain would invade us. It kept control over their minds, however, long after, and doubtless swayed Cromwell when he made the mistake of siding with France, rather than Spain, in the struggle for the supremacy of the Continent. South puts certain aspects of verbal magic with admirable skill when he says : 'Take any passion of the soul of man while it is predominant and afloat, and, just in the critical height of it, nick it with some *lucky* or *unlucky* word, and you may as certainly overrule it to your own purpose as a spark of fire, falling upon gunpowder, will infallibly blow it up.' In the same sermon—one of the most brilliant ever preached by South—he goes on to say that 'he who shall duly consider these matters will find that there is a certain bewitchery or fascination in words which makes them operate with a force beyond what we can naturally give an account of.' The thought is a true one, and would be well worth following up.

Words set in a special way, and with a peculiar knack, seem capable of producing a kind of mental intoxication. Junius possessed in a special degree this art of making words heady. Though the political controversies of his age are now cold and stale, and though we care little or nothing about Lord North and the Duke of Grafton, it is difficult for any person who is at all sensitive to literature to read them and not feel the effect. A person possessed of little or no historical knowledge described to the present writer how, when a mere lad, he took down 'Junius' from a bookshelf and began to read. He knew nothing about the characters, and in reality cared less ; but, said he, 'I read on eagerly and with delight, and when I closed the book I felt drunk.' But though, as we have pointed out, the phrases which seem to create great movements and to change men's minds are only pipes in which the waters, ready to overflow, are collected by the arts of verbal magic, we by no means desire to confine the phrase 'verbal magic' to the sleight of tongue which makes men think they are being led by those who are in reality following them.

Verbal magic plays a great part, not only in all personal intercourse, but in the influence which the politicians exercise over their supporters. The verbal magic used by the flatterer may seem an empty imposture to those against whom it is not directed, or who stand outside the circle in which the spell is cast ; but, if skilfully employed, its power is enormous. 'There is hardly any rank, order, or degree of men but more or less have been captivated and enslaved by words. It is a weakness, or rather a fate, which attends both high and low ; the statesman who holds the helm as well as the peasant who holds the plough.' So says South. He goes on to declare his belief in the impossibility of laying on flattery too thick in words which may fitly stand beside the remark attributed to Lord Beaconsfield—'All men like flattery, but in the case of Royalty you can lay it on with a trowel.' South asserts 'that if ever you find an ignoramus in place and power, and can have so little conscience and so much confidence as to tell him to his face that he has a wit and an understanding above all the world beside, and "that what his own reason cannot suggest to him, neither can the united reason of all mankind put together," I dare undertake that, as fulsome a dose as you give him, he shall readily take it down, and admit the commendation though he cannot believe the thing.' To put it otherwise, if only the spell is properly cast, the man, by verbal magic, may be made to believe that black is white.

But though the exercise of verbal magic and the concocting of heady phrases may do much to affect men and to take their minds captive, it is, after all, the plain words that go straight to the heart that have the most real and lasting effect. The man who thinks nothing of casting spells, or of how to apply his art magic, but speaks straight from the heart, if only he has in him sincerity, single-heartedness, and the passion of truth, will move the world most. South, again, has put this with great force and beauty in another of his sermons, for it is an instance of the irony of fate that the man who dealt in verbal magic more consistently than any of his contemporaries, and was always deep in spells and incantations cast with phrases, was the chief denouncer of verbal magic. After praising plainness of speech, he proceeds :—' This was the way of the apostles' discoursing of things sacred. Nothing here " of the fringes of the north star ; " nothing of " nature's becoming unnatural ; " nothing of the " down of angels' wings," or " the beautiful locks of cherubims ; " no starched similitudes introduced with a " Thus have I seen a cloud rolling in its airy mansion," and the like. No ; these were sublimities above the rise of the apostolic spirit. For the apostles, poor mortals, were content to take lower steps, and to tell the world in plain terms " that he who believed should be saved, and that he who believed not should be damned." And this was the dialect which pierced the conscience and made the hearers cry out, " Men and brethren, what shall we do ? " '

The truth is that the phrase ' With words we govern men ' must be amended and made to read ' With words we govern weak, vain, and foolish men.' No doubt, as a large part of mankind are weak, vain, and foolish, this is assigning a great importance to words ; but then it must be remembered that the weak, vain, and foolish are not the most active spirits, and that, even if they are captured, comparatively little has been obtained. No doubt we may splash up words, may juggle with them, and may make a great parade of their power, but in the end men are swayed not by the words, but by the thoughts on which the words rest. It is like the case of hypnotism. Theoretically, the best and most successful hypnotiser ought to be the greatest man in the world. His suggestions to the politicians and the capitalists should give him the command of society. Yet, as a matter of fact, the power of the hypnotiser is a dream, and cannot be employed in practice. So with the magician of words. His power is much more apparent than real. He can label the universal movements with his phrases, and can directly affect the weak and foolish part of the community ; but the label, though it may sell, does not make, the champagne.

A STUDY IN CONVERSATION

I

PEOPLE are rather too apt to regard discursiveness as the sign of a weak mind, and to suspect that a man who has something to say on every question, from the proper basis for actuarial calculations to the causes of fugitiveness in water-colour pigments, is never worth listening to, and is merely an idle prater. It is impossible, they argue, that a man should know anything worth knowing about so many subjects, and they go on to talk about 'Jack-of-all-trades and master of none,' and to speak of the mind being debilitated and the mental energy sapped by discursiveness. 'A man should talk about what he knows, and only about that. Then he may say something worth hearing. As regards other things, he should hold his tongue, and then he won't make a fool of himself.' So says the parlour oracle, and shuts his mouth with a snap. And no doubt the logical position is, or appears to be, a very strong one.

No man can know more than a very few things thoroughly. A man can only say what is worth hearing on things he knows thoroughly. A man should not talk except he says things worth hearing. Therefore a man should not be discursive, and should confine himself to his own subjects. Such is the outline of the syllogisms by which the discursive talker is put down, pulverised, and, if not reduced to silence, at any rate conclusively proved to be a babbling jackass. But in spite of the excellence of the logic, we all know that in fact the discursive talker can be, and often is, a most delightful talker. In spite of all the rules and all the schools, one may gain a great deal more not only of amusement, but of information, from the man who is not afraid of talking of anything in heaven above or the earth beneath than from the correct and pedantic gentleman who is always lying in wait for his own subject to turn up, and when it does turn up promptly blows it to pieces by discharging at its head an eighty-one-ton gun loaded to the muzzle, with facts and statistics. The discursive sportsman would have neatly put a bullet through the brain, and would have brought the game down unspoiled. The expert, who has bottled up his knowledge for a year, knocks it to smithereens, and leaves nothing but a few scraps of fur and feather.

Than the notion that the discursive talker is a weak-minded man none is more utterly and ridiculously absurd. Some of the hardest-headed of men have been the most ubiquitous talkers imaginable. Macaulay was one. Whatever game you might start, he would be ready to hunt it with you. He never chose the pedant's part or refused to let fly because, in the words of the Oxford don, the subject started ' was not in his period.' Instead, he would stand (as Fanny Kemble describes him) all day long on the hearth-rug of the library at Bowood and do battle with anybody and everybody on any conceivable topic.

We shall not, we trust, be passing the bounds of privacy in instancing Mr. Gladstone as another example of the great discursives. Read the account of a conversation held with him by that singular and attractive person John MacGregor (the hero of the 'Rob Roy' canoe), given in his Life. Mr. MacGregor records in his Diary how he met Mr. Gladstone and his daughter 'on board Lawton's yacht "Lenore."' 'Here had most intensely interesting confab with Chancellor of Exchequer on following subjects among others :—Shoeblacks ; crossing-sweepers ; Refuge Field-line ; translation of Bible ; Syria and Palestine Fund ; Return of the Jews ; Iron, brass, and stone age ; Copper ore, Canada ; bridges in streets ; arching over whole Thames ; ventilation of London ; *Ecce Homo* ; Gladstone's letter to author and his reply in clerk's hand to keep unknown ; speculation as to his being a young man who wrote it ; Language of Sound at Society of Arts ; Dr. Wolff's Travels ; Vambéry and his travels ; poster with Reform resolutions at Norwich ; use of the word "unscrupulously ;" marginal notes on Scripture.' The comment on this delightful entry is too good to be omitted. 'Took leave deeply impressed with the talent, courtesy, and boundless suppleness of Gladstone's intellect, and of his deep reverence for God and the Bible and firm hold of Christ.'

Our readers will note that these were not the sole topics, but only the subjects 'among others' touched on by Mr. Gladstone. Now, according to the principle which so many people profess to regard as the true one, Mr. Gladstone's opinion would have been only worth having on his own subjects—*i.e.* politics and theology,

and possibly philanthropy, as a mixture of the two.
He ought to have stood mute on the stone age, copper
ore, Canada, street bridges, and the converting of the
Thames into a great sewer.   Even the excursus on the
use of the word 'unscrupulously' in the Norwich poster
ought strictly to have been torn from·him and handed
over to a lexicographer.   But can any sane man declare
that Mr. Gladstone would not have been worth listening
to on all the subjects in the list, and that his acute and
supple mind would not have contributed something
noteworthy upon each and all of them?

Take again the two greatest talkers the world has
known—one of them an ancient, the other a modern—
Socrates and Dr. Johnson.   Socrates, no doubt, talked
on fewer subjects than Johnson, but that was only
because there were fewer subjects of conversation available.   The Athenian world was far smaller, simpler, and
therefore far less complex, than that of London in the
eighteenth century.   There were fewer books as well as
fewer men, and less technical knowledge had been
accumulated in the arts and sciences.   Socrates was as
discursive as he could be, considering his time and
opportunities.   Dr. Johnson's talk must have been quite
as discursive as that of any man who ever lived.   The
index to 'Boswell' is like that to an encyclopædia.
Analyse any of the great talks between Dr. Johnson
and his friends, and the subjects will not be found less
numerous or less varied than those recorded in the
extract from Mr. MacGregor's Diary.

In truth, discursiveness, instead of being the sign
of a weak mind, is the sign of a strong and active mind.
It is the torpid and unoriginal mind that sticks solely

to its own subject. The man of keen intellect and of that ample power of expression which usually, though not always, accompanies a keen intellect, can no more confine his mind, and so his tongue, to the one or two subjects in which he has special and peculiar knowledge than he can confine his vision to one or two objects. His mind travels over and takes hold of everything that comes within its reach, just as his eye does when it surveys a wide landscape. It is futile to say that the mind is demoralised by discursiveness. Instead it is sharpened and kept lively and active by dealing with a large number of topics.

The truth is that the pedantic and logical ideal of the great expert who is perpetually holding his mental nose hard down on the grindstone of ' the basis of ethics,' or the ' action of the optic nerve in blackbeetles,' or ' particular estates ' or ' contingent remainders,' and who never allows himself to express opinions on other subjects, is an absurdity. Let a clever man once get to know one subject thoroughly, and to put a fine edge on his mind by that study, and he is certain to try the blade on a dozen other subjects. It is impossible for a man of really great intellect to keep his mind from attacking all the subjects of interest which are in the air and the papers. If he is a very modest, or a somewhat suspicious, or, again, a pompous man, he may pretend in public not to have an opinion on the thousand and one topics of the day ; but depend upon it he has really a strong opinion in every case.

Lastly, it must not be supposed that the discursive man merely wastes his breath pleasantly and amusingly by talking at large. On the contrary, he very often adds to human knowledge, or else gives a stimulus to other minds. Most men of expert knowledge—specialists in abstruse subjects—will be able to give instances from their own experience of having talked over their own subject with a well-informed and able man of the discursive habit, and gained a good deal from doing so. ' Of course A has no special knowledge,' they will say ; ' but still he is so clever, and sees things so quickly, that if you supply him with the data it is ten to one that he will recombine them in some illuminating way, or draw some deduction which one might otherwise have missed.'

After all, science and knowledge of every kind go forward, not on the bare facts, but on the arguments drawn from the facts, and hence it may very well happen that the expert in argument and exposition, which the man of great discursive powers is apt to be, can give something to the specialist which is really valuable. No doubt there are plenty of discursive talkers who deserve to be shot at sight—men of feeble minds who twaddle about and around every conceivable topic, and of whom it is rightly said that there is nothing they touch which they do not becloud and obscure. But it is not the discursiveness of these persons which makes them bores. They would be just as bad if they had only one subject. Indeed, it may be said that in that case the horror they would make about the house would be even more intense. What they want is good sense and power, and this they will not obtain by concentration. No doubt there may be instances of men who talk badly when they are discursive, but well when they stick to one or two subjects, but we fancy that their number is very greatly exaggerated. There is in reality only one safe rule in conversation. Talk about what interests you. But if you are interested in a thousand things, which almost all men worth talking to are, you are sure to be discursive.

II

IT is reported of the late M. Renan that when anything was said to him with which he profoundly disagreed he invariably began his contradiction with the phrase, 'Vous avez raison mille fois.' With this for preface, he, in the gentlest and subtlest way, showed that his interlocutor was entirely wrong in his facts, or that he had propounded a theory which was utterly mistaken. In all probability M. Renan touched high-water mark in the art of discovering a right line in obliquity, and of making 'no' look like 'yes;' but there are, all over the world, hundreds of men who instinctively follow the same plan ; who cannot bear the slightest friction in social and intellectual intercourse ; and who always start a contradiction by pointing out that at bottom they entirely agree with you, though there is just one small and unimportant point on which they differ. You make a quotation or state a fact in the presence of a man of this type, and, knowing that it is his subject, ask whether you have 'got it right.' You have not ; but this does not in the least incline him to put you right plainly and simply. He assures you instead that your version is substantially correct, and then, by a series of subtle gradations, he manages to put into your mouth the true story.

A good illustration of this method of correction

is afforded by the story of the schoolmaster who was determined not to discourage his pupils by abrupt corrections. On the occasion of the story one of the boys was asked to give the English for the word 'Niger.' 'White' was the prompt reply. 'White,' answered the schoolmaster; 'yes, you mean a sort of grey, a misty colour, a dark neutral tint—in fact, black. Yes, quite right; "Niger," black. Go on, next boy.'

Is the social method of those who talk in the spirit of M. Renan, with his 'Vous avez raison mille fois,' or of the schoolmaster, with his subtle shadings of white into black, a good one? That is the question we desire to discuss. That there is a good deal to be said for it, when not carried to ridiculous extremes, we cannot doubt. Conversation is, after all, a sort of intellectual walk; and therefore anything which beats the path plain and makes going easy ought, *prima facie*, to be good. Sudden and abrupt contradictions are like sudden turns in a walk, and by no means pleasant. Perpetual agreement is, of course, the dullest thing in the world, and soon kills talk; but so does perpetual disagreement. Conversation between two men who, the moment they differ, or think they differ, contradict each other flat, is like walking over the big boulders on the moraine of a glacier.

If M. Renan was an example of the class of talkers who never contradict, and who, socially, always choose the line of least resistance, Lord Tennyson was a type of the opposing class. Though possessed of a personality lovable and attractive in a high degree, Lord Tennyson was a devotee of the abrupt method. He said what he meant straight out, and contradicted any statement with which he did not agree, or which he knew to be wrong, without compunction. He had, of course, whatever willingness to sink his own views was required by good manners, but within those limits he cared nothing for the line of least resistance. It was the same with the late Professor Freeman. It was difficult not to feel that he would as soon, if not sooner, disagree than agree with you. No doubt for many people this roughness has a great charm. Talking to a downright man has the attraction which belongs to a walk on rough ground, through gorse and heather, and over streams and rocks. The roughness and the variety stimulate, and give a sense of delight not to be found in an amble on an asphalted footpath. It may be easier to get on on the smooth ground ; but when that is not the primary object there is far more pleasure to most people in the rough going.

In truth, however, there is no possibility of coming to any definite decision as to which is the best conversational method. Some men are pleased and some disgusted with the talker who is always seeking for points of agreement, and making artificial ones when he cannot find them naturally. Again, there are some who abominate and some who delight in the blunt talker. It is, like so many things, a question of individual taste ; and though we may sympathise with one side more than the other, we are bound to admit that there is no absolute right or wrong in the matter. In the form of social intercourse we are considering—talking not to instruct, but to amuse—there is only one certain test of success : to ask whether the talk pleases. But, since what pleases A does not please B, it cannot be possible to commend one plan of talking to the exclusion of all others. He talks best who pleases most.

It is this fact, and this fact alone, which can guide the man who wishes to talk well and to gain the reputation of one from whose conversation no human being ever went away disappointed. The good talker does not convert his mind into a sort of intellectual sausage-machine, and, like Johnson or Carlyle, turn out his talk all of one pattern. Instead, he finds out what system of mental approach is most pleasing to his interlocutor, and employs that. If he sees that the man with whom he is talking likes the stimulation that comes from well-defined and well-persisted-in points of difference and the clash of mind with mind, he does not assail him with 'Vous avez raison mille fois,' but meets him in the open with a fair and square denial. If, on the other hand, our perfect talker finds the person with whom he talks to be of an irascible nature, unable to argue quietly, and thrown into a fit of indignation by a difference of opinion, he adopts the plan of dressing up his contradictions till they look almost like assents. Like the lady in Congreve—

> Whom he refuses [*to agree with*] he treats still
>   With so much sweet behaviour
> That his refusal, through his skill,
>   Looks almost like a favour.

It comes, then, back to this, that the most successful talker is he who moves on the line of least resistance ; but it is the line of least resistance properly and fully understood, and not the conventional line of least resistance. For example, in the case of a man who likes rough walking and enjoys an abrupt contradiction, the line of least resistance is not the line of pretending to agree. He sees through that artifice, and is not soothed, but irritated, by it. 'I don't want you to set me right by stealth,' is his feeling, 'but straight out.' Hence, in his case, to move along the line of least resistance is to stop him abruptly and contradict him flat. As we have said above, the only safe rule is to please. If both talkers in a conversation try to do that, and do it intelligently and not conventionally, they are pretty certain to arrive at what one of Mr. Rudyard Kipling's Mahommedan characters calls 'very good talk,' and to reach what Gibbon describes as 'the perfection of that inestimable art that softens and refines our social intercourse.'

III

WE can all tell a bore, male or female, when we see him or her, without instruction. An important point, however, is left over. That is—What is the particular quality that makes the bore and mars the man? It is evidently not what some people have supposed—the mere dwelling on dull subjects and the avoiding of entertaining topics. We have known men capable of making golf-shop interesting, and of holding their hearers spell-bound with the elaboration of the plans adopted by fire insurance offices for spreading their risks. Again, the man who takes up the most thrilling and diverting topics, and, mixing them with the mud in his thought, makes them stale, flat, and unprofitable, is only too familiar. Such a person seems to have a faculty the reverse of that possessed by the philosopher's stone. Everything with which his mind comes in contact is at once turned into lead. 'Marble I found them, and brickwork I left them,' is the epitaph that must be pronounced upon his attempts to deal with the most fascinating subjects of conversation ; and of him it is written, 'Nihil tetigit quod non degeneravit.'

But if boring does not consist in the subject talked about, but is a something brought by the bore himself, and quite independent of external considerations, what is it ? We believe that the essential part of boring is want of sympathy. Primarily, the bore is the person who preaches to an unsympathetic audience. Conversation—we are considering the conversational aspect of the bore, since that is the aspect in which he is best studied —is essentially a bilateral social function. It is not necessary for the two parties to talk equally, but there must be a reciprocal feeling set up between them. They are the carbon poles, and the light of true conversation does not burn unless the electric current of sympathy passes between them.

Now, the bore is unaware of this truth. He ignores the necessity for sympathy in his victim, and talks to the unwilling as eagerly as to the willing listener. He is incapable, that is, of telling whether his hearer is in sympathy with him or not. The man who is not a bore, if he hits on an uncongenial subject, very quickly leaves it. The bore rasps on, oblivious of the mental opposition which he is encountering. The bore has no notion of what is the line of least resistance. He does not pick the smoothest path he can find, but snorts with the utmost unconcern down the road of maximum friction. The man who is not a bore sees in an instant that the story of how the village pump was painted contrary to the orders of the vicar's churchwarden is not interesting to his audience, and immediately changes the subject. Not so the bore. He knows, or thinks he knows, what is a really good story ; and therefore, oblivious of the far-away look that has come into the eyes of Miss Jones and Mr. Smith, he makes them drink the anecdote to the dregs. Unaware that he is not sailing down a pleasant stream of talk, he does not spare the smallest detail, and recounts verbatim what the clerk said to the pew-opener or to the grocer's assistant, who sings alto in the choir. It is this fact—*i.e.* that lack of sympathy and of ability to enter into other people's feelings constitute the bore—that makes it possible for some men to be both bores and not bores.

If and when it happens that the bore's subject interests his hearers, owing to some special or individual circumstance, the bore may for a moment rise above boredom. This is, however, only true of the mitigated bore. The full bore, as we have said above, brings with him a plentiful supply of intellectual mud, and this he mixes so thoroughly with every thought in his brain that the man's whole intelligence is beclouded and bedraggled. The full bore, then, can manage to bore even the person who wants most to hear what he has got to say. Smith may know all about the Druidical remains in a particular neighbourhood, and Jones may desire intensely to hear about them. Yet, for all that, Smith's recital may inflict something very like physical agony on Jones.

We all know men of this type—men of whom we would gladly ask a question or two on this or that subject, but to whom we dare not administer the simplest interrogatory for fear of bringing down a veritable verbal avalanche. These are the men who will insist upon what they call clearing the ground—that is, on explaining twice over, and in language fit for an infant school, facts that one has known since one was knee-high. To make the thing 'clear to the meanest capacity' is their principle; and, in spite of the want of compliment to one's mental powers implied by the process, they carry it out remorselessly. The intermittent bore is produced by this want of ability to see what interests and what tires a hearer. The intermittent bore is the bore who, on ninety-nine questions, behaves and talks perfectly, but who, when one special subject is started, takes the bit between his teeth and starts madly down the line of most resistance. We have known men who could talk delightfully on every subject except metaphysics, but who, when once the conversation took a transcendental turn, would tear screaming down an inclined plane of acute boredom. Dr. Johnson had obviously been tried, and sorely tried, by an intermittent bore of this kind, or he would not, in his 'London,' have put such a passion of disgust into the lines—

> Here falling houses thunder on your head,
> And here a female atheist talks you dead.

Very possibly the female atheist is a capital talker on the stage, politics, or literature. Get her on theology, however, and there is not one of us who would not rather face the houses thundering on one's head. The phrase 'talks you dead' in Johnson's couplet is specially noteworthy, and shows that the bore, as known to us, does not greatly differ from the bore of the eighteenth century. The state of abject helplessness and misery to which a thoroughly practised and efficient bore will reduce one in two minutes could not be better described.

We must not forget, while dealing with the bore question, to say something about the false accusations of boredom which are occasionally brought against perfectly innocent people. For example, a crypto-bore, or an incipient, or potential, or intermittent bore will often say of some acquaintance that he or she is a bore, or bored him terribly. The accusation from a suspected bore must be received with the greatest caution. We will not discuss whether a bore can bore another bore, or whether there is such a thing as mutual boring. Those are difficult matters, and outside the scope of the present inquiry. There is, however, no doubt that A often accuses B of boring him merely because B has ventured to contradict A, or to differ from him on some point of controversy.

A story of Carlyle will supply the example we need. Carlyle took a friend and a much younger man out walking with him, and, in his usual way, indulged in a monologue, in which, nevertheless, his companion was much interested. Once or twice, however, the friend ventured to put in a word or two of objection in regard to something said by Carlyle. This annoyed Carlyle intensely, and when they reached home he turned upon his companion and addressed to him the following warning : 'Young man, I'd have ye to know that ye've the *capacity* for being the greatest bore in Europe.' The poor man had hardly spoken a dozen words ; but, since these had been critical, they had made him seem to Carlyle a potential bore of colossal proportions. Many men in this way get unjustly called bores. They venture to doubt some statement made in conversation, and are at once branded with the most terrifying of names. These unfortunate persons are, in truth, not bores at all, but merely the innocent detectors of the latent capacity of boring in others. Carlyle showed by his speech what was indeed the fact—that he, not his friend, possessed the potentiality of boring. It is true his great imagination generally saved him, but he often went perilously near the line. Had he not been the man of genius he was, he would assuredly have been the greatest bore in Europe.

LITERARY STUDIES

A STUDY OF LOUIS STEVENSON

I

ROBERT LOUIS STEVENSON AND HIS WORK

WHAT is it that makes Mr. Stevenson's literary work never wholly satisfying? What is the something in which his books fail to content, even when they most excite, the emotions? His romances are full of charm and of fascination. Nothing could be more vivid or more taking. The art is perfect, and dulness is banished from the page. And yet as one reads there grows the sense of some latent imperfection, some intangible fault of commission or omission which perplexes and astonishes. What can it be? Whence comes this sense that in the last resort we are cheated of the full inspiration? Scott was wholly without Mr. Stevenson's power of literary finesse, could be as clumsy and irrelevant as the author of 'Kidnapped' was careful and artistically true and exact; and yet Scott satisfies and contents and warms the heart and brain with the glow of animation, while Mr. Stevenson leaves them cold. 'Guy Mannering' edifies us in the truest sense of the word.

There is no such intellectual building up in Mr. Stevenson's work. There is a flaw somewhere in each and all of the fairy palaces of his creation, and when we most need his walls and towers to stand firm they fall in ruin about us.　We are finely touched, yet somehow not to fine issues.　It would not, perhaps, be fair to say that in spite of their apparent strength and fitness, there are traces of degeneration and morbidity, to borrow the medical phrase, in Mr. Stevenson's romances, but the expression conveys something of what we mean.　In Scott we get the beauty that comes of perfect health. In Stevenson that which is often to be found joined with the want of health and the variation from the normal.

One might spin many ingenious theories to account for this lack of the true soul-satisfying quality in Mr. Stevenson's work, but in all probability the explanation is a fairly simple one.　We believe that it is to be found in the way in which Mr. Stevenson approached and attacked the art of letters.　His original attitude towards literature was a very singular one.　Most men begin by an overmastering desire to say something—to tell a tale or write a poem—and then work out for themselves a style as adequate and as sound as they are able.　Mr. Stevenson, on the other hand, as he has told us himself, began at the other end—learnt first to write, and then looked out for something to write about.　Words and their skilful manipulation were to him an end in themselves.　He learnt to use them in the abstract, and did not regard them merely as a means.　He acted as a painter does when he studies drawing and attempts the acquisition of a technique.

In 'Memories and Portraits' Mr. Stevenson takes us fully into his confidence in this respect.　'All through my boyhood and youth,' he says, ' I was always busy on my own private end, which was to learn to write. I kept always two books in my pocket—one to read, one to write in. As I walked, my mind was busy fitting what I saw with appropriate words ; when I sat by the roadside I would either read or a pencil and a penny version-book would be in my hand to note down the features of the scene or commemorate some halting stanzas. Thus I lived with words, and what I wrote was for no ulterior use ; it was written consciously for practice.' His reading, too, was dominated by the desire to perfect his technique. When he came upon a passage that struck him as happy in phrase and style he ' must sit down at once and set himself to ape that quality.' Thus, he tells us, he ' played the sedulous ape to Hazlitt, to Lamb, to Wordsworth, to Sir Thomas Browne, to Defoe, to Hawthorne, to Montaigne, to Baudelaire, and to Obermann.' In a word, he worked at style as a student at the Slade or the Academy Schools works at his ' antique' and his ' life,' and makes studies in the way of Velasquez or Titian, or the great Dutchmen. Mr. Stevenson has told us in words of wonderful charm and eloquence what was the result of this conscious and laborious study of style ; and how, after such a training, the student of literary form could ' sit down at last, legions of words swarming to his call, dozen of turns of phrase simultaneously bidding for his choice, and he himself knowing what he wants to do and (within the narrow limit of a man's ability) able to do it.'

When Mr. Stevenson had thus taught himself to write he looked out for something to write about, just as a painter of the academic kind, when he has made himself master of his art, looks out for subjects which will enable him to show his skill and dexterity—his powers of eye and hand. Mr. Stevenson did not choose this or that topic because it was one which came naturally and inevitably to him. Instead, he selected a subject which would enable him to show what astonishing and delightful things he could do through his management of words. For example, he took the things he saw and the thoughts he thought on his journey with a donkey in the Cevennes and spread them out in phrases of perfect appropriateness and melody, linking each object or each abstraction with just the words that gave it what Hazlitt calls its 'exact, extreme, characteristic, impression.' . The result was enchanting. Such an occasion needed only perfect workmanship to produce a picture that was bound to delight all beholders.

The painter of consummate technique, when he is content to paint what he sees before him, and not to construct, is certain to please. The real test comes when the man who has approached his art from the academic standpoint has learnt to write in the abstract, and has then looked out for something to write about, begins to deal with the world of pure imagination, has to create and breathe life into men and women, and to deal with their passions and their joys and sorrows. It is then that we note the failure of the academic way of approaching literature. It is then that an ounce of humanity is seen to be worth a wilderness of exquisitely balanced phrases and of words that fall as softly as blown petals on the grass.

If Mr. Stevenson had remained an occasional essayist

his academic attitude would have done little or no harm to his art, and the want of which we have spoken would not have been apparent. When, however, he used in the land of romance the splendid power over words which he had so patiently acquired the flaw was visible. It was, of course, natural enough that he should desire to show his skill in the field of fiction, and we are heartily glad that he was not content to be nothing but an essayist, for we readily admit that without his romances the literature of our day would be poorer. Though we cannot help seeing the defects of his novels, we are more than ready to admit their charm. We do not desire to depreciate Mr. Stevenson's work, but only to find an explanation for the fact that his writing, though it comes so very near, never reaches the highest heaven of invention.

It must not, then, be supposed that we mean to imply that Mr. Stevenson was merely an exquisite weaver of words. He had also, no doubt, a brain that was full of thick-coming fancies and a great power of narration. What we contend is that he was first of all a word-wright, and that he used his story-inventing and story-telling faculty to set off his skill in words, just as he used his personal experiences on the canal or on the road. His fancies and experiences were selected and employed as means for displaying his style and his perfect taste in phraseology. At first people may be inclined to say that in reality this is what every poet or novelist does, but in truth it is not so. Scott, in his way, and Dickens and Thackeray in theirs, approached literature in an altogether different spirit. They, no doubt, were impelled to write by a desire for fame and money ; but they achieved success by opening out to the world the rich treasures of the human heart. They, we feel, are primarily concerned with unfolding the great drama of existence.

The question of style is with them quite secondary. No doubt without style and form and verbal melody Scott's work would have been defective and abortive ; but still it was not in these gifts, but in the humanity of the writer, that his literary work had its genesis. Scott wrote because he had something he wanted to say, and could at the same time find adequate expression for that something ; Mr. Stevenson, rather because he could weave words beautifully, and could also manage to find subjects which would bear ornamentation. The difference does not seem much, it is so narrow ; but it goes as deep as infinity. It is the difference between 'Redgauntlet' and 'Kidnapped.' How clumsy and ill-constructed and full of blotches and palpable slips is the first! How perfectly manipulated, how precise in language, thought, and construction is the second—how telling is every phrase and situation! Yet when General Campbell speaks those chivalrous words on the beach a whole world is affected. We are translated into a serener atmosphere, catch the clear accents, and learn the great language of a wide and noble humanity. In 'Kidnapped' we are never moved like this. We mark how fine are the colours ; 'we hear how the tale is told ;' it is 'art, triumphant art ;' but it is not, like the other, a piece of breathing satisfying human life.

It seems ungracious and churlish to leave Mr. Stevenson thus, and especially for one who, like the present writer, has obtained so much pure delight from the heavenly rhetoric of his pen, who has so often sung with him in spirit the song of the open road, who has marvelled again and again at the nicety of his judgments, whether of Pepys or Knox, or of Burns, who has so often joined the inimitable Pinkerton in the Dromedary Picnics, who has until seventy times seven sat with Morris while he drew up his debtor and creditor account, and who has not once, but a dozen times, seen with David and Catriona the first view of the Dutch coast and the merry windmills whirling on the shore. And yet it is most consistent with the spirit of the man we are criticising to speak out straight, and make no conventional and obituary phrases about his art. Mr. Stevenson was essentially sincere in criticism, and would have been the first to refuse mere lip-service. Manliness was one of his most cherished intellectual characteristics, and he therefore pays the great artist the truest respect who tries to judge his work fairly, openly, and without pretence.

II

Mr. Stevenson's Poetry

MANY of his friends and admirers, and perhaps even Mr. Stevenson himself, believed that his achievement in verse was by no means inconsiderable. Yet the greater public could never be induced to regard the author of 'Kidnapped' as a poet, and resolutely refused to look upon his poems as anything but interesting experiments in rhyme. That there was an implied compliment in this neglect may fairly be upheld. They would not call him a minor poet, and they could not call him a great one, so they would not think of him as a poet at all. Though we are far from insensible to the subtle charm which Mr. Stevenson knew how to weave into his numbers, we cannot doubt that here, as so often, the public judged rightly. Mr. Stevenson was not a poet, and they knew it; and he knew that they knew it, or, at any rate, thought it, and hence he never approached them quite confidently or whole-heartedly when he used rhyme and measure as his medium. If anything about so remarkable an artist could be amateurish, it was his verse.

But though we side with the public in holding Mr. Stevenson not to have had the real poetic gift, we admit that we cannot claim the public's happy franchise of giving no reasons for the faith that is in us. That which deems itself infallible—and public opinion certainly does that—need give no reasons for its judgments when it speaks *ex cathedrâ*; but the mere critic must be content to take lower ground, and to produce arguments and facts in support of his contentions. The attitude of 'he wasn't a poet, and there's an end of it,' is not for him.

No one can, of course, read Mr. Stevenson's verse and not acknowledge that at any rate he had much that goes to make up a poet. Note his power of phrase-making. Nothing could be more attractive than the way in which he clothes his thoughts with melodious words. Take the delightful poem called 'The House Beautiful,' which begins —

A naked house, a naked moor,
A shivering pool before the door,

and so soon falls into the exquisite couplet—

> Yet shall your ragged moor receive
> The incomparable pomp of eve.

'The incomparable pomp of eve,' that is one of those phrases to which belong Charles Lamb's remark on Landor's eight-lined poem to Rose Aylmer—'I lived on it for six months.' The remainder of the poem is hardly less delightful when it goes on to enumerate how the pageant of the hours and seasons shall enchant the house with beauty. 'The cold glories of the dawn' shall be around it, while 'the wizard moon' and 'the army of the stars' shall add to its delights. Charming, too, is the sober Puritanic ending, worthy of Vaughan, Herbert, or Quarles :—

> To make this earth, our hermitage,
> A cheerful and a changeful page,
> God's bright and intricate device
> Of days and seasons doth suffice.

But it was not merely in these touches of nature that Mr. Stevenson's verse was so happy. He could on occasion import a human interest into his poems which was both attractive and original, or, rather, as original as anything can be in a literature like ours. We find this in the little nameless poem about the spring, which begins—

> It is the season now to go
> About the country high and low,
> Among the lilacs hand in hand
> And two by two in Fairyland.

Again, that very attractive little poem entitled 'To H. F. Brown, written during a Dangerous Sickness,' has

lines in it that haunt the fancy like the snatches of song
in the Elizabethan dramatists.   It is in these lines, re-
ferring at once to his illness and to his desire to visit
Venice, that he tells us how ' his serener soul did these
unhappy shores patrol,'

> And wait with an attentive ear
> The coming of the gondolier.

But one might cover many pages with such extracts
as these.   Enough has been quoted to enforce the
question, What is it prevents this being poetry, or,
rather, the writer of such verse from being a poet ?   We
believe, that the chief, perhaps the only, element of
poetry which Mr. Stevenson lacks is that note of
inevitability which all true poetry must possess—the
note which makes us understand what Milton meant
when he spoke of

> The Muse that lends
> Her nightly visitations unimplored,

or what was in Mr. Watson's mind when he speaks of
the poet

> Who finds, not fashions, his numbers.

It is this note of inevitability, again, which makes us
feel that the exact thought, or rather mood, expressed
by the poet has and could have had no expression but in
poetry—that poetry alone would give the true emotional
representation of the writer's thought.   Now, in neither
respect do we meet with this inevitability in Mr. Stevenson's verse.   We feel, to begin with, most distinctly
that he has fashioned, not found, his verses, and indeed
his inspiration.   Still more do we find the lack of in-

evitability when we consider whether poetry alone could have given expression to the mood of the creator. Seldom, if ever, can we say that verse, and verse alone, could have been used to represent what he desired to represent.

Mr. Stevenson's poetry could not, perhaps, have been expressed better in prose, but certainly as well. There is nothing that seems to proclaim it as poetry through and through, or as unthinkable in prose. Curiously enough, we see this even in Mr. Stevenson's most successful set of poems, ' A Child's Garden of Verses.' The art is charming, but it is not inevitable poetry, but merely an extraordinarily clever analysis of a child's mental attitude towards the external world set forth in a semi-dramatic form. A prose essay would not have done the work so originally, but still it could have done it. That, however, could not be said of Wordsworth's ' Ruth.' There poetry, and nothing else, would have conveyed to us the desired mood, mental and emotional.

A curious feature of Mr. Stevenson's verse which cannot fail to be noticed by anyone who examines it closely and critically is its essentially imitative character Mr. Stevenson seems constantly to be borrowing some other bard's harp and playing on it after the original master's manner. No doubt the imitation is done with great tact and great discretion, and always with taste, but none the less the sense of imitation as opposed to originality is there. Mr. Stevenson, in the attractive account which he has given us of how he formed his prose style, narrates, as we have noted above, that he used to take some great writer—Hazlitt or Sir Thomas

Browne—and then for weeks play what he calls 'the sedulous ape'—*i.e.* imitate till he had mastered the secret of the author's style.   In prose, no doubt, Mr. Stevenson succeeded in distilling by this process a wonderful and original style of his own.   In his verse the last stage does not seem to have been reached—the stage which blends the compound into a new thing, and does away with the feeling that it is a mere unassimilated mixture.   In the verse signs of 'the sedulous ape' process are always cropping up.

For example, lines suggestive of Herrick, Marvell, and the seventeenth-century poets are constantly occurring, while echoes of Milton, Landor, Wordsworth, and even of Emily Brontë and Mr. F. Myers, assault the ear.   It would not, of course, be fair to speak as if Mr. Stevenson's verse is a mere mosaic of echoes.   It is never that; but still one is perpetually reminded of the sound of other singers' songs.   Yet so well done is the work of imitation that no one with the sense of letters can fail to get a great deal of interest and delight out of Mr. Stevenson's verse, if only for this reason.   Suppose we had a series of studies in oil made by Stevens the sculptor which contained attempts to paint now in the manner of Perugino, now of Mantegna, and again of Raphael, Correggio, and Guido, and the whole fine in workmanship.   We should not call them great pictures, but they would interest us profoundly, partly on account of the man who executed them, but also for their own sake.

We have based what has already been written chiefly on Mr. Stevenson's 'Underwoods' and the 'Songs of Travel,' collected now for the first time.   If, however, we take the verse where he was more or less bound to be original—*i.e.* his ballads—the failure to write real poetry, or, to put it in another way, verse on the same high level as his prose, is owing to the defect which comes from the want of inevitableness extraordinarily apparent. The nature of the form employed made it impossible to hide his weakness and to seek shelter in 'the perfection of that inestimable art' which was his in the region of prose. Take 'Ticonderoga.' The subject is a magnificent one for a ballad, and the artifice and language beyond reproach ; and yet no one's blood will ever be half as much stirred by it as, say, by 'Admiral Hozier's Ghost'—a composition, judged as literature, so infinitely its inferior. 'Heather Ale,' again, is a failure just where success might have been expected. One would have imagined Mr. Stevenson making a weird, half-magical ballad almost equal to some of the old ballads of elf-land, but somehow the result is quite stiff; while in 'Christmas at Sea' Mr. Stevenson again very palpably misses making a good sea-song. As for the Samoan ballads, one can only say that they are failures, in spite of the interesting local colour, the occasional beauty of the lines, and the capital stories they tell. They are very readable, but they are not good ballads.

To turn to the pages of 'A Child's Garden of Verses' is almost enough to make the present writer regret that he has assailed Mr. Stevenson's claim to be a poet and to retract all he had written.

But, after all, poetry is poetry, and 'A Child's Garden of Verses,' though it shows us the working of a child's mind by a delicious artifice of baby-rhymes,

is not poetry, but merely very delicate criticism and
analysis.   'C'est magnifique, mais ce n'est pas la
guerre.'   Because we like poetry, and because we like
Mr. Stevenson's verse, we must not assume that they
are one and the same thing.   No ; poetry is something
different from all this.   Perhaps Mr. Stevenson half
realised it himself when, in his poem ' To the Muse,' he
tells us—

> Resign the rhapsody, the dream,
>   To men of larger reach ;
> Be ours the quest of a plain theme,
>   The piety of speech.
>
> As monkish scribes from morning break
>   Toiled till the close of light,
> Nor thought a day too long to make
>   One line or letter bright,
>
> We also, with an ardent mind,
>   Time, wealth, and fame forgot ;
> Our glory in our patience find,
>   And skim and skim the pot.
>
> Till last, when round the house we hear
>   The evensong of birds,
> One corner of blue heaven appear
>   In our clear well of words.
>
> Leave, leave it then, Muse of my heart,
>   Sans finish and sans frame,
> Leave unadorned by needless art
>   The picture as it came.

III

MR. STEVENSON AS AN ESSAYIST

WE have pointed out above that Mr. Stevenson was invariably at his best when using his superlative gift of style and his mastery over words and phrases to describe something which had come within his own vision —in dealing, that is, with incidents of a simple nature, yet somewhat removed from the ordinary, such as came under his eyes when he tramped the highlands of the Cevennes with his donkey, or when he floated down stream on his canoe.   The first part of 'The Amateur Emigrant' exactly confirms this view of Mr. Stevenson's genius. He crossed the Atlantic in the 'second cabin' and mixed freely with the steerage passengers, and from this standpoint he has given us one of the most marvellous studies of the ways and modes of thought of a certain section of the British working classes that is to be found in literature.   We see the restless artisan, the man whose impulse it is when he has got down in the world to try his luck in a new country, portrayed with an insight and an accuracy which it would be an insult to describe as photographic, for there is none of the coldness, none of the faulty perspective, none of the lack of sympathy which belongs to the photograph, but which has at once all the nearness to life of a photograph and all the artistic and creative qualities of a great piece of painting.

Nor is the portraiture all.   The work is filled from the first page to the last with those happy inspirations in regard to commonplace things which charm and captivate in the best of Mr. Stevenson's work as an essayist. His moralisings on the life around him—we use the word 'moralising' in its true, and not its derived, sense—are veritable shafts of light thrown upon the habits and ways of thinking belonging to a class which, though in essentials so like that of their richer neighbours, remains in many ways so obscure.

For example, Mr. Stevenson tells us how at first he had his heart in his mouth when he watched the children of the steerage passengers 'climb into the shrouds or on the rails while the ship went swinging through the waves.' Yet their mothers 'sat by in the sun and looked on with composure at these perilous feats. "He'll maybe a sailor," I heard one remark; "now's the time to learn."' Mr. Stevenson had, he tells us, been on the point of running forward to interfere; but stood back at this remark reproved. And then comes the comment in which, and in the happy phraseology used to call up the scene, rests the secret of Mr. Stevenson's power. 'Very few in the more delicate classes,' he goes on, 'have the nerve to look upon the peril of one dear to them; but the life of poorer folk, where necessity is so much more immediate and imperious, braces even a mother to this extreme of endurance. And perhaps after all it is better that the lad should break his neck than that you should break his spirit.'

Here is real insight into the motive forces of life— the true moralisation of existence such as one finds in Shakespeare. One feels that Stevenson had to the full what De Quincey so well called the sympathy of comprehension as well as the sympathy of approbation.

There is plenty of the latter sympathy to be found on all sides. It runs riot in the world. But how few possess the former—the sympathy of comprehension! When, however, the two are combined in a man who can see and feel, and can make you see what he sees and feel what he feels, the result is often a real revelation of human nature.

Many of the sketches of men and of shipboard scenes are intentionally very much more vivid and realistic than that we have just noticed, and are intended to be, as it were, finished pictures. But they never depress us, as does the work of M. Zola and the French realists, by the feeling that they are nothing but pictures. Mr. Stevenson always bore in mind the great artistic as well as the great ethical truth that man is a moral being. That truth, as well as the truth that even on the animal side he is essentially what Sir Thomas Browne called him, 'a noble animal,' puts life into Mr. Stevenson's pictures. Even when he draws the sordid and the mean he contrives to strike somewhere and somehow the note which provides a solution and converts to worthier uses the pity and the terror, the indignation and the disgust, that his creation has evoked.

We are utterly at a loss to give, by means of quotation, any adequate account of the hundred or so of pages which contain the description of the voyage. Every page has something good in it, and each good thing is so welded into the text that it increases the interest of what precedes and follows, and of the whole The account of the two stowaways is quite exellent. One, named Alick, was a habitual malingerer in the battle of life, a clever, plausible, smooth-tongued, lying idler who boasted how easily he had been able to live by pretending to work and yet never working. The other stowaway was a Devonshire lad, hence called the Devonian, ready to work and honest, yet somehow, by a mixture of fate and fancy, a rolling stone. But though Alick was a man to be despised, there was in him 'a guiding sense of humour that moved you to forgive him.' 'It was more than half as a jest that he conducted his existence. "Oh, man," he said to me once with unusual emotion, like a man thinking of his mistress, "I would give up anything for a lark."' But we could not do justice to Alick and the Devonian under half a dozen pages, and so must leave them.

Unnoticed, too, must be the account of the art of conversation as practised among the steerage passengers, though it is one of the most luminous pieces of analysis on that interesting topic, the talk of uneducated people, that has ever been put on paper. We must, however, quote a few of the sentences that follow the remark that 'good talking of a certain sort is a common accomplishment among workmen.' 'Where books are comparatively scarce a greater amount of information will be given and received by word of mouth ; and this tends to produce good talkers, and, what is not less needful for conversation, good listeners.' Yet the talk was apt to be too dry. 'They pursue a topic ploddingly, have not an agile fancy, do not throw sudden lights from unexpected quarters, and when the talk is over they often leave the matter where it was. They mark time instead of marching. They think only to argue, not to reach new conclusions, and use their reason rather as a weapon of offence than as a tool for self-improvement.'

Again, we would fain, but must not, deal with what Mr. Stevenson says as to the workman's love of disconnected facts :—'One and all were too much interested in disconnected facts, and loved information for its own sake with too rash a devotion ; but people in all classes display the same appetite as they gorge themselves daily with the miscellaneous gossip of the newspaper.' How true this is of the working classes may be seen in the popularity of papers like 'Answers' and 'Tit-Bits,' which are in effect collections of disconnected facts—though, be it understood, facts of good report. Mr. Stevenson fastens on to this reflection an excellent gibe at the newspaper reader in general :— 'Newspaper reading, as far as I can make out, is often rather a sort of brown study than an act of culture.' The present writer at least pleads guilty. To him the evening newspaper is chiefly useful as a ready intellectual sedative.

Before we leave 'The Amateur Emigrant' we will quote from the chapter of 'Steerage Types' a portion of his inspired portrait of Mackay—a materialistic, drink-ruined working man of great natural ability :—

In truth, it was not whisky that had ruined him ; he was ruined long before for all good human purposes but conversation. His eyes were sealed by a cheap school-book materialism. He could see nothing in the world but money and steam-engines. He did not know what you meant by the word happiness. He had forgotten the simple emotions of childhood, and perhaps never encountered the delights of youth. He believed in production, that useful figment of economy, as if it had been real like laughter ; and production without prejudice to liquor was his god and guide. One day he took me to task—a novel cry to me—upon the over-payment of literature. Literary men, he said, were more highly paid than artisans ; yet the artisan made threshing machines and butter churns, and the man of letters, except in the way of a few useful handbooks, made nothing worth the while. He produced a mere fancy article. Mackay's notion of a book was Hoppus's 'Measurer.' Now, in my time, I have possessed and even studied that work ; but if I were to be left to-morrow on Juan Fernandez Hoppus's is not the book that I should choose for my companion volume. . . . Anything, whatever it was, that seemed to him likely to discourage the continued passionate production of steam-engines he resented like a conspiracy against the people. Thus, when I put in the plea for literature that it was only in good books, or in the society of the good, that a man could get help in his conduct, he declared I was in a different world from him. 'Damn my conduct,' said he ; 'I have given it up for a bad job. My question is, Can I drive a nail?' And he plainly looked upon me as one who was insidiously seeking to reduce the people's annual bellyful of corn and steam-engines.

One more quotation and we have done. It shall support our original contention in regard to Mr. Stevenson's happy faculty of moralisation :—

As far as I saw, drink, idleness, and incompetency were the three great causes of emigration, and for all of them, and drink first and foremost, this trick of getting transported over seas appears to me the silliest means of cure. You cannot run away from a weakness ; you must some time fight it out or perish ; and if that be so, why not now and where you stand? *Cœlum, non animum.* Change Glenlivet for Bourbon and it is still whisky, only not so good. A sea voyage will not give a

man the nerve to put aside cheap pleasure ; emigration has to
be done before we climb the vessel ; an aim in life is the only
fortune worth the finding, and it is not to be found in foreign
lands, but in the heart itself.

IV

'THE WRECKER'

MR. STEVENSON'S admirers may be divided into two
classes—those who like and those who do not like ' The
Wrong Box.' The former class will declare 'The
Wrecker' one of the happiest and most entertaining of
his romances, while the latter will probably place it
among his less successful books. The skeleton of the
story is a tale of the sea, full of shipwreck, murder, and
sudden death ; but interwoven with this narrative of the
strange and fateful things that happen 'to the suthard
of the line '—that region of romance where the rules
that govern this work-a-day and prosaic world of ours
are over-ridden and set at naught—are a series of
studies of men and manners in Paris, in Edinburgh, and
in San Francisco. In these studies Mr. Stevenson
shows a power of humorous and didactic delineation
which, though very different in style and manner from
that of Dickens, is yet, by its freshness, its bonhomie,
and its ability to hold the reader spell-bound over the
most prosaic details, suggestive of Charles Dickens.
Many of the characters and the incidents described are,
we fully believe, destined to make an impression on the
English-speaking world almost comparable to that produced by the creator of Mr. Micawber.

Especially is this true of Pinkerton. Mr. Stevenson has drawn in him a ' type ' which is characteristically American—the pushing business man whose heart is as true and his nature as generous as his mercantile transactions are shady, and who joins an intense love of his country and an eager desire for culture with a willingness to do almost anything but hurt a woman or injure a friend in order to further a bogus speculation or to advertise a worthless ' product.' Mr. Henry Adams, one of the ablest of living historians, has pointed out that the key-note of the typical American character is an intense belief and hope in regard to the future of America, and has shown how to this belief and to this hope is to be ascribed the American tendency to cat-sprawl, to bluff, to talk big, and to exalt a collection of mud huts into a city. The American, as we have already noted, is so sure of the greatness that awaits him and his, and lives so much in his speculations of the future, that the unimportant fact that the future as yet wants realisation is forgotten and put aside. But to make his dream complete the American wants the American man of enterprise to be the cleverest, the best, the most chivalrous, as well as the richest, on the face of the earth. Hence he is for ever thinking of how ' to build up the type,' to get culture, and to make the American citizen worthy of his noble heritage.

This alert, eager, boisterous spirit has been caught and transferred to his pages by Mr. Stevenson with an art that is beyond admiration. Without losing a point of humour, he has contrived to paint a picture which cannot be said to be exaggerated, and which is through-out sympathetic and attractive. Even when Pinkerton is engaged in his most objectionable speculations and is practising his worst barbarisms and vulgarities our hearts warm to him. At his worst every woman-reader will call him 'a dear' and every man 'a capital good fellow at bottom.' He first appears before us as an art-student in Paris, where he is hopelessly trying to become a painter, not because he has any turn for art, but because he thought his country needed more culture, and his soul burned within him to bring her the gift which would best help ' to build up the type : '—

Pinkerton's parents were from the Old Country ; there, too, I incidentally gathered, he had himself been born, though it was a circumstance he seemed prone to forget. Whether he had run away, or his father had turned him out, I never fathomed ; but about the age of twelve he was thrown upon his own resources. A travelling tin-type photographer picked him up, like a haw out of a hedgerow, on a wayside in New Jersey ; took a fancy to the urchin ; carried him on with him in his wandering life ; taught him all he knew himself—to take tin-types (as well as I can make out) and doubt the Scriptures ; and died at last in Ohio at the corner of a road. ' He was a grand specimen,' cried Pinkerton ; ' I wish you could have seen him, Mr. Dodd. He had an appearance of magnanimity that used to remind me of the patriarchs.' On the death of this random protector the boy inherited the plant and con-tinued the business. ' It was a life I could have chosen, Mr. Dodd ! ' he cried. ' I have been in all the finest scenes of that magnificent continent that we were born to be the heirs of. I wish you could see my collection of tin-types ; I wish I had them here. They were taken for my own pleasure and to be a memento ; and they show Nature in her grandest as well as her gentlest moments.' As he tramped the Western States and Territories, taking tin-types, the boy was continually getting hold of books, good, bad, and indifferent, popular and abstruse, from the novels of Sylvanus Cobb to Euclid's Elements, both of which I found (to my almost equal wonder) he had managed to peruse ; he was taking stock by the way of the people, the products, and the country with an eye unusually observant and a memory unusually retentive ; and he was collecting for himself a body of magnanimous and semi-intellectual nonsense which he supposed to be the natural thoughts and to contain the whole duty of the born American.   To be pure-minded, to be patriotic, to get culture and money with both hands and with [the same irrational fervour—these appeared to be the chief articles of his creed.   In latter days (not of course upon this first occasion) I would sometimes ask him why ; and he had his answer pat. ' To build up the type ! ' he would cry. ' We're all committed to that ; we're all under bond to fulfil the American Type ! Loudon, the hope of the world is there. If we fail, like these old feudal monarchies, what is left ? '

Pinkerton's account of his reasons for taking to art are too good not to be given. He gave them to Loudon Dodd, his American friend, the hero of the novel, who represents the opposite type of American humanity—the hyper-sensitive, over-cultivated type so familiar to us in the novels of Mr. Henry James and Mr. Howells :—

' Was it an old taste ? ' I asked him, ' or a sudden fancy ? ' ' Neither, Mr. Dodd,' he admitted.   ' Of course, I had learned in my tin-typing excursions to glory and exult in the works of God.   But it wasn't that.   I just said to myself, " What is most wanted in my age and country ? More culture and more art," I said ; and I chose the best place, saved my money, and came here to get them.'

As may be imagined, Mr. Pinkerton does not succeed as an artist, and is soon in San Francisco helping ' to build up the type ' by speculating wildly in everything, from brandy to agricultural implements, and in his spare time organising picnics on a commercial basis, buying up old wrecks, and running a variety of mad enterprises with the zeal of a saint and the energy of an election agent. While Pinkerton is thus engaged he generously invites to join him the shy, retiring Loudon Dodd, who has been left on the world by the bankruptcy and death of his father; but who is an artist to his finger-tips, and possessed with that intense horror of publicity and vulgarity which is to be found in the cultivated American. Loudon Dodd, in spite of the shame and agony which are often occasioned him by Pinkerton's vagaries, is devoted to Pinkerton, and Pinkerton worships Loudon Dodd as a person of his type always worships an artist and man of cultivation.

As may be imagined, the juxtaposition of the two men leads to some exceedingly humorous situations. When Loudon Dodd arrives at San Francisco to join his friend he finds the whole city placarded with advertisements announcing a lecture on 'Student Life in Paris, Grave and Gay, by H. Loudon Dodd, the Americo-Parisienne sculptor.' The 'knotted horrors of Americo-Parisienne' and the huge posters with his portrait make poor Dodd almost expire with vexation; but, finding it would break Pinkerton's heart to protest, and that he cannot get him to understand the depth of his objections—'If I had only known you disliked red lettering' was as high as he could rise—Dodd gives in, and consents to read the lecture, which has been written for him by a local pressman, Harry Miller. After that Dodd is gradually drawn into the vortex of Pinkerton's schemes, miserably protesting, but seldom able to do so effectually, because of the latter's feelings, and of his childlike devotion to his friend. Besides, Pinkerton supports Dodd, and how could he be so unchivalrous as to wound the man who cheerfully works to help him. Dodd, however, has no desire to be an idler, and asks his friend to let him work too. This is what he gets :—

'I've got it, Loudon,' Pinkerton at last replied. 'Got the idea on the Potrero cars. Found I hadn't a pencil, borrowed one from the conductor, and figured on it roughly all the way in town. I saw it was the thing at last ; gives you a real show. All your talents and accomplishments come in. Here's a sketch advertisement. Just run your eye over it. "*Sun, Ozone, and Music!* PINKERTON'S HEBDOMADARY PICNICS !" (That's a good, catching phrase, 'hebdomadary,' though it's hard to say. I made a note of it when I was looking in the dictionary how to spell *hectagonal.* "Well, you're a boss word," I said. "Before you're very much older I'll have you in type as long as yourself." And here it is, you see.) "*Five dollars a head, and ladies free.* MONSTER OLIO OF ATTRACTIONS." (How does that strike you ?) "*Free luncheon under the greenwood tree. Dance on the elastic sward. Home again in the Bright Evening Hours. Manager and Honorary Steward, H. Loudon Dodd, Esq., the well-known connoisseur.*" Singular how a man runs from Scylla to Charybdis ! I was so intent on securing the disappearance of a single epithet that I accepted the rest of the advertisement and all that it involved without discussion. So it befell that the words 'well-known connoisseur' were deleted ; but that H. Loudon Dodd became manager and honorary steward of Pinkerton's Hebdomadary Picnics, soon shortened, by popular consent, to The Dromedary. By eight o'clock, any Sunday morning, I was to be observed by an admiring public on the wharf. The garb and attributes of sacrifice consisted of a black frockcoat, rosetted, its pockets bulging with sweatmeats and inferior cigars, rousers of light blue, a silk hat, like a reflector, and a varnished wand. A goodly steamer guarded my one flank, panting and throbbing, flags fluttering fore and aft of her, illustrative of the Dromedary and patriotism. My other flank was covered by the ticket-office, strongly held by a trusty character of the Scots persuasion, rosetted like his superior, and smoking a cigar to mark the occasion festive. At half-past, having assured myself that all was well with the free luncheons, I lit a cigar myself, and awaited the strains of the 'Pioneer Band.' I had never to wait long—they were German and punctual—and by a few minutes after the half-hour I would hear them booming down street with a long military roll of drums, some score of gratuitous asses prancing at the head in bearskin hats and buckskin aprons, and conspicuous with resplendent axes. The band, of course, we paid for ; but so strong is the San Franciscan passion for public masquerade that the asses (as I say) were all gratuitous, pranced for the love of it, and cost us nothing but their luncheon.

We would willingly, had we space, quote more from the delightful half-dozen pages in which the story of the Dromedary Picnics is set forth. We must, however, leave these untouched, and leave also the wonderful picture of the old Scotch jerrybuilder. Mr. Stevenson is always happy in Scotland, but he has seldom done anything better than old Uncle Adam, with his belief in 'stuccy,' in 'plunths,' in the advisability of not paying too much attention to the theory of strains, and in the notion that Portland cement will go a long way if it is properly sanded.

Judged, however, as a whole, the 'Wrecker' is not altogether satisfactory. The character-drawing and the impressions of American and French life are excellent ; but the sensational story on which they are somewhat inartistically superimposed, though good enough as a piece of sensationalism, seems out of place. Here, too, we must make a protest against the shambles business in the last chapter. It is quite unnecessarily brutal. Still, in spite of any and every defect that can be urged against it, the book is in the fullest sense a delightful one, and is capable of giving three or four hours of pure enjoyment to thousands of men and women. Those who have not yet read it are indeed to be envied, almost as much as the man who has never read 'Treasure Island.'

V

MR. STEVENSON'S LAST ROMANCE

FULL of genius and of the glory of letters as is Mr. Stevenson's last romance, it confirms us in the opinion which we have ventured to express above—the opinion that though his novels have so many high qualities, and attract and delight from so many points of view, he was at his best as an essayist rather than as a writer of fiction.

'Weir of Hermiston' contains three or four studies of character which are in their way beyond praise. Our literature has few finer personal portraits than the picture of the hard, cruel, savage old lawyer who gives his name to the book, and who admittedly represents that most ruthless and violent of Judges, Lord Braxfield—the great Scotch Judge who out-Jeffreyed Jeffreys in his manners on the bench, but who was as brave, upright and honest in intent as Jeffreys was cowardly, dishonest, and corrupt. Hardly less striking is his weak, tearful wife, Mrs. Weir, a gentle, ineffectual creature, whose 'philosophy of life was summed in one expression—tenderness.' ' In her view of the universe, which was all lighted up with a glow out of the doors of hell, good people must walk there in a kind of ecstasy of tenderness.' She heard, and in a sense admired, the strenuous Calvinist divinity of her Minister. My Lord sat under him with relish, ' but Mrs. Weir heard him from afar off; heard him (like the cannon of a beleaguered city) usefully booming outside on the dogmatic ramparts ; and meanwhile, within and out of shot, dwelt in her private garden, which she watered with her tears.'

Contrasted with her is the elder Kirstie, the distant cousin, humble in rank though not in character, who fills the post of housekeeper to Mrs. Weir. ' Kirstie was a woman in a thousand, clean, capable, notable ; once a moorland Helen, and still comely as a blood-horse and healthy as the hill wind. High in flesh and voice and colour, she ran the house with her whole intemperate soul in a bustle, not without buffets.' Again, there is her niece, the younger Kirstie, the heroine of the tale, not quite so memorable a person as the aunt, but yet, as heroines go, a wonderful piece of womanhood. Mr. Stevenson, at any rate, never came so near success with a young woman as he does in drawing this wayward, impulsive girl—in love with love, with herself, and with her lover. Even the hero, Lord Hermiston's son, is attractive, though he has to play the difficult and ungrateful part of the high-minded young man. Many are the devices of authors to keep their heroes in virtue and good principle without degenerating into priggishness, and Mr. Stevenson has finely used the best of them. Other well-graced characters throng the book. The moorland brothers of the younger Kirstie, one a yeoman, one a local Burns, and the other a Glasgow merchant, show once again how subtle and how keen was their creator's power to pierce the secrets of human nature.

But the moral situations of the book are not less good than the characters. Mr. Stevenson touches finely the old and never-ending conflict between youth and age, between high and noble aspirations and hard, un-impassioned experience, between hot enthusiasm and cold worldly wisdom. We all know the tragedy of the son, who thinks, with tears of shame and misery, that his father cares nothing for the only things that matter in the world, high principle and truth and justice, and the father who regards his son as a weak, hare-brained idiot. To each the attitude of the other is an insult, and each feels that the other has wantonly wounded him to the heart. But 'to be wroth with one we love will work like madness in the brain,' and hence these quarrels, whatever their merits or excuse, are among the most terrible that man's heart can endure. Mr. Stevenson lays bare to us such a quarrel, and moralises it for us as he goes. With a rare, and in this case helpful, art he gives us the case for the older man. He shows us how the son is at last convinced that, after all, the duty of not quarrelling with a father who confessedly is not a mean or corrupt man is greater than the supposed sacred duty of violently championing certain of those great abstract principles of right and justice which seem worth the whole world to the fiery and feverish brain of youth. This episode is finely handled throughout. Lord Hermiston's son goes into Court and sees his father engaged in the, to him, most congenial task of 'hunting gallowsward with jeers' a poor, mean-spirited, trembling, commonplace criminal. The description of the Judge, and indeed of the whole trial, could not be better. After describing 'the panel'—*i.e.* the prisoner—Mr. Stevenson continues :—

Over against him my Lord Hermiston occupied the bench in the red robes of criminal jurisdiction, his face framed in the white wig.   Honest all through, he did not affect the virtue of impartiality ; this was no case for refinement ; there was a man to be hanged, he would have said, and he was hanging him.   Nor was it possible to see his lordship and acquit him of gusto in the task.   It was plain he gloried in the exercise of his trained faculties, in the clear sight which pierced at once into the joint of fact, in the rude, unvarnished gibes with which he demolished every figment of defence.   He took his ease and jested, unbending in that solemn place with some of the freedom of the tavern ; and the rag of man with the flannel round his neck was hunted gallowsward with jeers . . . The summing up contained some jewels. 'These two peetiable creatures [the criminal and the woman who betrays him] seem to have made up thegither, it's not for us to explain why.'—'The panel, who, (whatever else he may be) appears to be equally ill set-out in mind and boady.'—'Neither the panel nor yet the old wife appears to have had so much common sense as even to tell a lie when it was necessary.' And, in the course of sentencing, my lord had this *obiter dictum* : 'I have been the means, under God, of haanging a great number, but never just such a disjaskit rascal as yourself.' The words were strong in themselves ; the light and heat and detonation of their delivery and the savage pleasure of the speaker in his task made them tingle in the ears.

This hideous scene makes a terrible impression upon the Judge's son, Archie Weir, and when the day of execution comes he gives vent to wild words, denouncing the execution as a 'God-defying murder,' and afterwards makes a scene in a college debating society in regard to capital punishment in general. Of course, there is a scandal, and Lord Hermiston and his son have a deadly quarrel. In the course of the quarrel, however, Archie is made to see his fault by the kindly Lord Glenalmond— one of Lord Hermiston's brother judges, who, though his sympathies are with Archie, has a deep respect for the upright but savage man of the world. The talk between the man and the boy is quite delightful :—

'I could never deny,' he [Archie] began—'I mean I can conceive that some men would be better dead. But who are we to know all the springs of God's unfortunate creatures? who are we to trust ourselves where it seems that God Himself must think twice before He treads, and to do it with delight? Yes, with delight. *Tigris ut aspera.*'—'Perhaps not a pleasant spectacle,' said Glenalmond. 'And yet, do you know, I think somehow a great one.'—'I've had a long talk with him to-night,' said Archie.—'I was supposing so,' said Glenalmond.—'And he struck me—I cannot deny that he struck me as something very big,' pursued the son. 'Yes, he is big. He never spoke about himself ; only about me. I suppose I admired him. The dreadful part——'—'Suppose we did not talk about that,' interrupted Glenalmond. 'You know it very well, it cannot in any way help that you should brood upon it, and I sometimes wonder whether you and I—who are a pair of sentimentalists—are quite good judges or plain men.'—'How do you mean?' asked Archie.—'*Fair* judges, I mean,' replied Glenalmond. 'Can we be just to them? Do we not ask too much? There was a word of yours just now that impressed me a little when you asked me who we were to know all the springs of God's unfortunate creatures. You applied that, as I understood, to capital cases only. But does it—I ask myself

—does it not apply all through? Is it any less difficult to judge of a good man or of a half-good man than of the worst criminal at the bar? And may not each have relevant excuses?'—'Ah, but we do not talk of punishing the good,' cried Archie.— 'No, we do not talk of it,' said Glenalmond. 'But I think we do it. Your father, for instance.'—'You think I have punished him?' cried Archie. Lord Glenalmond bowed his head. 'I think I have,' said Archie. 'And the worst is, I think he feels it! How much, who can tell, with such a being? But I think he does.'—'And I am sure of it,' said Glenalmond.—'Has he spoken to you, then?' cried Archie.— 'O no,' replied the judge.—'I tell you honestly,' said Archie, 'I want to make it up to him. I will go, I have already pledged myself to go to Hermiston. That was to him. And now I pledge myself to you, in the sight of God, that I will close my mouth on capital punishment and all other subjects where our views may clash, for—how long shall I say? when shall I have sense enough?—ten years. Is that well?'—'It is well,' said my lord.—'As far as it goes,' said Archie. 'It is enough as regards myself; it is to lay down enough of my con- ceit. But as regards him, whom I have publicly insulted? What am I to do to him? How do you pay attentions to a —an Alp like that?'—'Only in one way,' replied Glenalmond. 'Only by obedience, punctual, prompt, and scrupulous.'— 'And I promise that he shall have it,' answered Archie. 'I offer you my hand in pledge of it.'

Surely a subtler and yet more helpful homily on the command 'Judge not' was never written. One could not do better than set a young man or woman bent on fighting a commonplace or a harsh parent to study that dialogue.

We cannot here follow the rest of the story or tell how the elder Kirstie half breaks her stormy heart over Archie, of how he and the younger Kirstie fall in love at first sight, or of how the villain of the piece comes on the stage. Nor, again, can we attempt to describe where the story leaves off or to discuss what was the ending intended for the tale. Our readers will find that out for themselves while enjoying a noble fragment of true literature. But though, as we have shown, there is so much good drawing of character and so many artful and stimulating situations in the book, the story is somehow or other not the success it ought to be. It is like those pictures in which the drawing, the colour, and the intention are alike excellent, and yet the work as a whole is disappointing. Whether, if Mr. Stevenson had lived, he would for the first time in his career have conquered this difficulty of composition, and have at last brought a story to perfection, it is of course impossible to say. It is conceivable that he might have done so. If he had, he would have produced a novel as great as anything in Scott, for of the stuff of which great novels are made here is enough and to spare. The parts of the tale are as near perfection as may be. We fear, however, that he would have failed in this drawing together of the material, this co-relating of the parts to the whole, this interfusion of a general harmony.

It is, indeed, this quality of harmoniousness which is lacking in 'The Master of Ballantrae,' in 'Catriona,' and in all Mr. Stevenson's other novels. That it is also lacking in 'Weir of Hermiston' is, we suspect, an essential, not an accidental, defect. But to say that this last work of a man of rare genius is not perfect is not to condemn it. It is full of a thousand things that stir the fancy and spur the imagination. The words, as in every great work of literature, are brimming over with meaning, and hurry us along in a torrent of eager and excited interest.

One more quotation we will give to exhibit this swift attraction of Mr. Stevenson's manner, here at its best. The last chapter describes a misunderstanding between Archie and his love.   He has to tell her that they must not see each other so often because people are beginning to talk.   Of course he does it very badly, and of course she resents his words as an insult:—

The schoolmaster that there is in all men, to the despair of all girls and most women, was now completely in possession of Archie.   He had passed a night of sermons, a day of reflection ; he had come wound up to do his duty ; and the set mouth, which in him only betrayed the effort of his will, to her seemed the expression of an averted heart.   It was the same with his constrained voice and embarrassed utterance ; and if so—if it was all over—the pang of the thought took away from her the power of thinking.   He stood before her some way off.   ' Kirstie, there's been too much of this.   We've seen too much of each other.'   She looked up quickly and her eyes contracted.   ' There's no good ever comes of these secret meetings.   They're not frank, not honest truly, and I ought to have seen it.   People have begun to talk ; and it's not right of me.   Do you see ? '—' I see somebody will have been talking to ye,' she said sullenly.—' They have, more than one of them,' replied Archie.—' And whae were they ? ' she cried.   ' And what kind o' love do ye ca' that, that's ready to gang round like a whirligig at folk talking ?   Do you think they havena talked to me ? '—' Have they indeed ? ' said Archie, with a quick breath.   ' That is what I feared.   Who are they ?   Who has dared———— ? '   Archie was on the point of losing his temper.   As a matter of fact, not any one had talked to Christina on the matter ; and she strenuously repeated her own first question in a panic of self-defence.   ' Ah, well ! what does it matter ? ' he said.   ' They were good folk that wished well to us, and the great affair is that there are people talking. My dear girl, we have to be wise.   We must not wreck our lives at the outset. They may be long and happy yet, and we must see to it, Kirstie, like God's rational creatures, and not like fool children. There is one thing we must see to before all. You're worth waiting for, Kirstie !—worth waiting for for a generation ; it would be enough reward.' And here he remembered the schoolmaster again, and very unwisely took to following wisdom. 'The first thing that we must see to is that there shall be no scandal about, for my father's sake. That would ruin all ; do ye no see that ?' Kirstie was a little pleased ; there had been some show of warmth of sentiment in what Archie had said last. But the dull irritation still persisted in her bosom ; with the aboriginal instinct, having suffered herself, she wished to make Archie suffer.

How difficult to bring out the inner meaning of such a situation, and to give their true value to the moral forces of the scene ! Yet how perfectly the work has been accomplished ! Assuredly the man who wrote this, even if he was not a great novelist, was among the greatest of writers.

———

VI

Mr. Louis Stevenson on Art

If a Roman patrician had been asked his opinion of the arts, and of the artists who work in words, in marble, or in pigments, the spirit of his reply would have been just that given by Mr. Louis Stevenson in his 'Letter to a Young Gentleman who proposes to embrace the Career of Art,' though doubtless the Roman would not have clothed his thoughts with a perfection of form such as the readers of English prose had hardly seen before the author of 'Kidnapped' elaborated, with skill consummate and complete, his golden gift of words. The

Roman feeling about Art was peculiar, and in absolute contrast to that of the Greeks. The Greek looked upon the poet, the sculptor, and the painter as obeying an impulse in its nature sacred. To him they were God-inspired men, and their work was a gift to the world which entitled them to veneration and respect as great as that bestowed upon the soldier or the statesman. To the Roman, on the other hand, neither poet nor artist was, in truth, aught but a skilled artificer—the cunning workman who with his ingenuity pleased either the mind or the eye. However great the skill, and however admirable and delightful the work produced, it could not raise the producer above the ranks of those who live merely to provide pleasure for others. To follow art seemed to the Romans in no sense a manly way of life, and no artist could, by excellence in his art, ever claim the praise and glory reserved for the generals, the lawgivers, or the rulers of men. To live to please —for in the artist's work they recognised nothing but the desire to please—appeared to them a sort of intellectual prostitution unworthy of a man.

This, apparently, was exactly Mr. Louis Stevenson's feeling. In the essay just mentioned he entirely accepts the Roman view, admits that the artist is nothing but the cunning artificer, and declares ' the end of all art is to please.' The artist, he says, must never forget this fact, nor must he fail to give the public what they want. If he is ' of a mind so independent that he cannot stoop to this necessity,' let him ' follow some more manly way of life.' ' I speak,' continues Mr. Stevenson, ' of a more manly way of life ; it is a point on which I must be frank. To live by pleasure is not a high calling ; it involves patronage, however veiled; it numbers the artist, how-ever ambitious, along with dancing-girls and billiard-markers. The French have a romantic evasion for one employment, and call its practitioners the Daughters of Joy. The artist is of the same family ; he is of the Sons of Joy, chose his trade to please himself, gains his liveli-hood by pleasing others, and has parted with something of the sterner dignity of man.'

Such is Mr. Stevenson's view, expressed with all the lucidity and directness which he knows well how to employ, and intended essentially to include the poet, for he singles out Lord Tennyson as a typical Son of Joy. Doubtless Mr. Stevenson was very proud of his frankness, and thought himself specially to be commended because he entertained no ' illusions ' on the subject of his art, though they might easily be so flattering to himself. Yet, for all that, Mr. Stevenson was entirely wrong, and his lucidity of language hides by refraction a very certain truth that lies below. The old Roman view is altogether false, and as barbarous as it is untrue. The Greek notion, the Hebrew notion—the prophet was the poet of the Jews—and the notion of the Teutonic races—the bards and the singers of the Eddas were as much esteemed as men as any jarl or viking—is the true one, as it is the noble one. The great poet or the great painter is as much a man as the warrior or the statesman.

But what, then, led so astute a critic as Mr. Louis Stevenson wrong, and what has made so many men of the present day dimly entertain and express the same feeling? The cause of the mistake is not very far to seek. Like all fundamental errors, its origin is simple enough. If the end of all art is merely to please, as

Mr. Stevenson supposes, then no doubt the men who live by pleasing alone are mere Sons of Joy. But to please is not the end of all art. Mr. Stevenson has confounded the end with the means. The means by which all the arts pursue their end must without question please; and the artist who attempts to work in any medium which does not in itself please will not produce a work of art. Pleasing, in a word, is the material in which the artist works. For pleasing to be the means of all art is, however, a very different thing from pleasing being the end of all art. The poet has something to tell the world, something which may neither please nor displease, something which is totally aloof from these conceptions. What he says, however, is said in a way which, if he is a true poet, will inevitably appeal to those sensations which we term pleasurable.

But though no man is a poet whose work does not please, the real poet has an end beyond the successful manipulation of the medium of his art. Doubtless many successful artists in words, like the painters of arabesques, the decorators of china vases, or the illuminators of the margins of the missals, never get beyond this perfection of their means—are content with merely using their pigments to their full advantage. The great artist, however, never stops here. He is solicitous beyond expression that the means he employs shall be used to perfection in order that the message to mankind which the song, the marble, the canvas, or the orchestra is to bear shall be conveyed with full effect; but to say, therefore, that to please is the end of Art is an absolute and total misconception.

Perhaps the best example of the great conscious artist in our literature is Milton. Milton never gave a line of verse, to the world on which he had not bestowed the most passionate labour. We may personally approve or condemn his style, but there can be no doubt that he endeavoured, with all the power of his sane and eager genius, to make his work please. Yet Milton would have scouted as an outrage on his art the notion that its end was merely to give pleasure. He recognised fully that the poet could only appeal to the world through a pleasure-giving medium, and that therefore poetry must please—did not Milton speak of 'poetry which is simple, sensuous, passionate,' the very constituent elements of pleasure ?—but he did not therefore fall into the error that the end of poetry was to please. Instead, when he said that the poet who would write worthily must make his life a true poem, he saw clearly that the end of his art, as of all the others, was in its highest conception to quicken men's minds to life, to raise them in intellectual stature, to console, to ennoble, to make life harmonious, and to give rest and peace to the soul. No ; the conception of the artist in words as the mere purveyor of pleasure is utterly impossible. And not only is the poet the harmoniser of life. He is not seldom in effect the doer of deeds—the man through whom action is, if not himself the man of action. Lord Tennyson, whom Mr. Stevenson instances as a Son of Joy, has said, and said truly—

> And here the singer for his art
>   Not all in vain may plead ;
> The song that nerves a nation's heart
>   Is in itself a deed.

No doubt we shall be told by those who cannot endure to give up the notion that all art is decorative meant only to please, and its end accomplished when the sensation of pleasure is aroused, that our separation of means and ends is not philosophical, and that we are beating the air with empty words and being misled with phrases. Still we are content. If we are wrong, at least we are wrong in good company, with Shelley and Sir Philip Sidney. Our fallacy, if it is one, is as old as the world, and likely to last as long, for, fortunately, if even the great artists grow infected with the heresy their works will give the lie to their theory.

Such, heaven be praised! is the saving grace of the highest art, that the man it inspires says often to those who hear him more than he actually purposes or intends. The inspiration of Art makes the artist, like the Pythoness at Delphi, speak all unconsciously the very words of God. Even Mr. Stevenson himself, though doubtless he is generally only a decorative artist, a worker in arabesque and cunning ornamentation rather than an artist who acts with a conscious purpose higher than that of using his medium to perfection, often unconsciously rises through the consummate perfection of his word-craft beyond the region of the mere Sons of Joy, and gives his hearers something far more real than pleasure. His single-hearted loyalty to his art and the sincerity and righteousness with which he obeys its commands make, for those who can see below the surface, the contemplation of his work an ennobling example of devotion to an ideal.

After all there is no better lesson a man can teach the world than that of obeying, without question and without reserve, the dictates of something spiritual and external to himself. This lesson the loyal artist teaches, even if he be unconscious of it. Thus Mr. Stevenson often denies his own assertion, and, discovering—to borrow Charles Lamb's illuminating phrase—'a right line in obliquity,' disproves that 'the end of all art is to please.' Let our readers turn to the Essay from which we have quoted—'A Letter to a Young Gentleman who proposes to embrace the Career of Art'—and they will find examples of what we mean. They will find there also many manly and many sensible things—for Mr. Stevenson's art is manly, whatever he may say.

EDGAR ALLAN POE

THE first thing which strikes one strongly in reading Poe in the mass is the extraordinary number of new artifices originated by him—artifices which were almost at once imitated and made the common property of writers of novels and stories, but which had never before been used, or, at any rate, systematically developed.   To no other man in the realms of romance has it been given to strike out so many new lines.   Not only was his genius prolific in itself, but it had the power in a high degree of rendering others prolific.

It is worth while to set out in order some examples of the new forms originated by Poe.   To begin with, he was the inventor of the 'detective novel,' which, in the hands of Wilkie Collins, Gaboriau, Du Boisgobey, and later Dr. Conan Doyle, has enchanted so many minds, and, as Mr. Andrew Lang sings, has sweetened many a weary mile of railway travel.   'The Murders in the Rue Morgue,' 'The Mystery of Marie Roget,' and the 'Purloined Letter' are perfect examples of the detective story.   There is in them all that literary chess-playing which so delights us in Wilkie Collins, and in them too we may find the prototype, or rather archi-type, of the famous Sherlock Holmes.   Poe's claim to have originated the novel of scientific imagination is equally good. Jules Verne's happy knack of mixing up the most daring flights of imagination with large doses of popular science was first worked out by Poe, and with wonderful success, in 'The Adventure of One Hans Pfaall.' Here the method of narrative is exactly that adopted thirty years later in 'The Journey to the Centre of the Earth' or 'The Voyage of the Nautilus.'

Another form of modern romance which may be said to have been originated by Poe is the type of story which is half a tale of travel and adventure in savage lands and half a tale of the marvellous. Mr. Rider Haggard, in books like 'She' and 'Allan Quatermain,' is the most conspicuous user of this form, but there have, of course, been hundreds of others who, though less successfully, have written of strange and magical peoples in unknown lands. In the 'Narrative of A. Gordon Pym' we get just this mixture. The end of this romance indeed, to put the cart before the horse, reads exactly like a piece out of one of Mr. Haggard's books. Very possibly Mr. Haggard never read the book ; but, even if he has not, it has affected him through the atmosphere of modern fiction. In the same way, consciously or unconsciously, Mr. Louis Stevenson was indebted to Poe for many of his most striking ideas. He did not, of course, plagiarise Poe any more than did Mr. Haggard, but cut many a graft from the fruitful stem of the American journalist. 'The Gold Bug,' with its memories of Kidd and his treasures, its Bishop's Hostel, and its map and cryptic directions, unquestionably suggested part of the machinery of 'Treasure Island,' though of course Mr. Stevenson infinitely improved what he borrowed.

Poe again originated what, for want of a better name, we must call the psychical story. 'William Wilson' is nothing like as good a story or as striking a piece of literature as the tale of Hyde and Jekyll, but its author's claim to have invented the method used by Mr. Stevenson is clear. Poe may, again, claim to have been before M. Zola or Flaubert in developing the realistic method. In nothing was he more skilful than in a minute and elaborate parade of detail, supported by a technical terminology exactly appropriate to the matter in hand, which gave an atmosphere of reality and of closeness to the object.

One might easily pile up other examples of the originating character of Poe's genius. He invented the romantic short story in which, though the hero and the other characters are modern men, they move in a dim world of crumbling castles and demoniac ladies, and hear, through magic casements opening on misty lakes, the thunders of the storm and the cries of the dying; while even above the roar of the tempest is heard the mutter of ancestral voices bewailing the ruin of their line. Such tales have been tried by many imitators in France and England; but in these strange, fantastic, and somewhat stagey horrors, Poe has always remained supreme. Those who have borrowed the light have never succeeded in making it burn the brighter, or, rather, with a more livid intensity of green and blue.

Lastly, in the matter of tales of pure horror, Poe was a pioneer. He first used, with anything like consciousness or success, the once effective but now somewhat threadbare artifice of suggesting a shame, a horror, a crime, too terrible, too awful for words. It must be confessed that Poe was extremely successful in his suggestions of the nameless horror. By taking care to be very specific in his narration as regards everything in his description of the room or the scene except the thing he does not describe, he contrives to create an atmosphere of reality which greatly heightens the effect. The bungler makes all misty and vague. Poe narrows his vagueness down to the one point where he must be vague. Of course the nameless, indescribable horror is only a literary conjuring trick. Still, Poe does the trick with great ability.

Though we have not been able to go deep enough into the matter to show the total sum of the debt which modern fiction owes to Poe, we have said enough to show how extraordinarily prolific was his genius in the work of originating new forms and new ideas in the art of narrative. After the question, ' Whom did Poe influence ? ' comes the question, ' Who influenced Poe ? ' There are, of course, many traces in his work of his readings among the mystical German books of the seventeenth and eighteenth centuries, and of our own writers during those periods. The problem we desire to solve, however, is not so much, ' whom did Poe borrow from ? ' as ' what greater writers of former times influenced him in style and thought ? '

Our own opinion, though we give it with diffidence, is that De Quincey, Swift, and Defoe affected him more deeply than any others. It is impossible not to notice how constantly he falls into De Quincey's way of attacking the subject of his thought. There is the same parade of his forces, the same pompous marshalling of the terminology appropriate to the occasion.

If the doctor prescribes quinine,—'Jesuit's bark is exhibited.' Again, the trick of describing some queer abnormal state of mind half in the language of the faculty and half in that of the metaphysicians is directly the result of De Quincey's teaching. Poe was also clearly influenced a good deal both by Swift and by Defoe. It is true that he was usually more florid in his use of words than either of these writers, but not seldom he shows that the benefits they conferred upon our tongue were fully appreciated by him. In the travel stories there are indeed plenty of passages where the debt to Swift is most obvious.

Before we leave the subject of Poe's tales we must take care to point out that when we insist upon the original character of Poe's genius we do not mean to represent his name as one of the great names in our literature. In spite of his gift of originating, of his intense love of beauty in all its forms, in spite of his mastery over language—his style was at once precise and melodious, clear and yet hauntingly suggestive of hidden things—and in spite, too, of his power to avail himself of human knowledge and human experience in every form, his stories cannot be said to be really great as literature. They may dazzle or horrify or amaze for a moment, but of permanent delight they contain little or nothing. What is the reason?

The reason is, we believe, to be found in the fact that Poe's tales contain nothing of true human interest. They never touch the heart or even the mind in the highest sense. At their best they move, or rather bewilder, the emotions, but that is all. With all his genius, Poe's characters move one less than the heroes

and heroines of the most ordinary three-volume novel.
His are not men and women, but phantoms seen in the
red glare of an unwholesome imagination. He cannot,
as could Mr. Stevenson, make Jekyll and Hyde real
persons. The two William Wilsons in their fur cloaks
'come like shadows, so depart.' And hence Poe's
tales, though so full of invention and of thick-coming
fancies, of ingenious surprises, of brilliant execution, and
of literary *tours de force*, in the end weary the reader.
He feels that he is marching over a desert of dry
sand. It is true that the sand is thickly specked with
gold, that the mysteries of eve and of the dawn are
with him, and that the mirage shows him its cloud-
capped towers, its shining castles, and its glowing
pageants of woods, wastes, and waters. It is not
enough. He thirsts for the running streams, for the
kindly works of men and oxen, for the wholesome faces
of human creatures, and the homely charities of the
green earth. Better the dullest, simplest, old-world
story than these terrible phantasmagoria.

Of course certain of Poe's tales will always be read
with delight for their ingenuity of plot and dexterity of
style ; but Poe can never hold even a second place
among the band which numbers Scott and Miss Austen,
Dickens and Thackeray—the sacred band of those who
have made life brighter and more interesting by
quickening human feeling and revealing man to himself
by insight and sympathy.

THE MELODY OF PROSE

To a carefully trained or to a naturally sensitive ear there is often a beauty of rhythm in prose as powerful as the most exquisite in verse. Indeed, on some natures the perfect harmony of the prose period produces an effect such as no measured cadence can ever achieve. Not that prose, however melodious, can affect the emotions or stimulate the imagination as poetry can. Only when the mere beauty of concordant or contrasted sounds is considered in isolation and apart from the higher emotional forces is it true that prose is capable of higher harmonies than verse. But if the supreme rhythm of prose is higher than the rhythms of verse, so is it far less common. The inner mystery has been divulged to few, and those few, save on rare occasions of inspiration, have been unable to cast the spell. Like the crowning accomplishment in all other arts, it can be better illustrated than defined.

That there is something divergent, almost antagonistic, to measure in the higher prose melody, is shown in the fact that the poets, however skilful in prose, have never quite reached it. Milton's poetry is beyond that of all others filled with the magnificent concord of sweet sounds ; but in his prose, splendid and sonorous as it is, we never find the true gem. The matrix is there, but swing; and in the 'Morte d'Arthur' there are a considerable number of passages of pleasant sound, but, taken as a whole, the higher harmony is entirely absent.   Maundeville's writings, too, have often a certain quaint melodiousness.   His description of the abbey of monks near the City of Camsay, where is the fair garden full of divers beasts, and where 'every day, when the monks have eaten, the almoner carries what remains to the garden, and strikes on the garden gate with a silver clicket that he holds in his hand, and anon all the beasts of the hill and of divers places of the garden come out to the number of three or four thousand,' is not without suggestions of great beauty.

The earlier writers are to a great extent debarred from the happiest effects by the use of an unvaried rhythm, which produces the same effect on the ear as measure, and so robs them of those changes which are essential to the best prose.   In the Romances, and in Lily the Euphuist, this is easily seen, and, though less marked, it is present in Latimer and Sidney, in Bacon and Isaak Walton.   Hooker, indeed, conquered the monotony; but he is content with clearing the stream of thought from affectations and obscurities, and with developing a style of eloquence and imagination. With Jeremy Taylor and Sir Thomas Browne there is, again, a monotony of cadence, though a beautiful monotony.

In the great writers of the end of the seventeenth and beginning of the eighteenth century the melody we seek for is not to be found.   Dryden and Swift, Pope and Addison had enough to do to make their style completely flexible and perspicuous.   They did all that was needed to render the instrument complete, but left it for others to draw from it its most perfect tones. Though Bolingbroke woke here and there a faint prelude, it was reserved for the nameless and mysterious writer of the greatest political satires that the world has ever seen first to achieve success. If Chatham could tell William Pitt to study 'Junius' as his model, and Coleridge give such great, if not unqualified, praise, there is no need for an apology for such a contention. When 'Junius' banters the Duke of Grafton on his connection with the University of Cambridge, and tells him that its admiration will cease with office, it is impossible not to recognise that a new element is present in English prose style :—

Whenever the spirit of distributing prebends and bishoprics shall have departed from you you will find that learned seminary perfectly recovered from the delirium of an Installation, and, what in truth it ought to be, once more a peaceful scene of slumber and thoughtless meditation. The venerable tutors of the University will no longer distress your modesty by proposing you for a pattern to their pupils. The learned dullness of declamation will be silent ; and even the venal Muse, though happiest in fiction, will forget your virtues.

The fall of the last sentence is, for sound, indeed, inimitable. Contemporary with, or somewhat earlier than 'Junius,' there are, however, writers whose work is capable of rhythms almost as melodious. There is Sterne, with the reflection on Uncle Toby's oath :—

The accusing spirit which flew up to Heaven's Chancery with the oath blushed as he gave it in, and the recording angel, as he wrote it down, dropped a tear upon the word and blotted it out for ever.

And, far deeper in sentiment, there is Johnson's lament in the preface to the dictionary, where he tells the story of his book, written ' not in the soft obscurities of retirement, or under the shelter of academic bowers, but amidst inconveniences and distractions, in sickness and in sorrow : '—

If the embodied critics of France, when fifty years had been spent upon their work, were obliged to change its economy, and give their second edition another form, I may surely be contented without the praise of perfection, which, if I could obtain in this gloom of solitude, what would it avail me ?   I have protracted my work till most of those whom I wished to please have sunk into the grave, and success and miscarriage are empty sounds.   I therefore dismiss it with frigid tranquillity, having little to fear or hope from censure or from praise.

Of course, Johnson did not always write like this. Too often the exquisite melody of such a phrase as ' this gloom of solitude' is exchanged for the mechanical, organ-grinding tones of the ' Rambler.' Personal feelings always inspired him.   He gets the same ring in the letter to Lord Chesterfield and in the passage on ' Paradise Lost,' where he is, in truth, comparing Milton's life with his own.

When Burke's hand touches the instrument, whatever of rigidity belonged to Johnson vanishes.   The passages in which the finer melody is found satisfy the ear as does De Quincey's best work.   For instance :—

Their prey is lodged in England ; and the cries of India are given to the seas and winds, to be blown about, at every breaking up of the monsoon, over a remote and unhearing ocean.

Or :—

Here the manufacturer and the husbandman will bless the just and punctual hand that in India has torn the cloth from the loom or wrested the scanty portion of rice and salt from the peasant of Bengal, or wrung from him the very opium in which he forgot his oppressions and his oppressor.

With the orators who were Burke's contemporaries it is not our purpose to deal, since the imperfect manner in which their speeches were reported makes it impossible to do them justice. Gibbon, then, next claims consideration. It is too much the fashion in these days to sneer at Gibbon's prose as monotonous and stilted. Yet, in truth, it was capable of great beauty of development. What could be more harmonious than the reflection on Julian at Paris ?—

If Julian could now revisit the capital of France he might converse with men of science and genius capable of understanding and of instructing a disciple of the Greeks ; he might excuse the lively and graceful follies of a nation whose martial spirit has never been enervated by the indulgence of luxury ; and he must applaud the perfection of that inestimable art which softens and refines and embellishes the intercourse of social life.

This has a serenity of cadence almost equal to the account, in the ' Autobiography,' of the writing of the last page of the last chapter of the ' Decline and Fall.' Yet neither can compare for beauty of sound with the final sentence of the well-known criticism of the consequences of the Reformation :—

The predictions of the Catholics are accomplished : the web of mystery is unravelled by the Arminians, Arians, and Socinians ; and the pillars of Revelation are shaken by those men who preserve the name without the substance of religion, who indulge the license without the temper of philosophy.

With the great prose writers of the beginning of the present century it is impossible to deal in detail. In many of them the true melody of prose, as we have attempted to show it by illustration, is present. In one of the greatest, if not the best known, it is easily discovered. Sir William Napier, in the 'History of the War in the Peninsula,' shows that he was a man blessed with an unusually fine ear for prose style. His description of the advance of the English infantry at the close of the Battle of Albuera is unrivalled :—

Nothing could stop that astonishing infantry. No sudden burst of undisciplined valour, no nervous enthusiasm weakened the stability of their order, their flashing eyes were bent on the dark columns in their front, their measured tread shook the ground, their dreadful volleys swept away the head of every formation, their deafening shouts overpowered the dissonant cries that broke from all parts of the tumultuous crowd, as slowly, and with a horrid carnage, it was pushed by the incessant vigour of the attack to the furthest edge of the height. There the French Reserve mixed with the struggling multitude and endeavoured to sustain the fight ; but the effort only increased the irremediable confusion ; the mighty mass gave way, and, like a loosened cliff, went headlong down the steep. The rain flowed after in streams discoloured with blood, and eighteen hundred unwounded men, the remnant of six thousand unconquerable British soldiers, stood triumphant on the fatal hill !

If for no other purpose than that of contrast, we might put side by side with this a passage from another military historian, whose work is among the best of histories in the English language, and is only not a classic because it is overwhelmed by the public ignorance of all things Indian. Captain Grant Duff's ' History of the Mahrattas ' contains a description of the advance of the Peshwa's army on the morning of the Battle of Kirkee which, for charm of literary skill, it is difficult to match, but which is just too elaborate for quotation. Instead we will quote his friend's account of a Mahratta charge. Mountstuart Elphinstone had himself admired the magnificence of the Mahratta onset, had witnessed ' the thunder of the ground, the flashing of their arms, the brandishing of their spears, the agitation of their banners rushing through the wind.'

In our own generation Mr. Ruskin is among the. most melodious of prose writers. One of Mr. Ruskin's happiest efforts is a description of Southern Italy :—

Silent villages, earthquake-shaken, without commerce, without industry, without knowledge, without hope, gleam in white ruin from hillside to hillside ; far-winding wrecks of immemorial walls surround the dust of cities long forsaken ; the mountain streams moan through the cold arches of their foundations, green with weed, and rage over the heaps of their fallen towers. Far above in thunder-blue serration stand the eternal edges of the angry Apennine, dark with rolling impendence of volcanic cloud.

A man who has written a passage such as this may claim to be forgiven any number of literary weaknesses and follies.

To write of melodious prose and not to quote from Newman or Carlyle seems an anomaly. The clear and liquid cadences of the one and the picturesque magnificence of the other have on some ears an effect hardly to be obtained from any other writing. To illustrate these qualities one has only to recall the passage on music from the ' University Sermons ' or the close of the ' Life of Sterling.'   A reference to the enchantments of the style of either passage must, however, suffice.

Among the orators of our time Mr. Bright alone can claim to have produced melodious prose.   The perorations of his speeches are indeed distinguished by a remarkable sweetness of cadence.

So inadequate and so hasty an attempt to exhibit by quotation the melody of English prose seems to need some apology.   Let us hope that those who know and love our literature will not be displeased to see the favourites of their reading quoted as they have been here ; and that they will pardon the omissions and the rejections.   In one respect at least our inquiry cannot be distasteful, for it serves to remind us how splendid, how wide, and how various is the field of English prose.

WILLIAM BARNES

THE Rev. William Barnes (known, where he was known at all, as the ' Dorsetshire Poet '), though he died at the age of ninety, cannot be said to have outlived his fame, for fame, in the sense of popularity or worldly applause, he never attained.   A little notoriety as the quaint preserver of an English dialect he no doubt did at one time achieve ; and a little curiosity among those who hunt for literary oddities was excited by the poet of the West Country vicarage who poured out from a full heart the love songs of a peasantry just losing their own character and sinking to the dull level of the English ' lower class.'   Beyond this his general reputation has not reached.

But though fame, in the sense of a recognition wide and popular, was not gained by Mr. Barnes, he nevertheless obtained for his songs what was to him perhaps more valued and more coveted—first, the appreciation of the simple folk among whom he lived, and then the sincere praise of that small circle of readers of verse who, though they cannot give popularity, yet know the true gold of poetry, and whose applause, once secured, ensure that the poet's works shall never utterly die. William Barnes's verse will always find an echo in the heart that is really open to the poet's voice.   He is not a poet because he writes in dialect; not merely note-worthy because he seized on what was beautiful in peasant life and expressed it in song. He, like Burns must have been a poet, in whatever language he had written, and whatever had been his theme. It happened that to the one the tongue of the Scotch Lowlands, to the other that of Dorsetshire and the West, was native ; but both are poets by a tenure, if not as great, at least as free and as secure as that of Shakespeare himself.

The Dorsetshire poet, again, like Burns, did not put on his dialect to sing in. It was the language of his daily life. In it he preached to the villagers in the parish church. In it he thought and spoke just as did the men and women with whom he mixed and with whom he peopled his songs.

To certain people, no doubt, the ' z's ' and ' w's ' of the poems simply cause a laugh. To them the refrain ' Lwonesome woodlands ! zunny woodlands ! ' or ' They evenèns in the twilight ' are nothing but ridiculous. To others the poems are merely a closed book. They see that some spirit of song is awake in the verses, but they cannot catch the music. The words are harsh and strange, and they dread the effort necessary to break through the hard rind and reach the mellow fruit within ; and very naturally, for the effort to like or understand is the death of pleasure. With the first class, the people who simply find the ' Poems of Rural Life ' laughable, it is useless to argue. We can only exclaim, with the despairing diplomatist obliged to associate with a minister more than ordinarily thick-headed, pompous, and opinionated—' Il est impossible de causer avec un mon-sieur comme ça.' It is not, however, mere waste of breath to try to get the others—those who think they cannot understand the dialect, and are terrified by it as they are by broad Scotch—to see his beauties.

The two especial merits of William Barnes's poetry, beyond its extreme dexterity of handling, grace and felicity of expression, and unforced music, are the wonderfully truthful painting of West Country scenery and the tenderness, the pathos, and the joy echoing delight with which he touches the loves and sorrows of simple country folk. To show the quality of his verse by quotation is almost impossible. It is necessary to read widely to feel the full enchantment of his numbers. The first stanza of the poem called ' The Love Child ' is exquisite in its quiet simplicity :—

> Where the bridge out at Woodley did stride
>   Wi' his wide arches' cool, sheäded bow,
> Up above the clear brook that did slide
>   By the popples befoamed white as snow :
> As the gilcups did quiver among
>   The deäsies a-spread in a sheet,
> There a quick-trippèn maid come along—
>   Aye, a girl wi' her light-steppèn veet.

It is almost an insult to set up a sign-post to the beauties of such a poem. Yet how faithful, how enchanting is the picture called before us ! Anyone who knows the West of England, and can picture the streams of Somersetshire or Dorsetshire, can call to mind just such a scene. The wide red sandstone arch, spanning the clear and shallow brook that runs away among the stones, and the flower-starred meadows on each hand, all rise before us in the poet's verse. How masterly and how certain of touch is the art that makes the

girl not an accessory of the landscape, nor the landscape a mere background to her figure, but blends and
interchanges the emotions that each evokes! Then
follows a verse in which 'the maid' asks, 'Is the road
out to Lincham on here by the meäd.?' and is told how
it goes, and after :—

> 'Then you don't seem a-born an' a-bred,'
>   I spoke up, 'at a place here about.'
> An' she answer'd wi' cheäks up as red
>   As a piny but leäte a-come out,
> 'No ; I lived wi' my uncle that died
>   Back in Eäpril, an' now I'm a-come
> Here to Ham, to my mother, to bide—
>   Aye, to her house to vind a new hwome.'

It is nothing short of a miracle that the simple greet-
ings and obvious questionings of country people can be
expressed so faithfully and yet in the language of the
purest poetic inspiration.   The peasants seem to talk as
they do in life ; yet somehow the poet's spirit fuses and
transmutes their words and deeds from the commonplace
of the realist into true poetry.

To find an analogy for such workmanship we must
seek a sister art.   Frederick Walker's painting has just
these qualities.   He is always the poet, always fusing
the mere metal of earth with the plastic fire of his
imagination, but yet always faithful to human nature.
He makes for us no strange, unreal, far-off realm of
beauty, but sets beauty itself like a star in our own natural
world of men and women. Just as the girl that treads
the almshouse path, the man that ships his oars at
Marlow Ferry, and the wayside wanderer across whom
the faint grey smoke-wreaths curl, are real and human

in all their grace and majesty of person, so the men and women of William Barnes's songs are as true as they are beautiful and delightful. The poem just quoted ends with a touch of pathos so delicate and so simple that it would be profane to set it out apart from the context. Yet, simple as the poem is, it is at the same time instinct with the spirit of a proudly conscious art. The few words that tell the story of the idyll were once, we are told, actually spoken to the poet. Yet they would have been none the less sincere if only in the singer's heart had they taken shape and substance.

As an example of a more Wordsworthian handling of Nature we may quote a stanza from 'The Woodlands:'—

> Oh, spread ageän your leaves an' flow'rs,
>   Lwonesome woodlands! zunny woodlands!
> Here underneath the dewy show'rs
>   O' warm-air'd spring-time, zunny woodlands!
> As when in drong or open ground,
> Wi' happy bwoyish heart I vound
> The twitt'rèn birds a buildèn round
>   Your high-boughed hedges, zunny woodlands!

In another way, the lines on the enclosure of the village common—'The Common a-took in'—are equally charming. How much the country life lost morally—though no doubt it gained materially—by the destruction of the commons and the open-field system of agriculture can be traced in such verse. The interest that the villagers took in the Manor Courts, in the appointment of the manorial officers, and in the discharge of their duties as 'the homage' was very real,

and, could it have been preserved, might have served as
a most valuable training for higher political action :—

> Oh, no, Poll! no!   Since they've a-took
> The common in, our lew wold nook
> Don't seem a bit as used to look.
>   When we had runnèn room.
> Gre't banks do shut up every drong
> An' stratch wi' thorny backs along
> Where we did use to run among
>   The vuzzen and the broom.
>
> .   .   .   .
>
> What fun there wer among us when
> The hayward come, wi' all his men,
> To drève the common, an' to pen
>   Strange cattle in the pound ;
> The cows did bleäre, the men did shout,
> An' toss their eärms and sticks about,
> An' vo'ks, to own their stock, come out
>   Vrom all the housen round.

'The Milkmaid o' the Farm' has in it the odour of
that wild pastoral rose that twines so gracefully yet so
artlessly as it sheds its shining petals, white and crimson,
across the poetry of the Elizabethan age.   The 'breath
of spring-time' that fans our cheeks in 'The Winter's
Tale,' in Jonson's masques, in Fletcher's lyric outbursts,
or in Heywood's songs is with us here as in that older
world.

In this context it is not impertinent to notice how
William Barnes uses the octosyllabic couplet in a way
that often reminds us of Greene, and sometimes even
of Shakespeare himself.   'The Stwonen Bwoy upon the
Pillar,' a poem that tells of the little archer of the classic

world standing, 'his bow let slack,' within some crumbling Hall's forgotten pleasance, is in this measure :—

> Upon the pillar, all alwone,
> Do stan' the little bwoy of stone ;
> 'S a poppy bud mid linger on,
> Vorseäken, when the wheät's a-gone.
> An' there, then, wi' his bow let slack,
> An' little quiver at his back,
> Drough het an' wet, the little chile
> Vrom day to day do stan' an' smile.
> When vust the light, a risèn' weäk,
> At break o' day do smite his cheäk.
>
> . . . .
>
> But oh ! thik child, that we do vind
> In childhood still, do call to mind
> A little bwoy a-call'd by death
> Long years agoo from our sad he'th.

If our readers have caught the spirit of the Dorsetshire poet in any of the quotations we have given they
will not fail to be charmed by the poem, ' Evenen, an'
Maidens out at door,' though in some ways its oddities
are more than ordinarily difficult to get over.   We quote
one verse :—

> Now the sheädes o' the elems do stratch mwore an' mwore,
>   Vrom the low-zinkèn zun in the west o' the sky ;
> An' the maïdens do stand out in clusters avore
>   The doors, vor to chatty an zee vo'k goo by.

The poem is as perfect an elegy as any in English ; or,
if the scornful reader will not allow us English, then as
any in the world.

Will the Dorsetshire poet's songs ever obtain their
true place in English literature by general acclamation ?
It is very doubtful. The readers of poetry too often

prefer to songs so strong and simple the prettier, softer,
more sugared cadences of a Muse that perhaps has
bought one-half of her clothes in Paris and stolen the
rest from the decadent poets of Greece and Rome.
Those who are thus beguiled will doubtless view the
'Poems of Rural Life' with indifference or contempt.
Is it worth while to attempt to convert them? Is it not
fitter to leave them, satisfied with the thought that, after
all, the loss is theirs? Or, in brave old Ben Jonson's
words :—

> If they love lees and leave the lusty wine,
> Envy them not their palates with the swine.

HERMAN MELVILLE

MR. STEVENSON would have deserved well of the republic of letters if he had done nothing but bring the South Seas back into fashion. Our fathers and grandfathers revelled in the stories of that wonderful region 'to the suthard of the line,' where, as De Quincey's sailor-brother declared, the best arguments against ghosts and the voices and strange shapes that haunt the vast solitudes of the sea are of no avail ; and where, as a later poet has told us—

> The blindest bluffs hold good, dear lass,
> And the wildest tales are true.

For some thirty years, however, a strange veil of dulness fell upon the face of the Pacific Ocean ; and if we heard at all of its islands and its surf-drenched reefs, it was in the prosaic narratives of Lady Brassey and other such long-distance tourists. A fortunate accident, however, took Mr. Stevenson to the South Seas, and at the magic of his voice the mists of commonplace gathered together and withdrew. With this renaissance of the South Seas it was inevitable that there should come a demand for the republication of 'Typee' and 'Omoo'—those wonderful 'real romances' in which the inspired usher, who passed his time between keeping school at Green Bush, N.Y., and sailing among the islands, told the world how he had lived, under the shadow of the bread-fruit trees, a life which, as far as sensuous delight and physical beauty were concerned, could only be compared to that of ancient Hellas. There, in vales lovelier than Tempe, and by waters brighter than those of the Ægean, he had seen the flower-crowned and flower-girdled Mænads weave the meshes of their rhythmic dance. He had sat at feasts with heroes whose forms might have inspired Lysippus and Praxiteles. He had watched in amazement and delight the torches gleaming through the palm groves while the votaries of mysteries, like those of Demeter or Dionysus, performed their solemn rites and meet oblations. Yet, in spite of all, he had yearned always with a passionate yearning for the pleasant fields of New England and the wholesome prose of modern life—the incomparable charities of hearth and home.

Though Melville has not the literary finesse of Mr. Stevenson, the description in 'Typee' of the life he led among a cannibal tribe in the Marquesas Islands has a charm beyond the charm of 'The Wrecker,' the 'Island Nights,' or those studies of the Marquesas which Mr. Stevenson contributed to the earlier numbers of 'Black and White.' 'Typee' is the 'document' *par excellence* of savage life, and a document written by one who knew how to write as well as to observe. We have inferred that Mr. Melville does not write as well as Mr. Stevenson, but this does not mean that he is not an artist in words. Mr. Melville is no mean master of prose, and had his judgment been equal to his feeling for form he might have ranked high in English literature on the ground of style alone. Unfortunately, he was apt to let the last great master of style he had been reading run away with him. For example, in ' Moby Dick '—one of the best and most thrilling sea stories ever written—Mr. Melville has ' hitched to his car ' the fantastic Pegasus of Sir Thomas Browne. With every circumstance of subject favourable it would be madness to imitate the author of ' Urne Burial.' When his style is made the vehicle for describing the hunting of sperm whales in the Pacific the result cannot but be disastrous. Yet so great an artist is Mr. Melville and so strong are the fascinations of his story that we defy any reader of taste to close this epic of whaling without the exclamation—' With all its faults I would not have it other than it is.' By an act of supreme genius, and by forcing his steed to run a pace for which he was not bred, Mr. Melville contrives, in spite of Sir Thomas Browne, to write a book which is not only enchanting as a romance, but a genuine piece of literature.

No one who has read the chapter on ' Nantucket ' and its seafarers, and has learned how at nightfall the Nantucketer, like ' the landless gull that at sunset folds her wings and is rocked to sleep between billows,' ' furls his sails and lays him to his rest, while under his very pillow rush herds of walruses and whales,' will have the heart to cavil at Melville's style. In ' White Jacket ' —a marvellous description of life on a man-of-war—we see yet another deflection given to Mr. Melville's style, and with still worse results. He had apparently been reading Carlyle before he wrote it; and Carlylisms, mixed with the dregs of the ' Religio Medici,' every now and then crop up to annoy the reader.   In spite, however, of this heavy burden, 'White Jacket' is excellent reading, and full of the glory of the sea and the spirit of the Viking.   And here we may mention a very pleasant thing about Mr. Melville's books.   They show throughout a strong feeling of brotherhood with the English. The sea has made him feel the oneness of the English kin, and he speaks of Nelson and the old Admirals like a lover or a child.   Though Mr. Melville wrote at a time when English insolence and pig-headedness and Yankee bumptiousness made a good deal of ill-blood between the two peoples, he feels that, on the sea at least, it is the English kin against the world.

We have left ourselves no time to quote, as we fain would, either the enchanting description of how Mr. Melville, while a prisoner in the 'island valley' of Typee, came upon the image of the dead chief seated in his canoe with his sails set, like a Viking for Valhalla ; or the exquisite picture of the forest glade, in which stood the great monoliths, placed there, like our own Druid stones, by some forgotten and perished people. Nor can we give his picture of Fayaway, the beautiful genius of the vale.   Typee and the South Seas our readers must explore for themselves.   Instead, we will quote the account of the Quaker whalers who sail out of the Island of Nantucket :—

Now, Bildad, like Peleg, and indeed many other Nantucketers, was a Quaker, the island having been originally settled by that sect ; and to this day its inhabitants in general retain in an uncommon measure the peculiarities of the Quaker, only variously and anomalously modified by things altogether alien and heterogeneous.   For some of these same Quakers are the

most sanguinary of all sailors and whale-hunters. They are
fighting Quakers ; they are Quakers with a vengeance. So that
there are instances among them of men who, named with Scripture names—a singularly common fashion on the island—and in
childhood naturally imbibing the stately dramatic 'thee' and
'thou' of the Quaker idiom ; still, from the audacious daring
and boundless adventure of their subsequent lives, strangely
blend with these unoutgrown peculiarities a thousand bold
dashes of character not unworthy a Scandinavian sea-king or a
poetical Pagan Roman. And when these things unite in a
man of greatly superior natural force, with a globular brain and
a ponderous heart ; who has also by the stillness and seclusion
of many long night-watches in the remotest waters, and
beneath constellations never seen here at the north, been led to
think untraditionally and independently ; receiving all nature's
sweet or savage impressions fresh from her own virgin,
voluntary, and confiding breast, and thereby chiefly, but with
some help from accidental advantages, to learn a bold and
nervous lofty language—that man makes one in a whole nation's
census—a mighty pageant creature, formed for noble tragedies.
Nor will it at all detract from him, dramatically regarded, if,
either by birth or other circumstances, he have what seems a
half-wilful, overruling morbidness at the bottom of his nature.
For all men tragically great are made so through a certain
morbidness. Be sure of this, O young ambition, all mortal
greatness is but disease. But as yet we have not to do with
such an one, but with quite another ; and still a man who, if
indeed peculiar, it only results again from another phase of the
Quaker modified by individual circumstances.

Nantucket itself must also claim notice. Here is the
description of the islanders and what they have
done :—

And thus have these naked Nantucketers, these sea-hermits,
issuing from their ant-hill in the sea, overrun and conquered the
watery world like so many Alexanders ; parcelling out among

them the Atlantic, Pacific, and Indian Oceans, as the three pirate powers did Poland. Let America add Mexico to Texas, and pile Cuba upon Canada ; let the English overswarm all India, and hang out their blazing banner from the sun ; two-thirds of this terraqueous globe are the Nantucketer's. For the sea is his ; he owns it, as Emperors own empires ; other seamen having but a right of way through it. Merchant ships are but extension bridges ; armed ones but floating forts ; even pirates and privateers, though following the sea as highwaymen the road, they but plunder other ships, other fragments of the land like themselves, without seeking to draw their living from the bottomless deep itself. The Nantucketer, he alone resides and riots on the sea ; he alone, in Bible language, goes down to it in ships ; to and fro ploughing it as his own special plantation. *There* is his home ; *there* lies his business, which a Noah's flood would not interrupt, though it overwhelmed all the millions in China. He lives on the sea. as prairie cocks in the prairie ; he hides among the waves, he climbs them as chamois hunters climb the Alps. For years he knows not the land ; so that when he comes to it at last it smells like another world, more strangely than the moon would to an Earthsman With the landless gull, that at sunset folds her wings and is rocked to sleep between billows, so at nightfall the Nan tucketer, out of sight of land, furls his sails, and lays him to his rest, while under his very pillow rush herds of walruses and whales.

If there is not high imagination and true literature in this, we know not where to find it.

THE PURITANS

L

I

ENGLISHMEN are admittedly ignorant of and careless about history. There is, however, one historical character in which they are universally interested, either on the side of praise or blame—Oliver Cromwell. You may find hundreds, nay thousands, of fairly educated men who have no opinion, good or bad, of even such great figures as William III. or the Earl of Chatham, but it is hard to discover one who has not a definite feeling in regard to the Protector, who does not love or hate the man, and to whom his story is not profoundly interesting. And what a story is that of the Huntingdonshire farmer-squire. First he inspired a troop of horse with a spirit that enabled them to encounter and overthrow 'gentlemen that have honour and courage and resolution in them,' and 'as one man to stand firmly and charge desperately,' making always, in their Captain's phrase, 'some conscience of what they did.' Next he so leavened a whole army with the same courage and the same enthusiasm that, looking back on the past, he could say of them, 'Truly, they were never beaten, and wherever they were engaged against the enemy they beat continually.' Lastly, and having subdued the foes of the Houses and the Word, he was raised, half by his own intention, half in his own despite, to be the greatest of European Sovereigns. Never in history has there been a General or a ruler more successful than 'The Protector of the liberties of England.' From the moment that he took in hand the sword to the day on which he breathed his last it is one continuous record of achievement in the field or in the council. In every action which he fought, great or small, he was victorious. He never led a charge but he routed the enemy, nor stood to receive an attack but he drove back his assailants. Every town that he besieged fell into his hands, every house he assaulted he stormed and captured. There was not an undertaking of his in dealing with troops in mutiny, with recalcitrant Parliaments, or with secret conspiracies in which he was not as completely triumphant. No less successful was his diplomatic action. The foreign Powers with whom he made treaties and alliances sought him as the arbiter of the fate of Europe, and the balance at once inclined to the scale in which he had thrown his sword.

II

IT is not, however, Cromwell's success that makes him so interesting to those who love him—and I cannot profess to be able to discuss him from any other standpoint. Cromwell, as I see him, is first of all the ideal Englishman, the man who represents, and in whom were incarnate all the strongest and most notable characteristics of the English race. If not in him, I know not where to find personified the Englishman's ideal of strength and moderation, courage and religious feeling, and that resoluteness, both in pride and humility, which makes men knowers of their own minds. On every side of him the typical Englishman emerges, the Englishman of compromises and common sense, the Englishman at once practical and illogical, who is yet pervaded with a certain ideality and a striving after higher things which seem the very negation of the superficial part of his character. His is the religious temper in the midst of worldly cares.

Cromwell's statesmanship shows the English standpoint in politics with all its virtues and defects. He is always a little too much inclined to be opportunist, and to think an accommodation may be made between ideas, however hostile and divergent. In the wonderful debates preserved for us in the 'Clarke Papers,' the contents of which I have described in another essay in the present volume, we are able to come extraordinarily close to Cromwell as a politician. We see him for ever trying to keep together the body in which he was sitting—the Council of the Army—to produce solidarity, and to prevent a centrifugal action. His attitude is always that of the typical good chairman of a Committee—' Don't you think, gentlemen, that by a very little concession on each side we could all agree on what ought to be done?' But at the same time there are very definite limits to Cromwell's opportunism. When the one or two great principles in which he believes are touched he becomes like iron. Again, if he considers that the welfare of the nation as a whole is endangered, and that patriotism requires such and such a thing to be done or left undone, there is no moving him.

Very typical, again, was Cromwell's attitude on the question of law and order. Though he loved liberty, he hated anarchy; and most characteristically thought and spoke of himself as the constable set to keep the peace in the parish of England. That is the Englishman all the world over. Let an Englishman get to the top, no matter where, from China to Peru, and his prime care will be to organise an efficient administration of law and order. Look, too, at Cromwell's treatment of the Socialists, Anabaptists, and Fifth Monarchy men. As long as they only talked he allowed them the utmost liberty, but when they tried to start the millennium by digging on somebody else's land, and infringing the legal rights of the commoners of Thames Ditton 'in a portion of the waste of the manor called St. George's Hill,' he soon let them know that England was not going to be turned upside down in order to try whether communism was a possible state of society. He, in fact, treated Socialism just as the plain man picked out of the next omnibus would treat it now. When it was in the air it had as good right to exist as any other theory. When it became a form of riot it was to be put down, not vindictively, but still with the necessary firmness.

Certain Englishmen have been grossly intolerant; but at heart the nation has always been tolerant —anxious, that is, not to limit the action of the human mind, or to constrain the conscience. Here Cromwell was prophetically typical. He first put into a tangible shape England's ideal of religious liberty—an ideal slowly and painfully, but resolutely pursued since his time. Nothing could be better than his words on toleration :—' Every sect saith : Oh, give me liberty! But give him it, and, to his power, he will not yield it to anybody else. Liberty of conscience is a natural right ; and he that would have it ought to give it.' On another occasion he says, even more definitely, ' I desire from my heart—I have prayed for it—I have waited for the day to see union and right understanding between the godly people—Scots, English, Jews, Gentiles, Presbyterians, Independents, Anabaptists, and all.'

In the matter of law reform Cromwell again showed himself extraordinarily English. He hated the rigmaroles and the common forms of the lawyers, and resented a great deal of our system of jurisprudence as pure barbarism. His feeling in favour of reform did not, however, induce him to make a clean sweep, like a French Jacobin, and to match the pedantries of abuse with the pedantries of innovation. Instead, he made his changes in the most conservative spirit, and never sacrificed the old unless he was sure that the new was better. It is curious to note how there swelled within him the fierce sense of indignation which two hundred years later swept away the old penal code and prevented hanging being any longer the commonest punishment of crime. Here are his actual words :—' The truth of it is, There are wicked and abominable Laws, which it will be in your power to alter. To hang a man for Six-and-eight-pence, and I know not what ; to hang for a trifle, and acquit murder—is in the ministration of the Law, through the ill-framing of it. I have known in my experience abominable murderers acquitted. And to see men lose their lives for petty matters : this is a thing God will reckon for.'

Englishmen, as a whole, do not find the military spirit very congenial to them. They are a little fretted by the sense of instant obedience which the soldier carries with him. But Cromwell managed so to be a soldier as not to forget he was a citizen. Great General as he was, and proud of his calling and of his men as he was also, he never offended the nation by even the faintest touch of 'the strut *en militaire.*' Though he gained power by the sword, and in effect held rule by the sword, he stood before the nation far more as a God-fearing country gentleman than as a man of war. In his bearing towards foreign nations Cromwell again exactly took up the attitude which the nation wanted and appreciated—the typically English attitude. He did not try to play the part of a Gustavus Adolphus or a Charles XII. or a Napoleon, or to conquer and subdue any of the Powers of Europe. He was content with making England feared and respected on the Continent, and with laying the foundations of Empire in the New World. He made England 'signify somewhat.'

In minor matters Cromwell was no less the quintessence of English manhood. Take his attitude towards art and music and literature. He was, like the nation as a whole, not very sensitive to the sense of beauty and refinement, but he could feel and give their proper value to the really great works of art. It was through his influence that the Commonwealth, though pressed sorely indeed for money, did not sell either the cartoons of Raphael or Mantegna's 'Triumph of Cæsar.' The fanatical Puritan would have condemned the cartoons as idolatrous and the Mantegnas as frivolous toys. Not so Cromwell. He saw the value and importance of these noble monuments of art.

Of his love for pictures there is a curious story told. When the Dutch envoys waited on Cromwell in March, 1653, they brought over with them some of Titian's paintings. The intercepted letter of a royalist (name unknown) has the following :—' One that was present at the audience given in the banquetting-house told me that Cromwell spent so much time looking at the pictures that he judged by it that he had not been much used heretofore to Titian's hand' (Thurloe, ii. 144). This is truly delightful. As Cromwell looked at the pictures it showed his brutal ignorance; if he had not looked it would have shown his utter disregard of things beautiful. The Cavalier has him both ways. The fact of Cromwell's saving the cartoons for the nation at the King's sale is well known. It is less well known that Charles II. tried to sell them to Louis XIV., and was only prevented by the fear of his Parliament. So much for Stuart patronage of the arts.

Cromwell's love of music is a matter of history, and in a musical age he was counted as being specially devoted to that art. Curiously enough, he says little about literature in his letters or speeches, but it is pretty clear that he was well read. In the matter of ceremonial he was very English. He does not seem to have cared for luxury or personal splendour in the least ; but when the occasion demanded a great ceremonial he took care that it should be unrivalled in magnificence. When Cromwell went in state, surrounded by his life-guards, he outshone in stateliness and grandeur all the Monarchs of Europe.

The English people have not long memories in history, but in a certain way they are strongly touched by past events. They always remember the Black Prince and Queen Elizabeth as national heroes. Strangely enough, both these great historical figures were, we know, held in loving remembrance by Cromwell. When he was at Canterbury it is said that one of his first acts was to put a guard over the tomb of the great knight who upheld the fame of England over sea. Again, in one of his speeches, a note of passionate patriotism comes into Cromwell's voice when he speaks of Elizabeth. ' That great Queen of happy memory, for so I must call her.'' It was the republican fashion not to use the conventional phrase of ' happy memory,' but all such pedantry must give way to the renown of the Sovereign who repelled the Armada. It may be a fancy, but it is worth noting, that Cromwell, in instituting, as he undoubtedly did, the plan of burying our great soldiers and sailors and statesmen in Westminster Abbey—he buried there Ireton, Blake, and Bradshaw—gave expression to the strong English sentiment which exists as to the place of sepulture. He saw prophetically how great an inducement to high deeds was Nelson's exclamation, ' A peerage or Westminster Abbey.'

Lastly, Cromwell is so typically English because he was essentially what we mean by an English gentleman, and an English gentleman is what every Englishman, rich and poor, gentle and simple, desires to be. No one who reads his letters and speeches can doubt that for a moment. Consider the following words, in which he described himself to his Parliament and showed his natural pride in being able to call himself an English gentleman :—' I was by birth a gentleman, living neither in any considerable height nor yet in obscurity. I have been called to several employments in the Nation—to serve in Parliament and others—and, not to be tedious, I did endeavour to discharge the duty of an honest man in those services, to God and his People's interest, and to the Commonwealth, having, when time was, a competent acceptation in the hearts of men, and some evidences thereof.'

But the character of a gentleman went deeper with Cromwell. It may be difficult to define the meaning of the phrase ' an English gentleman ' when used in the highest sense, but no one will doubt that he was an English gentleman who wrote the beautiful letter which told Colonel Valentine Walton of the death of his eldest son. ' Sir, God hath taken away your eldest son by a cannon shot. It broke his leg. We were necessitated to have it cut off, whereof he died. Sir, you know my own trials this way ; but the Lord supported me with this, that the Lord took him into the happiness we all pant for and live for. There is your precious child, full of glory, never to know sin or sorrow any more. He was a gallant young man, exceedingly gracious. God give you His comfort. . . . You may do all things by the strength of Christ. Seek that, and you shall easily bear. your trial. Let this public mercy to the Church of God make you forget your private sorrow. The Lord be your strength.' The free and gentle spirit of him who is born a true knight shows itself nowhere more clearly than in the offering of consolation to the afflicted. The vain, the foolish, the pompous, the insincere, the boorish exhibit themselves in their true colours when they have to write such a letter as that we have just quoted. The true gentleman alone is able to speak heart to heart, and to restrain and purify the grief of his friend.

III

IN Cromwell the sense of patriotism was deep and strong. He was, indeed, one of those rare men who feel for their country like 'a lover or a child.' England and English citizenship were with him a passion which, before his time, had never been possessed in anything like the same degree by any of our rulers or great Ministers. Indeed, the love of country in its most creative and passionate form may be said to have been the outcome of Puritanism. When Milton, when Mrs. Hutchinson, when Cromwell speak of England we feel that a spirit and a force are alive in their utterances which, though it may have found partial expression before in words with Shakespeare or in deeds with Raleigh and Drake, has for the first time become able to quicken and dominate the English race. When Cromwell spoke to the House of Commons 'of true English hearts and zealous affections towards the general weal of our mother-country,' he was using a language familiar enough now, but which before had hardly been felt as a great motive force among Englishmen.

It is impossible to read the history of the days of the Civil War and the Commonwealth without being struck by the extraordinary political sagacity and statesmanship with which Cromwell tempered his patriotism. It was owing to him, and to him alone, that the destruction of the Constitution, caused by the war and the dethronement of Charles, did not end in a period of anarchy and chaos such as took place in France during the period of the Fronde. At each step in his career Cromwell's dominant motive was the desire to prevent the country from going to ruin. He may have sometimes misjudged the necessities of the time, but his object was always to keep the ship of State from going on the rocks. No doubt he had other and lesser motives also, for Cromwell was a human being, and was no more above the emotions of ambition, anger, and the desire to see the triumph of his cause and the abasement of its enemies than his fellow-men. The ruling passion was, however, always that of patriotism. He may have wanted many things, some bad, some good, and some indifferent, but what he wanted most was the welfare of his country. He in very truth cared not to be great except that he might 'serve and save the State.'

If love of his country and the desire to keep her from harm was Cromwell's guiding star, his chief political characteristic was clearness and keenness of mental vision. No man ever saw more into the heart of a question, and fixed and fastened on the essential element, letting all the accidents, ornaments, and unrealities go as they would. A hundred instances might be marshalled to prove how he seized always and at once the main issue. One will serve as an example. The Earl of Orrery tried to get Cromwell to lend a favourable ear to the proposal that his daughter 'Frank' should be married to the King—*i.e.* Charles II.—and the Protector still remain the head of the army and the real ruler of the kingdom. Cromwell did not worry with the minor difficulties that forbade the proposal, but in refusing a scheme which superficially had so much to commend it, and which would have got him out of so many perplexities, stated the one insurmountable objection : 'He is so damnably debauched that he would undo us all.' This was the plain truth. Cromwell knew his man, and knew also that an arrangement which might have held with a Prince of honour, prudence, and discretion must have ended with a creature like Charles II. in ruin and disgrace. Even with the Puritan element in abeyance or under his feet, Charles's dexterous and unscrupulous opportunism could only just prevent the scandal of his life from producing a new revolution. Had he been yoked in an unnatural alliance with the party of the Saints a moral earthquake must have destroyed the compact before six months were over.

Cromwell had the statesman's capacity for seeing what was possible and what not. He carried this clearness of vision, this intellectual sincerity, into other regions than those of politics. That he was a deeply religious man there can be no sort of doubt. The notion that he was a worldly, hypocritical politician will not hold for a moment when examined in the light of the facts. But in Cromwell's day depth of religious feeling almost always went hand in hand with a fierce intolerance. The notion that it was possible to believe strongly and clearly, and yet allow other men to think differently, leaving the reconciliation of conflicting doctrines to the wisdom of God, was an idea that was as yet hardly born. Men somehow felt that not to persecute was to grow feeble in the faith. Cromwell, however, cut through these mists of paradox, or of mere logic, whichever we choose to call them, and saw that he who truly loved justice and truth must also be tolerant. Nay, more, he even saw the more difficult truth that toleration is *per se* a religious act, and not a mere convention based on convenience—a course of action founded on the principle of reciprocity. He saw that you must tolerate the faith of others, not merely to obtain toleration for yourself, but as part and parcel of your religious duty.

One cannot deal fairly with Cromwell as a statesman without mentioning the subject of Ireland. I will not attempt to deny that Cromwell did things there which, if not morally below the standard of his time, were below Cromwell's own standard. I confess, however, to feeling a sense of mystery as regards Cromwell in Ireland. Even the most favourable account of his actions will not fit in with the Protector's usual tender-ness of heart and moderation of conduct. He passed through Ireland in the spirit of a destroying angel, but this was a spirit utterly foreign to Cromwell's character. One feels as one reads the accounts of Cromwell's doings in Ireland as if the air had infected his brain, as if he had caught something of the headiness, ferocity, and lack of balance that seem native to the island. No doubt Cromwell's mind had been so inflamed by stories of the atrocities and massacres committed by the ' mere ' Irish during the rebellion that he worked him-self into the belief that the Irish soldiers and the priests who led them should be knocked on the head like wild beasts. But though this is an attitude for which, considering the circumstances, it is possible to find explanations and excuses, it is extraordinarily unlike the ordinary attitude of Cromwell. As I have said, the thing is a mystery, and we can only fall back on the somewhat fantastic idea expressed above—that Cromwell lost his head under the exciting influences that obtained then, as now, on the other side of St. George's Channel.

IV

A WORD as to Cromwell the man. Tenderness and amiability were the main characteristics of Cromwell's private character. As a contemporary observer said of him, 'he was naturally compassionate towards objects in distress, even to an effeminate measure,' and did 'exceed in tenderness towards sufferers.' In his dealings with his own family we see these qualities well illustrated. Even in the fulness of his greatness, when worldly state and power might well have been expected to harden him, the sufferings of his daughter so weighed upon his mind as to make him even unable to do the business of the State. In the middle of his Scotch campaign, he writes to the wife to whom he had been married thirty years with the tenderness of a lover: 'Truly thou art dearer to me than any creature. . . . My love to the dear little ones; I pray for grace for them. I thank them for their letters; let me have them often.'

There is something specially touching in the way in which Cromwell refers to his son Richard. The young man's indolence and love of pleasure meet with no mere cold, harsh rebuke, such as one might have expected from the typical Puritan. He treats his son's faults with a gentleness which is almost pathetic. Writing to Richard's father-in-law, he says: 'I envy him not his contents [*i.e.* pleasures]; but I fear he should be swallowed up in them.' No man whose heart was not of the kindliest mould could have felt the loss of his children as did Cromwell. The death of his eldest son Robert, when a schoolboy, made an indelible mark upon the father's nature. When his favourite daughter, Mrs. Claypole, died in the last months of his own life, the wound was reopened. Then, at his request, the verses from the Philippians were read to him which contain the words: 'I can do all things through Christ which strengtheneth me.' 'This Scripture,' said the Protector, 'did once save my life; when my eldest son died; which went as a dagger to my heart; indeed it did.' Of Cromwell's attention to his daughter, Mrs. Claypole, in her last illness, Thurloe tells us: 'For the last fourteen days his Highness has been by her bedside at Hampton Court, unable to attend to any public business whatsoever. . . . It was observed that his sense of her outward misery in the pains she endured, took deep impression upon him, who, indeed, was ever a most indulgent, tender father.'

Though Cromwell was in many ways a very humane person, there was also something demoniac in the man. John Aubrey, the Wiltshire antiquary, under the head of 'Impulses,' describes how at times Cromwell seemed as one possessed. 'Oliver Cromwell,' he says, 'had certainly this afflatus. One that I knew, and who was present at the battle of Dunbar, told me that Oliver was carried on with a divine impulse. He did laugh so excessively as if he had been drunk, and his eyes sparkled with spirits. He obtained on that occasion a great victory, though the action was said to be contrary to human prudence. The same fit of laughter seized him just before the battle of Naseby, as a kinsman of mine, and a great favourite of his, Colonel J. P., then present, testified.'

Cromwell's account in after days of what was passing in his mind at Naseby, as Mr. Waylen has pointed out, corroborates Aubrey's strange story. 'I can say this of Naseby,' he says, 'that when I saw the enemy draw up and march in gallant order towards us ; and we a company of poor ignorant men to seek how to order our battle (the General having commanded me to order all the horse), I could not, riding alone about my business, but smile out to God in praises, in assurance of victory ; because God would by things that · are not bring to nought things that are ; of which I had great assurance ; and God did it.' His letter to the Committee of the Cambridge Association in 1642 shows that he believed himself possessed by some exhilaration of spirit which was more than human. 'Verily I do think the Lord is with me. I undertake strange things, yet do I go through with them to great profit and gladness, and furtherance of the Lord's great work. I do feel myself lifted on by strange force, I cannot tell why. By night and by day I am urged forward in the great work.'

V

It is curious to note how many members of the governing class in modern times have Cromwell's blood in their veins. His descendants have given England a Prime Minister, Lord Goderich ; a Chancellor of the Exchequer, Sir George Cornewall Lewis ; a Foreign Secretary, Lord Clarendon ; a great reformer and champion of Free

Trade, Mr. Charles Villiers ; a Governor-General of India, Lord Ripon ; and a Viceroy of Ireland, Lord Cowper. It is true that Lord Goderich—' the transient and embarrassed phantom ' of Mr. Disraeli—was not a very Cromwellian figure, but, considering the manner in which the Cromwell family was ' kept under ' during the first hundred years after the Restoration, this record of eminence in the service of the country is very remarkable.

If one were to recapitulate the peers and baronets, the admirals and generals, and the persons distinguished in law or divinity, who had or have the blood of Cromwell, space would be required for a very formidable list. The living descendants of Cromwell already number many hundreds, and in another twenty years it is not impossible that they may have increased to thousands. Hence all fear that the line will ever become extinct may be banished. These descents are, of course, all through the female, the last male descendant, Mr. Cromwell of Cheshunt, having died in 1821. Since, however, the Queen only represents the kin of Cerdic, of Alfred, of William the Conqueror, of Henry Tudor, and of Charles Stuart through the female, it is absurd to speak of a Cromwellian descent through the female as something too remote to be worth remembering. It is stated, but whether accurately or not it is difficult to say, that, but for a piece of mean-spiritedness on the part of George III., we should still have a Cromwell by name as well as by blood. The last Mr. Cromwell was, it is said, anxious that his daughter and heiress should take his name and transmit it to her children. The following account of the circumstances which are alleged to have prevented his wish being carried out is given by Mr. Waylen in his curious book on 'Cromwell's Descendants.' After recounting the deaths of Mr. Cromwell's two sons, Mr. Waylen continues :—

Under these circumstances it is not surprising that Mr. Cromwell of Cheshunt should wish his daughter to carry it on, in accordance with the course usually pursued in such cases, by her husband's adopting the surname and arms of Cromwell either in addition to or in exchange for those of Russell. Such a procedure is technically said to be 'by royal permission ;' and though royalty seldom interferes in such matters, yet here was a case in which royalty's instincts seemed suddenly awakened to the susceptibility of an unaccustomed chord. True, it was a chord whose vibrations responded to the mere ghost of a name. But what a name ! Has it ever been other than a word of omen to royal ears during the last two centuries ? The issue of the affair is thus recorded by Mr. Burke the herald :—'Mr. Cromwell wishing to perpetuate the name of his great ancestor, applied, it is said, in the usual quarter for permission that his son-in-law should assume the surname of Cromwell ; when, to his astonishment, considering that such requests are usually granted on the payment of certain fees as a matter of course, the permission was refused. Such a course of proceeding is too contemptible for comment ' (*History of the Commoners*, vol. i., p. 433). The credit of the refusal has been variously ascribed to the old King, to the Prince Regent, and to William IV. Sir Robert Heron writing in 1812 makes mention of it thus,—'Within the last two or three years died the last male direct descendant of Oliver Cromwell. He was well known to my father and to Sir Abraham Hume, who lived near him. They represented him as a worthy man of mild manners, much resembling in character his immediate ancestor Henry the Lord Lieutenant of Ireland. Early in life his pecuniary circumstances were narrowed, but latterly he possessed a comfortable income

He was desirous of leaving his name to his son-in-law, Mr. Russell, and applied for His Majesty's permission that Russell should assume it ; but the old King positively refused it, always saying, 'No, no—no more Cromwells' (*Sir Robert Heron's Notes*). Another version of the affair is, that Mr. Cromwell becoming apprehensive that the change of name might, after all, prove a hindrance rather than otherwise to his grandchildren's advance in life, allowed the matter to remain in abeyance ; but that the scheme was revived by another member of the family in a memorial addressed to William IV. ; and that it was this King and not George III. who uttered the energetic veto above recorded.

This refusal may be regarded as the last attempt made to depress the Protector's family. Throughout the eighteenth century it is clear that the family suffered a good deal, and that it was usually thought prudent for its members to keep quiet. A pleasant story of the great Lord Hardwicke's conduct in checking the petty persecution of the Cromwells is worth remembering :—

Lord Chancellor Hardwicke once heard a suit in which the grandson of the Protector Oliver was a party. The opposing counsel thinking to make way with the jury by scandalising Oliver's memory, was running on in the accustomed style, when Lord Hardwicke effectually checked him by saying, 'I perceive Mr. Cromwell is standing outside the bar and inconveniently pressed by the crowd. Make way for him that he may come and sit on the bench.' The representative of the family accordingly took his place beside the Judge, and the orator changed his tone.

Before leaving the subject of Cromwell's descendants, it may be noted that Sir William Harcourt and the late Lord Lytton are both connected with the House of

Cromwell. The first Lady Harcourt was descended from the Protector, as is the widow of the late Lord Lytton. The curious circumstances of ' the inter-marriage in the fourth descent of Oliver's posterity and King Charles's,' and of the intermixture of Hyde and Cromwell blood must also be mentioned. What misery and humiliation would not the first Lord Clarendon have suffered, could he have known that his descendants would intermarry with those of the Usurper, and that the children of this intermixture would regard their descent from the Protector with far greater pride than that from the Chancellor of Charles II. !

A PURITAN GONE ROTTEN

IN the latest reprint of ' Pepys's Diary,' we are for the first time allowed to see all, or practically all that Pepys wrote in that marvellous daily confession where meanness, lubricity, and bright, eager interest in all that concerns man and the world stand side by side. Previous editors cut out first the coarse passages, and then what they thought the dull ones—those dealing with the details of Pepys's official life. The result was a considerable loss of local colour. Now we have the full-length portrait. It is true that the edges once turned down under the frame and now exposed to view do not alter the general character of the picture ; but at the same time they increase the total impression produced. That impression cannot but be a most unfavourable one to Pepys as a man. His nature was as loathsome a one as it is possible to conceive, for in spite of his ability, his keenness, his force, his pleasantness and his *bonhomie*, there ran through the man a deep strain of hypocrisy. ' Treacherous, lecherous, kindless villain.' The words are hardly too strong for this Puritan gone rotten, this Psalm-singing Roundhead who, though he wallowed as deep in the Caroline sty as any of his fellows, yet even in the privacy of his own Diary could not help turning up the whites of his eyes and lamenting all the sin and wickedness that was sending the country to the devil. He comes reeking from a squalid and adulterous amour to protest against the licentious talk and behaviour of the gallants of the Court. They cursed and swore and showed their vices in public, and this in Pepys's eyes was the greatest of crimes. Why could they not 'sin close' like himself, and not set so terrible an example to the vulgar?

It is impossible to read 'Pepys's Diary' and not feel a certain very disagreeable thought arise in the mind. Mr. Stevenson pointed out in his masterly essay on Pepys that but for the Diary our estimate of Pepys would be utterly different from what it is to-day. We should know him as a staid and capable official who in a dissolute and reckless age fulfilled a great public charge with zeal and discretion, a man who lived a long and happy married life, who loved learning and science, who was a prominent member of the Royal Society, and a noted musician who left a fine collection of books to his University, and who was at the end of his career a much respected Member of Parliament. To heighten this picture one may add the fact that Pepys appears in our literature as the author of a lettter to Dryden asking him to draw for the benefit of the public a picture of that most virtuous of virtuous figures—the worthy country parson. In a word, if we relied on what we know of Pepys from others we should think of him as one who did no discredit to human nature.

But, alas! we also know the man from the inside. We have a window to look into his very soul,—a window through which we see the black corruption of his nature. We see him lying and plundering and playing the profligate and the hypocrite, and hear his greasy protestations and unctuous excuses for his weakness. With such a contrast before us it is difficult to resist the question,—Are all men in reality like this one? Is the cynic right, and is there no such thing as truth and honesty and plain-dealing except among the frankly profligate? Would it be much the same story, we cannot help wondering, if we could get at the real man who lies behind the orderly, honourable, high-minded exterior of this or that great statesman or man of letters, soldier, or lawyer? Is it merely because we only see the outside that we pay so much honour to the men we fancy are of good report? Are they all modern Pepyses? It is all very well to say Pepys was an exception, but may not the world be full of such exceptions? Perhaps, after all, a hypocrite is not a monster, but merely a man unlucky enough to be found out! That is a natural train of thought after reading the Diary, but, thank God, it is not one which has a substantial basis. No, the cynic's point of view is not the true one. There are Pepyses, but they are rare, not common. That is the sober truth.

'Pepys's Diary' is a work of extraordinary interest from the point of view of the psychologist, but we are not sure that even greater interest does not attach to it as a work of literature. Without knowing it Pepys was a consummate artificer in words. He worked up no purple patches, he never wrote for effect, he cared nothing for showing off his gifts of style and knowledge, and yet in the art of composition he often does by instinct better than those who have laboured their writings to the extremest point.   Unless it be Dryden or South, no one in his age wrote so well as he.   He has to perfection the gift which Hazlitt, with the insight of genius, saw to be essential to the master of style.   He can make his words render up 'the extreme characteristic impression' of the thing written about.   And he does it, not to dazzle the town or win the applause of his contemporaries, but because it is natural to him so to write.   Take the wonderful account of his visit to the shepherd on Epsom Downs, so delightfully characterised by Mr Stevenson.   He jots it down in his subtle shorthand among his accounts and his love affairs, but the thing is one of the most perfect, because the least artificial, idylls ever written.   The old shepherd with his boy and his Bible and his crook and their eager interested worldly interviewer form a picture not to be surpassed in our literature :—

And so the women and W. Hewes and I walked upon the Downes, where a flock of sheep was ; and the most pleasant and innocent sight that ever I saw in my life,—we found a shepherd and his little boy reading, far from any houses or sight of people, the Bible to him ; so I made the boy read to me, which he did, with the forced tone that children do usually read, that was mighty pretty, and then I did give him something, and went to the father, and talked with him ; and I find he had been a servant in my cozen Pepys's house, and told me what was become of their old servants.   He did content himself mightily in my liking his boy's reading, and did bless God for him the most like one of the old patriarchs that ever I saw in my life, and it brought those thoughts of the old age of the world in my mind for two or three days after.   We took notice of his woollen knit stockings of two colours, mixed, and of his shoes shod with iron shoes, both at the toes and heels, and with great nails in the soles of his feet, which was mighty pretty ; and, taking notice of them, 'why,' says the poor man, 'the downes, you see, are full of stones, and we are faine to shoe ourselves thus ; and these,' says he, 'will make the stones fly till they sing before me.' I did give the poor man something, for which he was mighty thankful, and I tried to cast stones with his horne crooke. He values his dog mightily, that would turn a sheep any way which he would have him, when he goes to fold them ; told me there was about eighteen scoare sheep in his flock, and that he hath four shillings a week the year round for keeping of them ; so we posted thence with mighty pleasure at the discourse we had with this poor man, and Mrs. Turner, in the common fields here, did gather one of the prettiest nosegays that ever I saw in my life.

But Pepys's powers were not confined to the idyllic. He knew how to touch a note of tragedy as well, and could—so strange is this strange power of words—convey emotions which he was too base to feel. He was himself incapable either of patriotism or of devotion to a leader or friend, yet see how he describes the passionate scene round the bier of Sir Christopher Mings :—

Met with Sir W. Coventry and went with him into his coach, and being in it with him there happened this extraordinary case, —one of the most romantique that ever I heard of in my life, and could not have believed, but that I did see it ; which was this :—About a dozen able, lusty, proper men come to the coach-side with tears in their eyes, and one of them that spoke for the rest begun and says to Sir W. Coventry, 'We are here a dozen of us that have long known and loved, and served our dead commander, Sir Christopher Mings, and have now done the last office of laying him in the ground. We would be glad we had any other to offer after him, and in revenge of him.

All we have is our lives ; if you will please to get His Royal
Highness to give us a fireship among us all, here is a dozen of
us, out of all which choose you one to be commander, and the
rest of us, whoever he is, will serve him ; and, if possible, do
that that shalt show our memory of our dead commander and
our revenge.'   Sir W. Coventry was herewith much moved (as
well as I, who could hardly abstain from weeping), and took
their names, and so parted ; telling me he would move His
Royal Highness as in a thing very extraordinary, which was
done.

We might add plenty of other examples to show how
great was the literary gift of Pepys,—for instance, the
immortal description of how he buried his brother. The
passage there about the grave-digger is worthy of
Shakespeare. We have quoted enough, however, to
show that he had born in him the magic of style. It is
indeed this magic which makes the Diary what it is.
Without it the book, in spite of its psychological interest,
its record of strange pages in history, and even its
quaintness, would be a dead thing. Because it has style
as well as these, Pepys's Diary is one of the great books
of English literature.

A PURITAN TURNED SOUR

I

IF Pepys was a Puritan gone rotten, Swift was a Puritan turned sour. The rock bed of Swift's nature was essentially Puritan. He was a Puritan in his humanity, in his fierce seriousness, in his intellectual ardour, and in his inability to look at the world except from the moral point of view. But the corruptions of the age in which he was bred and something in the man's own heart turned his Puritanism sour. He kept untainted the pride, the independence, and the self-respect of the Puritan, but he kept little else from contamination. The rest went rancid, and suffered a change which helped to make Swift one of the strangest and most pathetic figures in the annals of mankind.

II

' Never anyone living thought like you,' said to Swift the woman who loved him with a passion that had caught some of his own fierceness and despair. The love which great natures inspire had endowed 'Vanessa' with a rare inspiration. Half consciously she has touched the notes that help us to resolve the discord in Swift's life. Truly, the mind of living man never worked as Swift's worked. That this is so is visible in every line, in every word he ever wrote. No phrase of his is like any other man's ; no conception of his is ever cast in the common mould. It is this that lends something so dreadful and mysterious to all Swift's writings. Merely to read his life, even in its most exaggerated form, is not to realise this to the full. To understand it perfectly is to feel for once the spirit that breathes in his works. Its quality may want a name as it wants a parallel, but none the less is it distinct and unmistakable.

Indignation has rightly been described as the key-note of Swift's character ; but its quality was something more than human. In changing in degree from ordinary human indignation, his temper changes in kind. Swift's indignation is as universal as it is intense. He tears the mask off human nature not merely to reveal some particular hypocrisy, some special pretence, but to show that there is nothing, and can be nothing, below the mask but madness and lust, cruelty, and meanness. When he loses a friend, his indignation is loud, not so much that the best die, but that so many wretches live. He regrets that he ever loved a friend, because of the pain of loss. In his fierce nature, the poet's noble consolation, ''Tis better to have loved and lost than never to have loved at all,' finds no echo. When in later life he turns the pages of that most brilliant of satires, 'The Tale of a Tub,' it is not with pleasure in viewing so masterly a creation ; but with the despairing cry, 'Good God ! what a genius I had when I wrote that book !' Happiness with him is the 'perpetual possession of being well deceived.' 'You should think and deal with every man as a villain, without calling him so, or flying from him, or valuing him less. This is an old, true lesson.'

Swift did not so much show man's errors that he might amend them, as deny with curses the possibility of reformation. Add to this that he poured filth and contempt in abundance upon the whole relation of sex ; that his works are deliberately intended to produce in his readers' minds a physical loathing for themselves and for the rest of mankind—and it seems at first sight incredible that the world should delight in, or even tolerate, his writings. Is not the answer to be found in this unhuman quality of Swift's spirit which has been suggested before ? What would have been mere railing, intolerable from its nastiness, if spoken by an ordinary mortal, the world has been willing to accept from Swift, because he has conceived his thought in no mere human manner. It will take from him what it would not take from another, for the compulsion of genius is irresistible.

III

THE best and most illuminating things said of Swift were said by himself. In one of his letters he tells us that 'a person of great honour in Ireland'—how characteristic is the phrase, for Swift, after a magnificent and terrific fashion of his own, was a sort of Titanic snob—used to tell him that his mind was like 'a conjured spirit that would do mischief if he would not give it employment.' This demoniac quality is one of the essential things to remember about Swift. Equally important is it to bear in mind that what Swift lusted after was not power, or wealth, or fame, or happiness, but worldly consideration. This, again, we have from his own lips. 'All my endeavours from a boy,' he confessed to Pope, 'were only for want of a great title and fortune that I might be used like a lord by those who have an opinion of my parts ; whether right or wrong is no great matter.'   ' To be used like a lord,' not to be counted the greatest genius of the age, or to exercise a mighty influence in politics, was Swift's ambition. Since he was born poor and in humble circumstances, he could only get himself 'used like a lord' by achieving a great place in literature. He never pretended, however, that he sought the glory of letters for itself. That was only useful as a stepping-stone to social consideration. To gain this, he sacrificed all hope of personal happiness,—everything, in a word, but in-dependence of character. That he did not sacrifice this was due in no small measure to the.fact that his clear and great intellect told him that if he gave up his per-sonal independence he would be giving up the very thing he desired.

A great many subtle and ingenious explanations have been given of the motives which induced Swift to act as he acted towards women ; but the simplest and most intelligible is usually forgotten. Swift, a bachelor, could live on a couple of hundred a year, and yet mix on terms of equality with all the great people in London ; therefore Swift, poor and single, might force men to use him like a lord. Swift, poor and married to Stella must at once have sunk into a lower social stratum. Hence his whole nature resented the notion of marriage with an intensity so frenzied that those who ignore this key to his character have been led into a labyrinth of theory and conjecture. Other causes may very likely have helped to fix his determination, but the knowledge that marriage would socially have pulled him down was, we cannot doubt, the chief and original ground for the cruelty he showed to the women who loved him. As has been said above, Indignation is the word which best sums up the spirit that tore his heart. But here too the phrase is Swift's own. In the epitaph which he ordered to be cut on the black marble tablet over his tomb, in large letters deeply cut and strongly gilded, occur the memorable words *Sæva indignatio*. Those words express exactly the mental temper of the man who, on the day of his birth, never neglected to read and appropriate to himself the third chapter of the Book of Job. In spite of the fact that he had wrung from the great world the consideration he so fiercely desired, and had gratified his pitiful ambition to be used like a lord, it was in all sincerity that he cursed 'the night in which it was said there is a man-child conceived.' 'Let that day be darkness ; let not God regard it from above, neither let the light shine upon it. Let darkness and the shadow of death stain it ; let a cloud dwell upon it.' These were imprecations which the whole life of Swift tells us must have been used by him in the deadliest earnest.

But though this desire to be used like a lord gives us the ruling passion in Swift's nature, much in his life remains, and must continue to remain, unexplained. How was it that the man in whose presence no one ever dared to use a coarse or indecent word filled his pages with filth which would have been thought disgraceful in the days of Petronius Arbiter ? How was it that a man who in personal matters hated to do an unkindness deliberately tortured the two women who loved him and whom he loved ? Swift was a man who saw through everything and everyone, and who would not endure for a moment the thought of double dealing. Yet Swift acted before the world in regard both to Stella and Vanessa an elaborate imposture. Again, Swift was, as Lord Bolingbroke said, in everything the exact reverse of a hypocrite—a man who could not endure that others should think him what he was not. But this being so, what are we to think of his religious views—views which could not for a moment have stood the tests which Swift employed in the case of other men's professions?

IV

OF all Swift's works 'Gulliver's Travels' is the most satisfactory, complete, and characteristic. The book is shot through and through with fierce irony. Yet what has been its fate? A volume meant to hurl humanity on to a muck heap has become the delight of babes. How would Swift have regarded the fact that his great satire, not on England or his own times alone, but on mankind in general, has become a favourite child's book; that the work of which he said himself, 'Upon the great foundation of misanthropy the whole building of my travels is erected,' is read by boys and girls, who care nothing about misanthropy, and who miss the point of every magnificent stroke that falls on Walpole and the Whigs?

In re-reading 'Gulliver,' while the enthusiasm and delight for the imaginative creation remain unimpaired, there is added the pleasure evoked by vivid and penetrating satire, by the keenest irony, by the most finished rhetoric, and the nicest criticism. Where is there to be found a piece of satire more perfect than Gulliver's description of the discoveries as to the secret springs of history which he made among the Ghosts of Laputa :—

Here I discovered the true course of many great events that have surprised the world ; how a whore can govern the back-stairs, the back-stairs a council, the council a senate. A General confessed in my presence, that he had got a victory purely by the force of cowardice and ill conduct ; and an Admiral, that, for want of proper intelligence, he beat the enemy, to whom he intended to betray the fleet. Three kings protested to me, that in the whole of their reigns they never did once prefer any person of merit, unless by mistake, or treachery of some minister in whom they confided : neither would they do it if they were to live again ; and they showed with great strength of reason, that the royal throne could not be supported without corruption, because that positive, confident, restive temper which virtue infused into a man was a perpetual clog to public business.

Perhaps the most consummate instance of Swift's irony in our language is to be found in Gulliver's conversation with the King of Brobdingnag. The Englishman offers to tell his Majesty the secret of the use of gunpowder, in order that he may thus be able to make himself absolutely supreme in his kingdom, and enforce his commands at pleasure. Such, however, were 'the miserable effects of a confined education,' that the king not only refuses with horror, but declares that rather than know such a secret he would lose half his kingdom, and further commands Gulliver, as he values his life, never to mention the subject again. Then follows Gulliver's reflections on conduct so extraordinary :—

A strange effect of narrow principles and views, that a prince possessed of every quality which secures veneration,

love, and esteem ; of strong parts, of great wisdom, and pro-
found learning ; indued with admirable talents, and almost
adored by his subjects, should, from a nice, unnecessary scruple,
whereof in Europe we can have no conception, let slip an
opportunity put into his hands that would have made him
absolute master of the lives, of the liberties, and the fortunes of
his people ! Neither do I say this with the least intention to
detract from the many virtues of that excellent king, whose
character, I am sensible, will, on this account, be very much
lessened in the opinion of an English reader ; but I take this
defect among them to have arisen from their ignorance, by not
having hitherto reduced politics to a science as the more acute
wits of Europe have done.

Equally good as an example of this peculiar mixture
of satire and irony is the character of a Minister given
by Gulliver to his horse-master :—

I told him that a first or chief minister of State, who was
the person I intended to describe, was a creature wholly exempt
from joy and grief, love and hatred, pity and anger ; at least,
makes use of no other passion but a violent desire of wealth,
power, titles ; that he applies his words to all uses except to the
indication of his mind ; he never tells a truth, but with the
intent that you should take it for a lie ; nor a lie, but with the
design that you shall take it for a truth ; that those he speaks
worst of behind their backs are in the surest way of preferment,
and whenever he begins to praise you to others, or to yourself,
you are from that day forlorn. The worst mark you can receive
is a promise, especially when it is confirmed with an oath ;
after which every wise man retires, and gives over all hope.

Many reflections scattered up and down ' Gulliver's
Travels ' show how clear and sane was Swift's insight
into the world around him. Take, for example, the
famous description of the action-at-law which he gave
to his master in the land of the Houyhnhnms, and the

definition of legal precedents ; or the criticism on our system of female education.

It would be possible to multiply to any length instances of each form of literary artifice to be found in the pages of this extraordinarily various book. The style alone, though it will drive the student to despair if he fancies it possible to imitate, will in every other way well repay the most careful analysis. Its characteristics cannot be better given than in Swift's own description of the Brobdingnag literature. 'Their style is clear, masculine, and smooth, but not florid ; for they avoid nothing more than multiplying unnecessary words or using various expressions.' And with such words it may be well to close an attempt to reinvite those who have not read 'Gulliver's ·Travels ' since childhood, to study once more one of the profoundest and most brilliant of satires, one of the greatest of imaginative creations, and one of the noblest models of style in the English language.

MILTON'S PROSE

I

THERE is no doubt that if we take Milton's prose as a whole it cannot be called good.   It did nothing for the development of English style.   Full as are his writings of magnificent outbursts of eloquent rhetoric, the instrument he uses is very imperfect and very carelessly handled.   It is just the antithesis of his poetic manner. One of his greatest glories as a poet is the magnificent equality of his style—an equality not of a medium, but of a superlative excellence.   In prose he is always in danger of falling to the level of the contemporary tract; and though he rises, none higher, it is only at intervals.   In truth, the pedestrian passages in his prose writings have no style at all.   They might, except for the sense and learning, have as well been written by any hack pamphleteer.   No human being could read twenty lines of Milton's most ordinary verse —though such a phrase is a misnomer—and not recognise, before he recognised any other beauty, that he was reading the works of one of the great masters of expression.   There are pages in Milton's prose works which those most susceptible to the charm of style may read without an emotion.   Of course they will not turn very many pages in this mood.   Before long they must come to one of those magnificent outbursts in which the rushing splendour of words bears down all criticism. But to have written such passages is not to be a great prose-writer. A great prose-writer must be judged by the ordinary level of his writing. Dryden was a great prose-writer, though he never wrote in prose any passage of really magnificent sound or transcendent appropriateness of expression. Milton's ordinary level of writing was too often in the following strain [1] :—

Nevertheless, there be in others, beside the first supposed author, men not unread, nor unlearned in antiquity, who admit that for approved story, which the former explode for fiction ; and seeing that ofttimes relations heretofore accounted fabulous have been after found to contain in them many footsteps and relics of something true, as what we read in poets of the flood, and giants little believed, till undoubted witnesses taught us that all was not feigned ; I have therefore determined to bestow the telling over even of these reputed tales, be it for nothing else but in favour of our English poets and rhetoricians, who by their art will know how to use them judiciously.

This enormous sentence, which, to use Mr. Mark Pattison's phrase, does not stop with the sense, but only because the writer is out of breath, is by no means an extreme example.

Compare for a moment Dryden's fluent idiom in a few sentences from his ' Dedication of the Æneid : '—

If sounding words are not of our growth and manufacture, who shall hinder me to import them from a foreign country?

---

[1] This passage occurs in the *History of England*, a work which is said to have been forty years in writing, and therefore may more fairly be taken than the hurried compositions which he threw forth in the moment of an instant political need.

I carry not out the treasures of the nation which is never to return ; but what I bring from Italy, I spend in England ; here it remains, and here it circulates ; for, if the coin be good, it will pass from one hand to another. I trade both with the living and the dead, for the enrichment of our native language. We have enough in England to supply our necessity ; but if we will have things of magnificence and splendour, we must get them by commerce. Poetry requires ornament ; and that is not to be had from our old Teuton monosyllables. Therefore, if I find any elegant word in a classic author, I propose it to be naturalised, by using it myself ; and if the public approve of it, the bill passes.

II

BUT to insist that Milton was not a great prose-writer, and to point out that he did not create for himself a great prose manner which he could use indifferently for common subjects, is not to disparage Milton, but only to show that the development of English style runs from Bacon and Hooker through Dryden, and leaves Milton a side-eddy in the stream. This granted it may be admitted that Milton's writings contain passages which for splendour of sound, for grandeur of thought, and for appropriateness of expression, have no equals in the English language. Even the peroration of Mr. Bright's greatest speech on the Crimean War, magnificent as is the flow of its period, will not stand in comparison with the passage in the ' Areopagitica,' which contains the metaphors of the strong man rousing himself after sleep, and of the eagle ' mewing her mighty youth.'

The ' Areopagitica,' indeed, abounds with such passages. How spirit-stirring is the invocation—for

the 'Areopagitica' is really an oration—which begins—
'Lords and Commons of England, consider what
nation it is whereof ye are, and whereof ye are the
governor'—an invocation which continues with the
praises of our country conceived in the highest vein of
patriotism and of oratory. Proud is the Puritan spirit
which, after reciting the praises of that learning which
'has been so ancient and so eminent among us,' goes
on—'Yet that which is above all this, the favour and
the love of Heaven, we have great argument to think in
a peculiar manner propitious and pretending towards
us.' Then follows the famous regret that, but for the
'obstinate perverseness' of our prelates in suppressing
Wicklif, 'the glory of reforming our neighbours had
been completely ours ;' and the boast that God is now
again revealing Himself to His servants, 'and, as His
manner is, first to His Englishmen.' The address to
London—perhaps the one instance in which the great
city has inspired a feeling in a poet akin to that which
Athens, Rome, and Florence inspired—is conspicuous
for its swift and ringing cadences :—

Behold now this vast city, a city of refuge, the mansion-
house of Liberty, encompassed and surrounded with his pro-
tection, the shop of war hath not there more anvils and
hammers working, to fashion out the plates and instruments of
armed justice in defence of beleaguered truth, than there be
pens and heads there, sitting by their studious lamps, musing,
searching, revolving new notions and ideas wherewith to present,
as with their homage and their fealty, the approaching Reformation ; others as fast reading, trying all things, assenting to
the force of reason and convincement.

Milton's irony is not generally conspicuous, for his
temper was too thoroughly English. In one place

however, in this tract he indulges it. He tells the Parliament that if they license printing they must also license music. ' It will ask more than the works of twenty licencers to examine all the lutes, the violins and the guitars in every house ; they must not be suffered to prattle as they do, but must be licensed what they may say.' ' Who,' he goes on, ' shall silence all the airs and madrigals that whisper softness in chambers ? ' Perhaps one of the most remarkable characteristics of Milton's prose when compared with that of his contemporaries, is the number of short, telling phrases which are only not epigrams because they have no after-thought. Take as examples the celebrated definition ' Poetry which is simple, sensuous, and passionate ; ' the declaration that the poet ' ought himself to be a true poem,' or the dicta—' Opinion is but knowledge in the making,' ' As good almost kill a man as a good book ; ' or ' The State shall be my governors, but not my critics.'

But Milton's fine passages are not composed solely of happy phrases or outbursts of glowing rhetoric. Every now and again, the crabbed and parenthetical stream of some pedantic diatribe will be lit up by a passage of such exquisite grace, that our delight for the moment overweighs all the regret that the magic at his command was not used less sparely. Milton, in his apology against a pamphlet called ' A Modest Con-futation,' has given us his ' Biographia Literaria,' and told us how he learned to prefer ' the two famous renowners ' of Beatrice and Laura :—

And long it was not after, when I was confirmed in this opinion, that he, who would not be frustrate of his hope to write well hereafter in laudable things, ought himself to be a true poem, that is, a composition and pattern of the best and honourablest things, not presuming to sing high praises of heroic men or famous cities, unless he have in himself the experience and the practice of all that which is praiseworthy. . . . Next, for hear me out now, readers, that I may tell ye whither my younger feet wandered, I betook me among those lofty fables and romances which recount in solemn cantos the deeds of knighthood founded by our victorious kings, and from hence had in renoun over all Chrisendom. There I read it in the oath of every knight, that he should defend to the expense of his best blood, or of his life, if it so befell him, the honour and chastity of virgin or matron. From whence even then I learnt what a noble virtue chastity ever must be, to the defence of which so many worthies by such a dear adventure of themselves had sworn. And if I found in the story afterwards any of them by word or deed breaking that oath, I judged it the same fault of the poet as that which is attributed to Homer to have written undecent things of the Gods. Only this my mind gave me, that every free and gentle spirit without that oath ought to be borne a knight, nor needed to expect the gilt spur, or the laying of a sword upon his shoulder, to stir him up, both by his counsel and his arm, to serve and protect the weakness of any attempted chastity. So that even those books which to many others have been the food of wantonness and loose living, I cannot think how, unless by divine indulgence, proved to me so many incitements to the love and steadfast observation of virtue.

It is worth while to put in contrast with this a passage from one of those lofty romances which so deeply enchanted Milton that he nearly substituted the Court of Logress or of Lyoness for the fields of Heaven, the Knights of the Round Table for Abdiel Raphael and Satan. The following description of how Vivian enchanted Merlin is from the 'Suite de Merlin.' Milton's prose shows evident traces of the influence of such writings as these :—

So they sojourned together longtime, till it fell on a day that they went through the forest hand in hand, devising and disporting, and this was in the forest of Brocheland, and found a bush that was fair and high of white horthorne full of flowers, and there they sat in the shadow, and Merlin laid his head in the damsel's lap, and she began to taste softly till he fell on sleep; and when she felt that he was on sleep she arose softly, and made a cern with her whimple all about the bush and all about Merlin, and began her enchantments so as Merlin had her taught, and made the cern nine times, and nine times her enchantments; and after that she went and sat down by him and laid his head on her lap, and held him there till he did awake, and then he looked about him and him seemed he was in the fairest tower of the world, and the most strong, and found him laid in the fairest place that ever he lay beforn; and then he said to the damsel, 'Lady thou hast me deceived, but if ye will abide with me for none but ye may undo thy enchantments;' and she said, 'Fair sweet friend, I shall oftentimes go out, and ye shall have me in your arms and I you; and from henceforth shall ye do all your pleasure;' and she him held well couenaunt for few hours there were of the night one of the day but she was with him. Ne never after come Merlin out of that fortress that she had him inset; but she went in and out when she would."

III

THE Miltonic ideal of that to which a man of letters should attain was both sane and noble. With him the poet is never to fall to the author. Before all things he must be the good citizen, not presuming to praise high deeds, unless he is himself a sharer in their accomplishment. His life must be of the real world and a true poem; and though singing and the lore that strives to make life harmonious is his duty, yet he must not flinch, if the love of his country and of what is right and dear to him in the fabric of society prompt him to take his share in the strife of the world.   This was Milton's ideal. , This he fearlessly put before him and followed.   Milton was a man first—a man of noble courage and of high resolve —who, though he was born with the divinest gift of verse, yet saw clearly that not by sinking the man for the singer, but by claiming and using all his duties as a man, would he make his life that true poem which is the poet's.   And this is why Milton's fame as a man and fame as a poet can never be separated, but unite to give him that incomparable renown which he was too truthful ever to doubt his due.

A PURITAN COURTSHIP

NO more delightful account of the liberal side of the Puritan spirit can anywhere be found than in the charming story of Colonel Hutchinson's courtship, which is set out with loving minuteness of detail in the 'Memoirs' by his wife.

When Mr. Hutchinson, son of Sir Thomas Hutchinson, and Margaret, daughter of Sir John Biron, of Newstead, had finished his education at the University of Cambridge, where for his exercise he practised tennis and for his diversion music, he stayed for a short time in his father's house at Owthorpe; and then going to London, began to study law at Lincoln's Inn. The harsh studies of the men who were perfecting the details of that strange and inglorious structure, the family settlement, were, however, little to his taste, and he thought it more profitable to exercise himself in 'dancing, fencing, and music.' One day Mr. Hutchinson, tired of the town, and not knowing how to dispose of himself, was wondering whether to accept the invitation of a French merchant to take a journey to France. While undecided, his music-master came in and recommended that instead he should go to the music-master's house at Richmond, at which place 'there was very good company and recreations, the King's hawks being kept near the place, and several other conveniences.'

Mr. Hutchinson determined to accept this offer. Fortunate choice ; for had he not, Lucy Hutchinson's 'Memoirs' would never have been written. But he was not to go without a warning, delightfully characteristic of his age, and prescient of what was to be his own fate. One of his friends, hearing of the intended visit, told him how fatal for love was Richmond, and how he would never return thence a free man. To confirm it, the friend told a tale of a gentleman who, going there to lodge, had found all the people he saw 'bewailing the death of a gentlewoman that had lived there.' 'Hearing her so much deplored he made inquiry after her, and grew so in love with the description that no other discourse could at first please him, nor could he at last endure any other ; he grew desperately melancholy, and would go to a mount where the print of her foot was cut, and lie there pining and kissing of it all the day long, till at length death in some months' space concluded his languishment.'

'This story,' says Mrs. Hutchinson, ' was very true.' At least it breathes the spirit of the Duke in ' Twelfth Night,' of ' Philaster,' of Ford's ' Lover's Melancholy,' and shows how the dramatists chose plots of melancholy no more fantastic than the stories of everyday life. Mr. Hutchinson was not daunted, however, by this tale, and went to Richmond, and since he ' tabled ' or boarded in the house of a musician, was plunged into the element he loved most—music and singing. Not only did the king's musicians meet there to practise new airs, but ' divers of the gentlemen and ladies that were affected with music came thither to hear.' The handsome young boarder made friends easily. And no wonder, unless his description belies him. His fair complexion, his beautiful light-brown hair, 'very thick set in his youth, softer than the finest silk, and curling into loose great rings at the ends,' and his grey eyes 'full of life and vigour,' his well-made person, his active and graceful movements, and that 'most amiable countenance, which carried in it something of magnanimity and majesty mixed with sweetness,' must together have made up a very pleasing person. And if we say that 'he had an exact ear and judgment in music,' and 'often diverted himself on the viol, on which he played masterly,' we shall hardly want to add the beauty and propriety of his dress, for which he was famed, to explain his popularity in a musical society ; or that, as Mrs. Hutchinson says, with truly feminine candour and discernment, he was 'nobly treated, with all the attractive arts that young women and their parents use to procure them lovers.'

But Mr. Hutchinson was not to be caught by 'their fine snares ; ' and, though 'without any taint of incivility,' reproved the pride and vanity of these too attentive young persons. His time, however, was soon to come. In the house where he boarded was also 'a younger daughter of Sir Allen Apsley, late Lieutenant of the Tower, tabled for the practice of her lute till the return of her mother, who was gone into Wiltshire.' The cause of the mother's journey into Wiltshire was one which was by no means strange in the seventeenth century,—the accomplishment of a treaty for marrying her elder daughter, who had also gone with her mother. The sister, left at Richmond, though quite a child, was so excellent a musician that Mr. Hutchinson 'took pleasure in hearing her practice, and would fall in discourse with her.' The acquaintance ripened. ' She, having the keys of her mother's house some half a mile distant, would sometimes ask Mr. Hutchinson when she went over to walk along with her. One day when he was there, looking upon an odd shelf in her sister's closet, he found a few Latin books. Asking whose they were, he was told they were her elder sister's; whereupon, inquiring more after her, he began first to be sorry she was gone before he had seen her, and gone upon such an account that he was not likely to see her. Then he grew to love to hear mention of her, and the other gentlewomen who had been her companions used to talk much to him of her, telling him how reserved and studious she was, and other things which they esteemed no advantage.'

All this, however, only inflamed Mr. Hutchinson the more, and gradually he fell in love with her very report, so fatal for love was Richmond. Every circumstance tended to plunge him deeper. One day he heard a song which rumour gave out as 'Mrs. Apsley's' composition. This the cautious Mr. Hutchinson could not at first believe possible, for he fancied 'something of rationality in the sonnet beyond the customary reach of a she-wit.' The rumour, however, was shown to be true. Then, said Mr. Hutchinson, ' I cannot be at rest till this lady's return, that I may be acquainted with her.' The gentleman who had vouched for the authorship of the song replied, ' Sir, you must not expect that, for she is of a humour she will not be acquainted with any of mankind ; and however this song has stolen forth, she is the nicest creature in the world for suffering her

perfections to be known ; she shuns the converse of men
as the plague ; she only lives in the enjoyment of
herself, and has not the humanity to communicate that
happiness to any of our sex.' 'Well,' said Mr.
Hutchinson, 'but I will be acquainted with her.'

It is difficult, as we read this, to realise that we are
reading Puritan memoirs, with such admirable skill is
the lover's idyll recounted. So dramatic, too, is the
situation that it seems that the whole story must be the
creation of Fletcher's muse. However, the course of
true love was not altogether to run smooth. Soon after
the episode of the song, as the company were at dinner
in the musician's house, 'a footboy of my lady her
mother came to young Mrs. Apsley' [Mrs. and Miss
were then interchangeable] 'saying that her mother and
sister would soon return.' When they asked the mes-
senger if Mrs. Apsley were married, 'having been instructed to make them believe it, he smiled, and pulled
out some bride-laces, and told them Mrs. Apsley bade
him tell no news, but give them the tokens, and carried
the matter so that all the company believed she had been
married.' On hearing this poor Mr. Hutchinson 'immediately turned pale as ashes, and fell a fainting to
seize his spirits.' With difficulty concealing his condition, he left the table. When alone he himself began
to remember the story told him, and 'to believe that
there was some magic in the place which enchanted
men out of their right senses.' Make what effort he
would, 'the sick heart could not be chid nor advised into
health ; ' and it was not till he had cross-questioned the
foot-boy and discovered the fraud that his spirits
revived. While now in better hope and waiting to see

his unknown mistress he was one day invited to 'a noble treatment at Sion Garden.' While there it was announced to young Mrs. Apsley that her mother and sister were really come. The solution of this situation, so admirably worked up by Mrs. Hutchinson, must be told in her own inimitable language,—for it would be a profanation to abridge the charm of her description of the lovers' first interview :—

She (young Mrs. Apsley) would immediately have gone, but Mr. Hutchinson, pretending civility to conduct her home, made her stay till the supper was ended ; of which he eat no more, now only longing for that sight which he had with such perplexity expected. This at length he obtained ; but his heart being prepossessed with his own fancy, was not free to discern how little there was in her to answer so great an expectation. She was not ugly in a careless riding-habit ; she had a melancholy negligence both of herself and others, as if she neither affected to please others nor took notice of anything before her ; yet in spite of all her indifferancy, she was surprised with some unusual liking in her soul when she saw this gentleman, who had hair, eyes, shape, and countenance enough to beget love in any one at the first, and these set off with a graceful and generous mien which promised an extraordinary person. He was at that time—and, indeed, always—very neatly habited, for he wore good and rich clothes, and had a variety of them, and had them well suited and every way answerable, in that little thing showing both good judgment and great generosity—he equally becoming them and they him, which he wore with an equal unaffectedness and such neatness as do not often meet in one. Although he had but at evening sight of her he had so long desired, and that at disadvantage enough for her, yet the prevailing sympathy of his soul made him think all his pains were paid, and this first did whet his desire to a second sight, which he had by accident the next day, and to his joy, found that she was wholly disengaged from that treaty which he so much feared had been accomplished. He found withal that, though she was modest, she was accostable and willing to entertain his acquaintance. This soon passed into a mutual friendship between them ; and though she innocently thought nothing of love, yet was she glad to have acquired such a friend who had wisdom and virtue enough to be trusted with her councils, for she was then much perplexed in mind.

Mrs. Hutchinson goes on to tell us with loving minuteness the details of her courtship, and of 'the opportunity of conversing with her' that was afforded to Mr. Hutchinson 'in those pleasant walks, which at that sweet season of the spring invited all the neighbouring inhabitants to seek their joys ; where, though they were never alone, yet they had every day opportunity for converse with each other, which the rest shared not in, while everyone minded their own delights.' She recounts also the wicked machinations of the other ladies of Richmond to make mischief between the lovers, and whose ' witty spite represented all her faults to him, which chiefly terminated in the negligence of her dress and habit, and all womanish ornaments, giving herself wholly up to study and writing.' So ends the story of Mr. Hutchinson's courtship.

The extraordinary felicity with which it is told does not, however, exhaust Mrs. Hutchinson's literary powers. In political satire, in historical narrative, in fervent disquisition, her style—fine, plastic, and glowing, fits closely round her subject, and expands or contracts, in eloquent rhetoric or in terse narration, just as she requires it. Her sketch of English history has a vigour of expression marvellous when compared with the ordinary historical writing of her age. What could be better than her description of Edward the Confessor as 'that superstitious prince who, sainted for his ungodly chastity, left an empty throne to him that could seize it ;' or her proud boast against the wild ambition of princes and their flatterers, which in England 'could never in any age so tread down popular liberty but that it rose again with renewed vigour, till at length it trod on those that trampled it before ?'

ABRAHAM LINCOLN—THE LAST OF THE PURITANS

I

THE English-speaking world will never read the story of the Rebellion of the Southern States without a thrill of pride and exultation. The achievement of the Puritans in throwing off the tyranny of the Stuarts, and establishing in its place, not license or anarchy, but a wise and liberal polity, was heroic and inspiring. But the veiling hand of time diminishes for modern men its distinctness and reality. With the defence of the Union it is different. We almost hear the reverberations of the cannon at Vicksburg, and our hands may still clasp the hands of those who overthrew embattled treason at Gettysburg and Chattanooga. The glory won by the English race is so near, that it still stirs the blood like a trumpet to read of the patriotism of the men who fought at the call of Lincoln.

Nothing is more admirable, as nothing is more dramatic in recorded history, than the manner in which the North sprang to arms at the news that the nation's flag had been fired on at Fort Sumter. It is all very well to hire soldiers at so much a day and send them to the front with salutes and rejoicings, but the action of the Eastern and Western States meant a great deal more than this. It meant a voluntary sacrifice on the part of men who had nothing to gain and everything to lose by throwing over a life of ease or profit to shoulder a musket or serve a gun. A continent was on fire. It is one of the greatest of Lincoln's claims to admiration, that though he sympathised with the fervour and enthusiasm of his countrymen, he was never carried away by it. He was one of those rare men who can at once be zealous and moderate, who are kindled by great ideas, and who yet retain complete control of the critical faculty. And more than this, Lincoln was a man who could be reserved without the chill of reserve. Again, he could make allowance for demerits in a principle or a human instrument, without ever falling into the purblindness of cynicism. He often acted in his dealings with men much as a professed cynic might have acted ; but his conduct was due, not to any disbelief in virtue, but to a wide tolerance and a clear knowledge of human nature. He saw things as a disillusionised man sees them, and yet in the bad sense he never suffered any disillusionment. For suffusing and combining his other qualities was a serenity of mind which affected the whole man. He viewed the world too much as a whole to be greatly troubled or perplexed over its accidents.

To this serenity of mind was due his almost total absence of indignation in the ordinary sense. Generals might half-ruin the cause for the sake of some trumpery quarrel, or in order to gain some petty personal advantage ; office-seekers might worry at the very crisis of the nation's fate ; but none of the pettinesses, the spites, or the follies could rouse in Lincoln the impatience or the indignation that would have been wakened in ordinary men. Pity, and nothing else, was the feeling such exhibitions occasioned him. Lincoln seems to have felt the excuse that tempers the guilt of every mortal transgression. His largeness and tenderness of nature made him at heart a universal apologist. He was, of course, too practical and too great a statesman to let this sensibility to the excuses that can be made for human conduct induce him to allow misdeeds to go unpunished or uncorrected. He acted as firmly and as severely as if he had experienced the most burning indignation ; but the moment we come to Lincoln's real feelings, we see that he is never incensed, and that, even in its most legitimate form, the desire for retribution is absent from his mind. *Tout comprendre, c'est tout pardonner*, was the secret of his attitude towards human affairs. In a word, Mr. Lincoln possessed intellectual detachment in its highest and purest form. The test of intellectual detachment is the possession of the true sense of justice, and this he had if ever man had it. No more truly just man ever walked this earth. There is no hate in justice, though hate, we are willing to admit, is often more of a virtue than a vice. But Lincoln was not unmanned, as most men would have been, by his lack of hate. It is almost inconceivable and yet true, that he carried on his death struggle with the South without ever feeling the passion of hate, and yet without ever faltering in his course. Many a General has neglected to hate his enemies ; but that has usually been due to indifference to the cause of the war, or to a cynical disbelief in such a thing as righteousness. Lincoln had a fervent belief in the justice of his actions, and yet could view the South without a trace of hatred. His attitude can be best illustrated by quoting the sublimest passage from that sublimest of modern speeches—the Second Inaugural. We know not, if not there, where to find an example of the higher mental detachment :—

Both parties deprecated war ; but one of them would make war rather than let the nation survive ; and the other would accept war rather than let it perish. And the war came. One-eighth of the whole population were coloured slaves, not distributed generally over the Union, but localised in the Southern part of it. These slaves constituted a peculiar and powerful interest. All knew that this interest was somehow the cause of the war. To strengthen, perpetuate, and extend this interest was the object for which the insurgents would rend the Union, even by war ; while the Government claimed no right to do more than to restrict the territorial enlargement of it. Neither party expected for the war the magnitude nor the duration which it has already attained. Neither anticipated that the cause of the conflict might cease with, or even before, the conflict itself should cease. Each looked for an easier triumph, and a result less fundamental and astounding. Both read the same Bible, and pray to the same God ; and each invokes His aid against the other. It may seem strange that any men should dare to ask a just God's assistance in wringing their bread from the sweat of other men's faces ; but let us judge not, that we be not judged. The prayers of both could not be answered – that of neither has been answered fully. The Almighty has His own purposes. 'Woe unto the world because of offences ! for it must needs be that offences come ; but woe to that man by whom the offence cometh.' If we shall suppose that American slavery is one of those offences which, in the providence of God, must needs come, but which, having continued through His appointed time, He now wills to remove, and that He gives to both North and South this terrible war, as the woe due to those by whom the offence came, shall we discern therein any departure from those divine attributes which the believers in a living God always ascribe to Him ? Fondly do we hope—fervently do we pray—that this mighty scourge of war may speedily pass away. Yet, if God wills that it continue until all the wealth piled by the bondman's two hundred and fifty years of unrequited toil shall be sunk, and until every drop of blood drawn with the lash shall be paid by another drawn with the sword, as was said three thousand years ago, so still it must be said, ' The judgments of the Lord are true and righteous altogether.' With malice toward none ; with charity for all ; with firmness in the right, as God gives us to see the right, let us strive on to finish the work we are in ; to bind up the nation's wounds ; to care for him who shall have borne the battle, and for his widow, and his orphan—to do all which may achieve and cherish a just and lasting peace among ourselves, and with all nations.

Notice how the sense of justice saves Lincoln from confusing and confounding right and wrong. Though the South were not necessarily wicked, there was a real question of right and wrong involved, which must never be lost sight of. The man with only the lower intellectual detachment, had he attempted to write as Lincoln wrote, would probably have ended by blurring the moral outlook, and would have lost touch of the cause of the war. Lincoln, because he possessed the higher intellectual detachment, was able to be perfectly just to the South, and yet never to confuse the moral issue. Right and wrong were not the same to him, though he could see so well, and understand so completely, the attitude of the South. This is the intellectual detachment which is indeed worth having, and against which the graces of the lower intellectual detachment weigh like thistle-down in the balance.

So much for the intellectual side of Lincoln's nature. Behind it was a personality of singular charm. Tenderness and humour were its main characteristics. As he rode through a forest in spring-time, he would keep on dismounting to put back the young birds that had fallen from their nests. There was not a situation in life which could not afford him the subject for a kindly smile. It needed a character so full of gentleness and good temper to sustain the intolerable weight of responsibility which the war threw upon the shoulders of the President. Most men would have been crushed by the burden. His serenity of temper saved Lincoln. Except when the miserable necessity of having to sign the order for a military execution took away his sleep, he carried on his work without any visible sign of over-strain. Not the least of Lincoln's achievements is to be found in the fact that though for four years he wielded a power and a personal authority greater than that exercised by any monarch on earth, he never gave satirist or caricaturist the slightest real ground for declaring that his sudden rise to world-wide fame had turned the head of the backwoodsman.

Under the circumstances, there would have been every excuse for Lincoln, had he assumed to his subordinates somewhat of the bearing of the autocrat he was. It is a sign of the absolute sincerity and good sense of the President that he was under no sort of a temptation to do so. Lincoln was before all things a gentleman, and the good taste inseparable from that character made it impossible for him to be spoiled by power and position. This grace and strength of disposition is never better shown than in the letters to his generals, victorious or defeated. When they were beaten, he was anxious to share the blame; when victorious, he was instant to deny by anticipation any rumour that he had inspired the strategy of the campaign. If a general had to be reprimanded, he did it as only the most perfect of gentlemen could do it. He could convey the severest censure without inflicting any wound that would not heal, and this not by using roundabout expressions, but in the plainest language. 'He writes to me like a father,' were the heart-felt words of a commander who had been reproved by the President. Throughout these communications, the manner in which he not only conceals but altogether sinks all sense that the men to whom they were addressed were in effect his subordinates, is worthy of special note. 'A breath could make them, as a breath had made,' and yet Lincoln writes as if his generals were absolutely independent.

II

LINCOLN'S PROSE STYLE

WE have said something of Lincoln as a man, and as the leader of a great cause. We desire now to dwell upon a point which is often neglected in considering the career of the hero of the Union, but which, from the point of view of letters, is of absorbing interest. No criticism of Mr. Lincoln can be in any sense adequate which does not deal with his astonishing power over words. It is not too much to say of him that he is among the greatest masters of prose ever produced by the English race.   Self-educated, or rather not educated at all in the ordinary sense, as he was, he contrived to obtain an insight and power in the handling of the mechanism of letters such as has been given to few men in his, or, indeed, in any age.   That the gift of oratory should be a natural gift is understandable enough, for the methods of the orator, like those of the poet, are primarily sensuous, and may well be instinctive.   Mr. Lincoln's achievement seems to show that no less is the writing of prose an endowment of Nature.   Mr. Lincoln did not get his ability to handle prose through his gift of speech.   That these are separate, though co-ordinate faculties, is a matter beyond dispute, for many of the great orators of the world have proved themselves exceedingly inefficient in the matter of deliberate composition.   Mr. Lincoln enjoyed both gifts.   His letters, despatches, memoranda, and written addresses are even better than his speeches ; and in speaking thus of Mr. Lincoln's prose, we are not thinking merely of certain pieces of inspired rhetoric.

We do not praise his prose because, like Mr. Bright, he could exercise his power of coining illuminating phrases as effectively upon paper as on the platform. It is in his conduct of the pedestrian portions of composition that Mr. Lincoln's genius for prose style is exhibited.   Mr. Bright's writing cannot claim to answer the description which Hazlitt has given of the successful prose-writer's performance.   Mr. Lincoln's can.   What Hazlitt says is complete and perfect in definition.   He tells us that the prose-writer so uses his pen ' that he loses no particle of the exact, characteristic, extreme, impression of the thing he writes about ; ' and with equal significance he points out that 'the prose-writer is master of his materials,' as 'the poet is the slave of his style.' If these words convey a true definition, then Mr. Lincoln is a master of prose. Whatever the subject he has in hand, whether it be bald or impassioned, businesslike or pathetic, we feel that we 'lose no particle of the exact, characteristic, extreme, impression' of the thing written about. We have it all, and not merely a part. Every line shows that the writer is master of his materials ; that he guides the words, never the words him. This is, indeed, the predominant note throughout all Mr. Lincoln's work. We feel that he is like the engineer who controls some mighty reservoir. As he desires, he opens the various sluice gates, but for no instant is the water not under his entire control. We are thus sensible in reading Mr. Lincoln's writings that an immense force is gathered up behind him, and that in each jet that flows every drop is meant. Some writers only leak ; others half flow through determined channels, half leak away their words like a broken lock when it is emptying. The greatest, like Mr. Lincoln, send out none but clear-shaped streams.

The Second Inaugural—the concluding portion of which we have just quoted—well illustrates our words. Mr. Lincoln had to tell his countrymen that after a four years' struggle, the war was practically ended. The four years' agony, the passion of love which he felt for his country, his joy in her salvation, his sense of tenderness for those who fell, of pity mixed with sternness for the men who had deluged the land with blood—all the thoughts these feelings inspired were behind Lincoln pressing for expression. A writer of less power would

have been overwhelmed.   Lincoln remained a master of
the emotional and intellectual situation.   In three or
four hundred words that burn with the heat of their
compression, he tells the history of the war and reads
its lesson.   No nobler thoughts were ever conceived.
No man ever found words more adequate to his desire.
Here is the whole tale of the nation's shame and misery,
of her heroic struggles to free herself therefrom, and of
her victory.   Had Lincoln written a hundred times as
much more, he could not have said more fully what he
desired to say.   Every thought receives its complete
expression, and there is no word employed which does
not directly and manifestly contribute to the development of the central thought.

As an example of Lincoln's more familiar style, we
may quote from that inimitable series of letters to his
generals to which we have made allusion already.
The following letter was addressed to General Hooker
on his being appointed to command the Army of the
Potomac, after mismanagement and failure had made
a change of generals absolutely necessary :—

I have placed you at the head of the Army of the Potomac.
Of course I have done this upon what appears to me to be
sufficient reasons, and yet I think it best for you to know that
there are some things in regard to which I am not quite
satisfied with you.   I believe you to be a brave and skilful
soldier, which, of course, I like.   I also believe you do not
mix politics with your profession, in which you are right.   You
have confidence in yourself, which is a valuable, if not an in-
dispensable, quality.   You are ambitious, which, within reasonable bounds, does good rather than harm ; but I think that
during General Burnside's command of the ·army, you have
taken counsel of your ambition, and thwarted him as much as

you could, in which you did a great wrong to the country and to a most meritorious and honourable brother-officer. I have heard, in such a way as to believe it, of your recently saying that both the army and the Government needed a dictator. Of course, it was not for this, but in spite of it, that I have given you the command. Only those generals who gain successes can set up dictators. What I now ask of you is military success, and I will risk the dictatorship. The Government will support you to the utmost of its ability, which is neither more nor less than it has done and will do for all commanders. I much fear that the spirit, which you have aided to infuse into the army, of criticising their commander and withholding confidence from him, will now turn upon you. I shall assist you as far as I can to put it down. Neither you nor Napoleon, if he were alive again, could get any good out of an army while such a spirit prevails in it. ' And now beware of rashness. Beware of rashness, but with energy and sleepless vigilance go forward and give us victories.

It is possible that this letter may sound too severe in tone when read without the context. If, however, the condition of the army at the time and the intrigues of the various commanders are considered, it will be recognised as erring in no way on the side of harshness. As a piece of prose it is inimitable. The complete mastery over his materials possessed by the writer is everywhere apparent. Each touch of irony, of humour, of feeling, is laid exactly where it ought to be laid, and exactly where Mr. Lincoln meant it to be laid. Flaubert after his thirty years of study could not have controlled the mechanism of writing better, or indeed so well.

A PURITAN MICAWBER

IN the second series of the 'Verney Papers,' one of the most delightful of the Memoirs of the Cromwellian period, we get a full-length picture of a person who was nothing more nor less than a Puritan Micawber.

Tom Verney, the Puritan Micawber, a warrior always in pawn to some small tradesman, and yet always designing mining speculations, and waiting for something to turn up in the Barbados or elsewhere, is one of the most amusing figures in the romances of real life. Poor Tom suffered from a perpetual and apparently entirely incurable lack of shirts, clothes, and other conveniences and necessaries. He was for ever bombarding his highly respectable and much-tried brother with letters, begging for clothes. These letters are every bit as monumental as those of Mr. Micawber, and read with the same mouthy amplitude of phrase. Note how in the following is reproduced the immortal Micawber's magnificent parade of financial exactitude, as well as the splendour of language :— Weekly instalments of 3*s*. each ! and then the exquisite touch as to his 'cloudy condition : '—

To imitate historians in putting prefaces to their books, I conceive I need not, for I am confident you are so very sencible

of my want of clothing. Sir my last request to you is for a
slight stuff sute & coat against Whitsontide, which may stand
you in 50*s.*, the which I will repay you by 3*s.* weekly till you be
reimburst. In former times my own word would have passed
for such a summ, but now *they* [*they* is good] require securitie
of mee, becaus I live in soe cloudy a condition. God put it
into your hart once to releive my nakedness & you shall find
a most oblidgeing brother of Sir, your humble servant,

THOMAS VERNEY.

When Tom is thinking of going to the West Indies, he
does not, like the Micawbers, discourse on the habits
of the kangaroo, because he did not live in a scientific
age. His environment was theological, hence when he
drew up the list of things which his family were to provide for his journey, it is in the following style :—

First for a provision for my soul—Doctor Taylour his holy
liveing & holy dyeing both in one volume. 2ly the Practise of
Piety to refresh my memery. The Turkish Historye, the
reading whereof, I take some delight in. Now for my body.

A list follows of provisions of all kinds, Westphalian
hams, Cheshire cheeses, Zante oil, beef suet, everything
to be ' of the very best quality.' He will not ask for
' burnt clarett or brandy,' though he requires it, ' for I
must not, Sir, overcharge you, for you have been highly
civill to me ! '

Unfortunately, however, Tom in one thing was not a
true Micawber. He was a rogue, and a heartless one,
and also a habitual liar, and not a mere pompous waiter
on the something which never turned up. But, though
this must be said, we will not dwell on the darker side
of Tom's character. Let us return to the true Micawber

vein, and learn how he apprises his elder brother that his greatest stock has come to one poor groat, 'and how I am able to subsist five months with one groat I appeal to you and all rationeull and judicious persons.' His great archetype could not have bettered this appeal to the opinion of the rational and the judicious. When he was confined in the Fleet Prison, Tom wrote the following admirably expressed letter to his brother. Mark how he stands outside himself, and is favourably impressed by the chance of his own conversion :—

You are that founetaine, from whence all my joy, delight, and comfort comes, and long may you live to see, what you principally aime att, my amendment. He goeth farr that never turnes. Wors livers than my self have seen their errors and have returned home like the prodigall : why may not I? God hath endued mee with a reasoneable understanding ; and I question not a reall conversion, since I have soe courteous, soe kind, and so tender a harted brother to help mee up before I am quite downe. . . . In relation to my inlargement, I begg the continueance ·of a weekly supply dureing my restraint. Eighteene pence a day, which amounts in the week to 10s. 6d., is as low as any one that is borne a gentleman can possibly live att, let my wants be supplied by noon, that I may have a dinner as well as others.

He is bailed out before noon, but alas! he is re-arrested, and is back again by dinner-time. This fact, however, only stimulates his literary faculty, and he pens the same day a second letter to his brother, which ends, ' I must submit if so you have decreed, and if I perish I perish.' He does not perish, however, and three days after is inditing to his brother-in-law, Dr. Denton, an admirable plea for clean sheets to be obtained from a cruel jailer at two shillings ' per payre.' Tom is ultimately released, and then comes the eternal question of where he shall go. At first Malaga was proposed, because, as the ingenuous warrior confessed, 'he had a wife at Malaga :'—

He promised if he reached Malaga to send Sir Ralph 'the knowledge of my wive's and my greeting, together with the scitueation of the place, there manner of government, and with what else that I shall esteeme worthy your reading.' . . . But he has no special preference for Malaga. He next desires 'to be transported in a shipp that is bound for the Barbados. . . . Courteous Brother, That Island, and all the Indies over, doth wholly subsist by merchandizeing : and that person that aimes to live in creditt and repute in those parts must be under the notion of a merchant or factor, planter, or overseer of a plantation, and he that lives otherwise, is of 'little or noe esteeme. . . . I could (soe it might not occasion an offence) prescribe you a safe way how to send mee thither, like a gentleman, like your brother, and allso to equall my former height of liveing there : but you may perhapps find out a way (unknowne to mee) how I may subsist and have a being like a gentleman till you can heare I am safely arrived there or noe.'

Tom's real preference, however, was for spending the summer on a Dutch man-of-war, because, as he fervently remarked, 'Noe damned bayliff nor hellish sergent can or dares disturb my abode there.' (How Shakespeare would have loved the fellow ! Here is the very air of Ancient Pistol and his mates !)

The eternal clothes question and the instant need of shirts sends Tom into heroics :—

'I doe know of a garment that would last mee to eternity, and it is to be purchased for less than forty shillings ; which is a grave ; and *that* I cannot have neither as yet ; in time I shall, then I shall have a requiem sung unto my soul, and purchase a releas from this my miserable life to enjoy one more glorious; soe I thought to have made an end of this my sad complaint, but before I soe doe I make it my request to you, if I have either by writeing, or by word of mouth abused you, or spoken evilly of you (which to my knowledge I never yet did) as to bury it in the grave of oblivion, and to weigh those words of mine as proceeding wholly from a person drunk with passion, and overwhelmed with miseries.' Sir Ralph sends him shirts, but refuses to advance any money, or to discuss his claims to enter upon a 'glorious' life, in a more appreciative world than here below.

But it would take a whole book to thoroughly depict the Puritan Micawber. Fain would we tell, but cannot, how Tom took to speculating in mines in Wales and elsewhere, and how these, though magnificently successful as commercial ventures, were always in need of a little money to go on with. Alas! the mines went smash, and Tom, like a modern director, had to come into court :—

'It is truth' [he writes to his brother] ' the jury brought mee in guilty; but of what ? not of the fact, but of too much indiscretion and rashness; which caused the judge and the major part of the justices to declare in open court, that they did really beleeve mee to be a person meerely drawne in, and they hoped it would be a warneing to mee for the future. Sir, when Sir Thomas Thinn understood the sence of the Bench, and that I was acquitted, paying my fees, he cunningly arrested mee in the face of the court, charging mee with an action of 500*l*. the which I have [word torn out] bayle too. It will not be long till he hath lex talionis, and soe we shall make it a cross action.'

With one more quotation we must leave Tom. We all know how people without money take vast journeys solely for the sake of economy. Tom did the like. 'My intentions,' he tells us, 'are both for cheapness and privacy to journey into North Wales into a place called Anglesey, some two hundred and fifty miles.' Of a truth, Tom was a perfect character, and gladly indeed would we believe, as he assured his incredulous relatives, that he was not 'naturally inclined to evill.'

PURITAN POLITICS

I

THE PURITANS AND THE RISE OF MODERN DEMOCRACY

IT is often said that even if the French Revolution produced a slush of lust and blood, into which courage, virtue, freedom, and good faith were cast and trampled under foot, it at least gave birth to new ideas, taught men rights before unknown, and proclaimed, if it did not secure, human liberty. At the Revolution dawned the ideas and the beliefs that have overthrown tyranny and oppression throughout the world. That is the claim made on behalf of the movement which ended in the Consulate and the Empire. In truth, it is the vulgarest of vulgar errors. All reasonable men must of course admit that, besides doing a great amount of good in France, the Revolution testified to certain truths which underlie the best forms of popular government and secure liberty of body and soul. But these truths were not born in Paris. They did not flow from the guillotine, nor were they inspired by the orgies of the Carmagnole. They had been born long before among the English race across the Channel or in the settlements of New England.

Of the French Revolution it is exactly accurate to

say that its principles were both new and true. Unfortunately, however, those which were new were not true, and those which were true were not new. The ideas of liberty of conscience, of liberty of the person, of equality before the law, of the sovereignty of the people, of the abolition of privilege, were great and fruitful ideas, but they had, every one of them, been not merely suggested but fully stated either in the Long Parliament, among the so-called Levellers or ideal Republicans of Cromwell's army, or in the course of the foundation of the communities which the Puritans created on the north-east coast of America. What was good in the French Revolution, and what has since enlightened the continental world, was altogether anticipated by the political workings of the Puritan spirit. Doubtless the Revolution gave a fiery advertisement to freedom, and doubtless this was important, but this was all it did. Burke's famous phrase, describing the work of the Jacobins, should be made to read : ' Their errors were fundamental ; their improvements superficial—and borrowed from the Puritans.'

The previous existence in England of the Democratic ideas which have been claimed as the product of the French Revolution is shown by a study of the ' Agreement of the People,'—the constitution which the Army endeavoured to force on the Long Parliament directly after the final overthrow of the King's power. Let no one suppose that this was an anarchic or levelling document, though the so-called Levellers were supposed to have inspired it. It is merely an attempt by the Army to get a constitution or fixed scheme of government as a security for the liberties they had just won, and to provide against the fruits of their labours being swept away by a sudden Act of Parliament. The Army saw, in fact, what political philosophers are beginning to see now, that it is not well to have the 'fundamentals' of government always at the mercy of a scratch majority in Parliament, and they drew up their Agreement in order to get this evil remedied. The Agreement 'proposed by the agents of the five regiments of Horse, and since by the general approbation of the Army, offered to the joynt concurrence of all the free Commons of England,' begins by declaring how needful it is for them to provide against any return 'into a slavish condition.' Accordingly, after declaring in favour of a Redistribution Bill, the abolition of Rotten Boroughs and Biennial Parliaments, they make the following very remarkable declaration :

That the power of this, and all future Representatives of this Nation, is inferior only to theirs who chuse them, and doth extend, without the consent or concurrence of any other person or persons, to the enacting, altering, and repealing of Lawes ; to the erecting and abolishing of Offices and Courts ; to the appointing, removing. and calling to account Magistrates, and Officers of all degrees ; to the making War and Peace, to the treating with forraigne States :   And generally, to whatsoever is not expressly, or implyedly reserved by the represented themselves.

Which are as followeth,

(1.) That matters of Religion, and the wayes of God's worship, are not at all intrusted by us to any humane power, because therein wee cannot remit or exceed a title of what our Consciences dictate to be the mind of God, without wilfull sinne : neverthelesse the publike way of instructing the Nation (so it be not compulsive) is referred to their discretion. (2.) That the matter of impressing and constraining any of us to serve in the warres, is against our freedome ; and therefore we do not allow it in our Representatives ; the rather, because money (the sinews of war) being alwayes at their dis- posall, they can never want numbers of men, apt enough to engage in any just cause. (3.) That after the dissolution of this present Parliament, no person be at any time questioned for anything said or done, in reference to the late publike dif- ferences, otherwise than in execution of the Judgments of the present Representatives or House of Commons. (4.) That in all Laws made, or to be made, every person may be bound alike, and that no Tenure, Estate, Charter, Degree, Birth or place do confer any exemption from the ordinary Course of Legall proceedings, whereunto others are subjected. (5.) That as the Laws ought to be equall, so they must be good, and not evidently destructive to the safety and well-being of the people. These things we declare to be our native Rights, and therefore are agreed and resolved to maintain them with our utmost possibilities, against all opposition whatsoever, being compelled thereunto, not only by the examples of our Ancestors, whose blood was often spent in vain for the recovery of their Free- domes, suffering themselves, *through fraudulent accommoda- tions*, to be still deluded of the fruit of their Victories, but also by our own wofull experience, who having long expected, and dearly earned the establishment of these certain rules of Government are yet made to depend for the settlement of our Peace and Freedome, upon him that intended our bondage, and brought a cruell Warre upon us.

It would be difficult to draw up a better list of funda- mentals than these, and their moderation strongly testifies to the good sense of the Army ' Agitators,'— *i.e.* agents or, as we might say, commissioners. Yet the ' Agreement of the People,' when presented to the House of Commons, was at once declared seditious and destructive to the authority of Parliament. It will be remembered by readers of Carlyle that when the two regiments mutinied and arrived at Ware without orders, they wore in their hats copies of the ' Agreement of the People,' with the motto, ' England's Freedom and Soldiers' Rights,' in capital letters outside. ' Cromwell rode up : " Remove me that paper," he said. The soldiers refused, and began to complain, whereupon he roughly rode his horse among the ranks, and commanded that the leaders should be arrested. Then, convoking a Council of War upon the spot, he had three condemned to die, and one of the three, chosen by lot, immediately shot at the head of his regiment.' But the agitation for a fixed Constitution did not die out. Later, another and enlarged version of the ' Agreement of the People ' was presented to Parliament. This document is specially remarkable from the circumstance that it contains what is, in fact, a proposal for the Referendum to be used as the safeguard of the Constitution. The men who drew up this Agreement recognise that with mere acts of a single House, people can say, ' We have no bottom,' and they therefore desire a Constitution accepted by the people, and made unalterable thereby,—a rock-foundation of government. So remarkable is the wording of the document in this respect that we shall quote it, in spite of the fact that it is to be found at length in Mr. Gardiner's ' Documents of the Puritans' Revolution :'

Now, to prevent misunderstanding of our intentions therein, we have but this to say, that we are far from such a spirit, as positively to impose our private apprehensions upon the judgments of any in the kingdom, that have not forfeited their freedom, and much less upon yourselves, neither are we apt in anywise to insist upon circumstantial things, or aught that is not evidently fundamental to that public interest for which you and we have declared and engaged, but in this tender of it, we humbly desire : (1.) That, whether it shall be fully approved by you and received by the people, as it now stands or not, it may yet remain on record, before you, a perpetual witness of our real intentions and utmost endeavours for a sound and equal Settlement, and as a testimony whereby all men may be assured what we are willing and ready to acquiesce in ; and their jealousies satisfied or mouths stopt, who are apt to think or say, We have no bottom. (2.) That, with all the expedition which the immediate and pressing great affairs admit, it may receive your most mature consideration and resolutions upon it ; not that we desire either the whole, or what you shall like in it, should be by your authority imposed as a law upon the kingdom, for so it would lose the intended nature of an 'Agreement of the People ; ' but that, so far as it concurs with your own judgments, it may receive your seal of approbation only. (3.) That, according to the method propounded therein, it may be tendered to the people in all parts, to be subscribed by those that are willing, as petitions and other things of a voluntary nature are, and that, in the meanwhile, the ascertaining of these circumstances, which are referred to commissioners in the several counties, may be proceeded upon in a way preparatory to the practice of it ; and if upon the account of Subscriptions (to be returned by those Commissioners in April next), there appears a general or common reception of it amongst the people, or by the Well-affected of them, and such as are not obnoxious for Delinquency, it may then take place and effect, according to the tenour and substance of it.

To show how clearly these Puritan Constitution-makers realised the principles of government and the nature of their work, we must make one more quotation. Here is a passage to be found in the 'Appeal to the English Nation,' which serves as an introduction to the scheme of the sixteen regiments—one of the many forms of the agitation connected with the ' Agreement of the People :'

If any shall inquire why we should desire to joyne in an agreement with the people, to declare these to be our native Rights, and not rather to petition to the Parliament for them ; the reason is evident : No Act of Parliament is or can be unalterable, and so cannot be sufficient security to save you or us harmlesse, from what another Parliament may determine, if it should be corrupted ; and besides Parliaments are to receive the extent of their power and trust from those that betrust them ; and therefore the People are to declare what their power and trust is, which is the intent of this Agreement.

The need of a Constitution which shall not lie always open to the will of Parliament could not have been better put.   How admirable alike as citizens and soldiers were these russet-coated dragoons! When it came to the 'shock,' none could resist the Puritan troopers. Yet in council the men who charged harder and fought fiercer than any soldiers before or since, were as wise, as reasonable, and as acute as if they had been trained in a university. Most soldiers would say ' Heaven help an army whose privates are amateur professors of constitutional law ! ' But who would dare to say it of the New Model ? The typical Ironside, the God-fearing, freedom-loving dragoon of whom Cromwell said, with such pride and pathos, ' They were a lovely company ; truly they were never beaten,' is, all men must allow, one of the most interesting figures in history. For some of us, indeed, he is the most interesting—more memorable even than the Greek in arms or in the Agora, than the Roman in the Comitia, or than the Hebrew defending the Temple. Here is the Englishman at his best;

the citizen who fights to defend his liberties, and yet does not fall into the lower estate of the soldier, but remains the citizen—the man who can use the sword, yet does not demand the orgies and the license in which the perils of the field so often ask to be paid—the guardian and upholder of what is best worth having in life—the true knight of freedom.

II

CONSTITUTION-MAKING UNDER THE PURITANS

IT is not too much to say that the 'Clarke Papers,' lately issued by the Camden Society, constitute one of the most interesting contributions ever made to English history at its most interesting period—the period of the Commonwealth. This sounds exaggerated, but let our readers pause a moment before they condemn us for overdoing our praise. Think of what the Papers consist! They are mainly the shorthand reports of the debates which took place at the 'Council of the Army' in regard to the drafting of a Constitution for England. At these debates were discussed such questions as the veto of the House of Lords, the possibility of having a part of the Constitution put out of the reach of the House of Commons and made changeable only by consent of the people, the problem of natural rights, the proper extent of the franchise, the subject of redistribution of seats, and a hundred other vital points such, for instance, as Centralisation, Particularism, and Socialism.

The men who took part in the debates, and whose words are preserved verbatim, were Cromwell, Ireton, and Fairfax. Surely it cannot be wrong to say that the opinions of such men, expressed on such subjects, are of paramount interest not only historically but politically.

And not only do these debates show us what was thought by leaders like Cromwell. We get also the opinions of the plain soldiers—representatives of whom attended the Council. Generally, these stern, hard-headed troopers of the New Model seem to have been content to let those officers who were in sympathy with them be their spokesmen, but every now and then 'Buffecoate' or 'A Soldier' (as the reporter, who apparently could not remember the names of any one below the rank of Colonel or Captain, heads their remarks) puts in some plain but shrewd and forcible observation. In a word, these reports show us what the Puritan was in council, eminently a political creature, full of sound sense, and as far separated, even when most extreme, from the heady word-drunken Jacobin of the French Revolution, as he was from the ordinary pleasure-loving, devil-may-care soldier of fortune such as the Continent knew to its misery during the seventeenth century.

It may be as well to remind our readers shortly how it happened that the 'Council of the Army' came to be debating the sort of points that were debated by the Convention that drew up the Constitution of the United States of America, or that were debated a year or two ago, when the delegates of the Australian Colonies drew up their remarkable draft Bill for constituting the Australian Continent into a Commonwealth. It happened, roughly speaking, in this way. When the King had been taken prisoner and the first Civil War was over, the men of the New Model and of the other victorious armies of the Commonwealth were determined not to disband till a settlement of the nation had been arrived at, and a Constitution devised and accepted by Parliament which should make it clear that the soldiers had not fought in vain, and should serve as a bulwark against tyrannies, new and old—Monarchical and Parliamentary. But the House of Commons seemed in no mood to give the soldiers satisfaction on this point. Hence grew up in the Army, both among the officers and the men, a demand for a proper settlement of the Government. This demand was taken up by the 'Council of the Army,' at which the chief officers and representatives of the regiments were present, and they debated, clause by clause, various constitutional proposals.

This is only a rough and imperfect sketch of the position, but we cannot attempt here to do more than indicate how and why the Council of the Cromwellian Army came to turn itself into a constitutional Convention. We have said enough, however, to indicate the general contents of the 'Clarke Papers.' It only remains to be said that Major Clarke was Secretary to the 'Council of the Army;' that he took notes of the proceedings, that the notes were preserved at Worcester College, Oxford, and that they have been given to the world through the enterprise of the Camden Society.

The first thing that strikes one in reading these debates is the mental characteristics of Ireton. It is little less than a revelation to find that the famous soldier was a constitutional lawyer of great ability and no little learning. His instincts were extraordinarily conservative, but at the same time he was no doctrinaire. Though the rights of property were his sheet-anchor, though he loathed the idea of universal suffrage, and though he held the notion of 'natural rights' in the utmost contempt, he was not incapable of seeing the other side, and was always for compromise and a fair and reasonable agreement wherever possible. What he wanted was a redistribution of seats on a numerical basis and a freehold suffrage. A freeholder was, he argued, a person who could not decamp and leave the country if he had muddled its affairs, as might the man who had only movables. Still, he was content to agree to household suffrage for people who paid rates to support the poor, provided that they were in an independent position, and not under the influence of any one else. Here are the terms of the franchise clause agreed to by the Army under the influence of Ireton :—

That the electors in every division shall be natives or denizens of England, not persons receiving alms, but such as are assessed ordinarily towards the relief of the poor ; not servants to and receiving wages from any particular person. And in all elections except for the Universities they shall be men of 21 years of age or upwards, and housekeepers dwelling within the division for which the election is.

Ireton also was in favour of the House of Lords being maintained. He agreed, however, to modify its veto by a clause which he thus explained :—

Col. Rainborow : That some thinges in the Agreement were granted there. To Debate whether or noe when the

Commons Representative doe declare a law itt ought nott to passe without the Kinge's consent.—Com. Ireton : Truly this is all ; whether honour, title, estate, liberty, or life, [if] the Commons have a minde to take itt away by a law [they can do so] ; soe that to say you are contented to leave them all, this [negative] being taken away, is as much as·to say you are to allow them nothing. Consider how much of this dispute is saved, [by] this that is read to you. It gives the negative voice to the people, noe lawes can bee made without their consent. And secondly itt takes away the negative voice of the Lords and of the Kinge too, as to what concernes the people ; for itt says that the Commons of England shall be bound by what judgements and alsoe [by] what orders, ordinances, or lawes shall bee made for that purpose by them ; and all that followes for the King or Lords is this,·that the Lords or King are nott bound by that law they passe for their owne persons or estates as the Commons are, unlesse they consent to itt. Therefore what is there wanting for the good or safety of the Commons of England ?

That is but a poor example of Ireton's power of constitutional exposition, but it must stand, because of the special interest of the subject-matter.

Cromwell's intervention in the debates is most curious and instructive. He seems to have taken far less interest in the details of constitutional lore than Ireton. His main idea seems to have been to keep the Council together, to pour oil on the troubled waters, and to prevent violent disagreements. He only flamed up when there was anything like Particularism in the air. Then, indeed, the first and greatest of Unionists showed himself no Gallio. Here is an excellent Unionist sentiment. Cromwell is insisting upon the danger of throwing the Constitution headlong into the melting-pot. New Constitutions, all equally plausible, will follow each other in quick succession :—

And if so what do you think the consequence of that would be ? Would it not be confusion ? Would it not be utter confusion ? Would it not make England like Switzerland, one county against another as one canton of the Swiss is against another ? And if so what would that produce but an absolute desolation—an absolute desolation to the nation ?

Here is another curious example of Cromwell's Unionism :—

And truly, this is really believed : if wee doe nott indeavour to make good our interest there [*i.e.* in Ireland], and that timely, wee shall nott only have (as I said before) our interest rooted out there, butt they will in a very short time bee able to land forces in England, and to putt us to trouble heere. I confesse I have had these thoughts with myself that perhaps may bee carnall and foolish. I had rather bee overrun with a Cavalerish interest [than] of a Scotch interest ; I had rather bee overrun with a Scotch interest then an Irish interest ; and I thinke of all this is most dangerous. If they shall bee able to carry on their worke they will make this the most miserable people in the earth, for all the world knowes their barbarisme —nott of any religion, almost any of them, butt in a manner as bad as papists—and you see how considerable therin they are att this time. Truly itt is [come] thus farre, that the quarrell is brought to this state, that wee can hardly returne unto that tyranny that formerly wee were under the yoake of, which through the mercy of God hath bin lately broken, butt wee must att the same time bee subject to the Kingdome of Scotland, or the Kingdome of Ireland, for the bringing in of the Kinge. Now itt should awaken all Englishmen, who perhaps are willing enough hee should have come in uppon an accomodation, but [see] now [that] hee must come from Ireland or Scotland.

We have only space to make one more quotation from these delightful volumes. It shall be from a speech by Cromwell. It is on that great principle of politics ; and any Government is a good one as long as you stick to it and work it reasonably, *i.e.* there is no abstract right or wrong in the matter ; what is wanted is to know the real wish of the people :—

If I could see a visible presence of the people, either by subscriptions, or number [I should be satisfied with it] ; for in the Government of Nations that which is to bee look't after is the affections of the people, and that I finde which satisfies my conscience in the present thinge. [Consider the case of the Jews.] They were first [divided into] families where they lived, and had heads of families [to govern them], and they were [next] under judges, and [then] they were under Kinges. When they came to desire a Kinge, they had a Kinge, first Elective, and secondly by succession. In all these kindes of Governement they were happy and contented. It you make the best of itt, if you should change the Governement to the best of itt, it is butt a morall thinge. · Itt is butt as Paul sayes 'Drosse and dunge in comparison of Christ ;' and why wee shall soe farre contest for temporall thinges, that if wee cannott have this freedome wee will venture life and livelihood for itt. When every man shall come to this condition, I thinke the State will come to desolation. Therfore the considering of what is fitt for the Kingedome does belonge to the Parlia-ment—well composed in their creation and election—how farre I shall leave itt to the Parliament to offer itt. There may bee care—That the elections or formes of Parliament are very illegall, as I could name butt one for a Corporation to chuse two. I shall desire, that there may bee a forme for the electing of Parliaments. And another thinge as the perpetuity of the Parliament that there is noe assurance to the people, butt that itt is perpetuall, which does [not] satisfie the Kinge-dome ; and for other thinges that are to the Kinge's Negative vote as may cast you off wholly, itt hath bin the resolution of the Parliament and of the Army—If there bee a possibility of the Parliament's offering those thinges unto the Kinge that may secure us I thinke there is much may be said for the[ir] doing of itt.

It is impossible to speak of the 'Clarke Papers' without a word of thanks to Mr. Firth for the masterly way in which he has edited them. When is he going to give us what we have a right to demand at his hands because no one could do it better than he, a full, final, and complete Life of Cromwell, a life which shall give us the man, the whole man, and nothing but the man? It is a great opportunity, for no such book exists; but it is by no means an occasion too great for Mr. Firth's powers.

HUMOURS OF THE FRAY

STUDIES IN OFFICIAL DIGNITY

I

STRAW HATS AND JUDICIAL DIGNITY

THE 'Daily Telegraph,' we suppose on good authority, once declared that the County Court Judges of England had come to a momentous decision. It announced that the County Court Judges had passed a new rule enabling them, "without loss of dignity, to wear straw hats during the hot weather.' Many people no doubt read this paragraph with amusement. County Court Judges, like Bishops, policemen, and rural Deans, are for some unexplained reason always surrounded with a faint nebulous envelope of humour. Why there should be what the Latin grammar calls 'a tending' to laugh if not at, at any rate in connection with, these useful and important classes, is a very puzzling question ; but we cannot expect that the form of the ' Daily Telegraph's ' announcement will check the merriment, ' be the same a little more or less,' which naturally centres in their Honours. One need not be very waggish to wonder how the new arrangement will prevent a loss of dignity, or to speculate by what cunning device of drafting the enabling rule is made to operate as a bar to a waste of dignity only in the hot weather. A plain man might imagine that the way the hat was worn would have more to do with the loss of or gain of dignity than any rule ever drawn. For example, a straw hat worn at the back of the head, or set well on the side, as Mr. Toole set his in ' Walker, London,' or pulled down over the left eye, seems at first sight so terrible a non-conductor of dignity that nothing could neutralise it. Apparently, however, the rule acts as a kind of talisman, and ' during the hot weather ' is a final and complete estoppel to any accusation of want of dignity.

We confess we would give a great deal to see the actual words of the rule. Does it, we wonder, define a straw hat? It surely ought to do so, for nothing is more of the essence of the question than the kind of straw. Much as we believe in the innate dignity of the average County Court Judge, both in hot and cold weather, and ready as we are to admit the efficacy of a well-drawn rule in determining matters of convention, we hold, and are prepared to stick to our opinion, in spite of all opposition, that there are forms of the straw hat which it is a mere infamy to put on one's head—hats which even the senior County Court Judge could not wear, with the thermometer at 102°, without an entire loss of dignity, nay, of the right to human consideration. We shall not describe these particular hats too minutely, lest some depraved and misguided man, drawn by the dreadful attraction of bottomless evil, should be led to wear them. Suffice it to say, that they are made of a kind of scaly straw only fit for a fish-basket, and that they are surrounded at the top by a hideous clere-story—probably to introduce the air to the top of the head. It is this clere-story—this abomination of ventilation—which constitutes their peculiar vileness, and makes it harmful merely to see them. No County Court Judge could touch such a hat and not be defiled, and we sincerely trust that they have been scheduled as in no case within the rule.

Another form of straw hat which we hold to be very doubtful wear for County Court Judges is the large-brimmed Panama. It is a very comfortable type of hat no doubt, but no one who reflects for a moment can doubt that it is distinctly unsuited to a Judge. It has far too melodramatic an air about it. Judge Lynch might wear it as he rode his fiery mustang to string up a dozen or so of negroes, but not a man on his way to administer indifferent justice in a small-debts court. A man with such a hat on his head feels fit for serenades, poker across an empty rum-barrel, a ten-mile ride in the moonlight, and any and every sort of wild and reckless deed. For his Honour Judge —— to wear it down to Court would be to invite trouble and confusion. Who, after putting on such a head-gear, could sit down soberly to consider whether somebody's conduct had not been ' negligence amounting to fraud,'—we believe the phrase is legally a little *passé*, but let it stand. Why, the very essence of Panama straw is negligence and abandonment of all the more prosaic duties. A man who acted up to the spirit of his hat, and every man is liable to do that at times, might commit an act of daring self-sacrifice and heroic devotion, might swim a flooded creek, or leap a ' canyon ' to save an old lady's favourite cat, but he could not help scorning to pay his just debts, and would distinctly refuse to pay damages for acts of wilful neg-lect. How then could a County Court Judge, with his head hot from contact with a Panama straw, hope to be able to perform his duties in a satisfactory manner ?   It would be absurd to expect it of him.

Equally unsuitable would be that sort of cheap, loose straw hat sold in English village shops.   The hats are innocent enough in spite of their picturesqueness, but they are not in character, and would be very likely if not to deflect the mind of the Judge, to make substantial tradesmen and other persons of local importance in the Circuit think less well of him.   They are hats which belong of right to the sentimental village · artisan. They would be appropriate, too, for a male pupil-teacher in very hot weather, or for a photographer, except when taking a group at a diocesan synod or other clerical gathering.   For County Court Judges they are distinctly too unsubstantial, and could not be worn with any propriety.   The true wear for a County Court Judge, if he must wear a straw hat—a proposition which, we think, has hardly been sufficiently proved—is undoubtedly a plain, thick straw, with a straight, stiff brim, moderately high in the crown.   The plait of the straw should not be excessively broad or again excessively narrow, but a good compromise—something which should instinctively suggest, as it were, ' Pay 5s. now, and 2s. 6d. a week for the next ten weeks.'   One would not like to insist that the straw should be mixed black and white in colour, but unquestionably it would be exceedingly appropriate, and it might indeed become a principle that the more the black predominated the more orthodox the hat.

But though one may pretty easily arrive at the ideal make of straw hat, one has not by any means accomplished the whole task.   One of the great difficulties connected with straw hats—a difficulty which we do not doubt was felt by the Committee of County Court Judges who drafted the rule—is the fact that straw hats involve ribbons, and ribbons open a vast and fertile field of difficulty and danger. If straw hats stood alone it would, as we have shown, be comparatively plain sailing when once the main principle had been accepted, but the ribbon problem, inseparably connected as it is with the straw-hat problem, is of terrible dimensions. We sincerely trust that the Council added some directions on the ribbon question. It would have been sheer downright cruelty to let the County Court Judges loose on a world of ribbons unrealised, and, to a great extent, unrealisable. Without some hard-and-fast rule to guide him in the selection of a ribbon—and a ribbon he must have on his straw hat unless he is to look positively disreputable—the County Court Judge is as good as lost.

The reason is plain, though it may not seem so at first sight. When a hatter or haberdasher sells you a straw hat he brings out a neat box of ribbons and asks you to choose. You hesitate, and he holds them up one after the other, placing the cheek of the roll of ribbon affectionately against the side of the hat, and asking you if you do not think that they go very nicely. It seems a simple and innocent transaction enough, and yet there is a snare for the County Court Judge in every one of those rolls. How is that? In this way. Say the Judge chooses a neat blue-and-white check ribbon, and then the temperature having risen to the prescribed height—we do not know what the degree is, but of course it is laid down in the rule, no body of lawyers would leave a phrase so vague as 'hot weather' undefined—

goes down to hold a Court in a distant part of his circuit.
It is not too much to say that the new hat and ribbon
which he wears so lightly may ruin his influence with the
suitors of the Court, and inspire them not with the respect which men should feel towards a Judge, but with
exactly the opposite feeling. The reason is this. It
may easily happen that this innocent ribbon shows the
colours of a local boating, cricket, or cycling club of anything but good repute. Instantly people will ask, Why
has the Judge joined the 'Pedbury Hornets,' or the
'Dunsbury Grasshoppers'? as the case may be, and a
hundred objectionable answers and reflections will be
made. The Nonconformist conscience will begin to build
a marvellous fabric on the ribbon. Elders, after chapel,
will ask each other, How comes it that one in so high a
position should encourage young men in smoking,
betting, profane swearing, and record-cutting? The
local preacher will recall how, when he admonished
young James Jones, 'the son of one of the friends at the
other end of the parish, now no more,' for belonging to
an ungodly society, the unhappy lad replied : 'Why,
ain't old Judge Blank a bloomin' " Hornet," himself?
I see'd him with the club ribbon on this werry
morning. What's good enough for him is good enough
for me : so stow it, old Stiggins !—His very words, I
assure you, dear Mr. Johnson.'

Every sort of danger lurks in colours. One Judge
will try a plain yellow-and-pink ribbon, and stumble
into the racing colours of some noble owner. The
result will be that half the district will take tips from
his hat. The chief tipster at the 'Boar and Blunder-
buss' will whisper in the bar that he has got 'a moral'

this time, and will go on to explain how he came to get hold of it. 'Did you notice the old Judge this morning? You did. Well, then, did you see what he'd got in 'is 'at? Lord X's colours, and no mistake. Well, and what do that mean? It means to a certainty that " Armadillo " 'll win the Great Peddlington Handicap! Mark my word, the old boy has got a pot on and wants to show he ain't ashamed of it!' Such talk is certain to follow an incautious use of the ribbon.

Depend upon it, the County Court Judges have a most difficult task before them. In our opinion, safety lies only in one direction. They must appoint a committee and design a County Court Judge's ribbon, and let its tints and pattern be known to the world. Then a Judge will be known by his ribbon, the hat will become official, and there need be no scandal. A plain straw hat and an official ribbon—that is the only possible outcome of a rule which we suspect has been somewhat hastily entered upon. Such things as hats and ribbons seem, no doubt, mere things of form, but unless the County Court Judges take care, they will find them, as Bacon said, 'things of substance.'

II

CYCLES AND EPISCOPAL DIGNITY

THE papers have lately been busy with rumours of a bicycling Bishop. It is stated that the Bishop of —— intends, when proficient, to ride a bicycle along the roads of his diocese, and we are assured that, though his lordship has not yet ventured outside his own gates, he has for some weeks been engaged in practising on the gravel-paths and down the carriage-drive. How this knowledge has been obtained is not stated. Possibly it was by what on the Continent is called an 'officious' *communiqué* to a press agency—one of those curious pieces of literature which have a style all their own, and wrap up a statement of fact just as a precious china image is wrapped up in cotton-wool. More probably, however, the information was acquired by the less regular but far more ancient way of looking over the hedge. In primitive societies that is the universal method of collecting news, and we should not be surprised if it still held its own in ——. These great primal instincts of the race die hard in the provinces.

It requires no enormous stretch of the imagination to call up the way in which the news got out. One sees an eager group of small children and workmen returning from their toil flattening their noses against the gate of the Bishop's palace—even the most ordinary of villa residences is a palace when lived in by a Bishop; the cowl may not make the monk, but the Bishop will make anything short of furnished lodgings a palace—or squeezing their heads between the iron railings, while in the gathering gloom a dark figure flits up and down the drive, now swooping like some great bird into a flower-bed, now shaving the stable wall by a hair's breadth, and now charging full-tilt into a laurustinus-bush. What more natural than that the reporter of the local paper on the prowl for 'copy' should be passing that way and should join the watchers? The mere look of the silent and absorbed row of backs, or the exclamation from one of the boys, ' Oh, Lor', he did go a oner that time,' or ' Won't his shins be sore, neither,' would be enough to make him join the group and look over the head of the smallest girl to see what was the cause of the excitement. A word of explanation, or the sight of the Bishop himself coming down the last ' lap,' amid the cheers maybe of his wife and daughters on the front-door step, would be quite sufficient to put the journalist instantly *au fait* with the situation. In a moment his note-book would be in his hand, and a vivid, terse impression of the scene be recorded.

In America, of course, an interview, fictitious or otherwise, according to the Bishop's temper, would be added to the description of the scene, and such appropriate head-lines as, ' He will not be beaten by a— Wheel,' ' Practises in the Parlour on Wet Days,' and ' Does not Believe that "Coasting" is Contrary to Scripture,' would be displayed with all the typographical resources of the office. In England the reporter must be content with a ' spicy par,' and with the knowledge that in the silly season every newspaper in the kingdom will copy his piece of cycling intelligence and deck it out with a delightful variety of titles, from ' The Bishop and the Bicycle ' to ' The Bench on Wheels.'

The fact that at last a Bishop is about to become a bicyclist has been the signal for a great deal of controversy, and the whole problem of official dignity, and what infringes it and what does not, has been raised in its acutest form. It has long been admitted that curates, vicars, and rectors may ride a cycle, and even Rural Deans are by common consent allowed to do their visitations on a 'safety.' As, yet, however, the line has been drawn, and drawn strictly, at Rural Deans. Above that rank it has not been considered consistent with ecclesiastical dignity to go a-wheel. Archdeacons, Deans, Bishops, and Archbishops have all been ruled out of the delights and conveniences of pedalling. A vicar may run all over his parish on a tandem with his curate, but the notion of a Bishop 'cutting about' his diocese on a bicycle seems utterly abhorrent to many minds.

And yet there is something peculiarly arbitrary and unreasonable in maintaining this .'taboo.' We prescribe for all the greater dignitaries of the Church a costume which specially lends itself to the cycle, and yet we try to forbid them the use of the wheel. To put a man into neat black gaiters is to subject him to a daily temptation to take to a bicycle. The absence of trousers is a tacit but perpetual invitation to the road. The curate and the rector before they go for a spin must deal with their trousers in one of the many, but all of them difficult and tiresome, ways relied on by those who do not use breeches or knickerbockers for riding. They must either tuck their trousers into their socks—a Bohemian expedient hardly to be recommended to the clergy—or they must use some form of steel clip, for the employment of india-rubber bands, though occasionally practised by men of letters, is far too untidy for those who want to set a good example in the parish. An Archdeacon, a Dean, a Bishop, or an Archbishop need be troubled by none of these troublesome devices. At any and every moment of the day he is ready equipped to spring upon the saddle. The maximum of preparation required by him is to give a slight reef to his apron, and even this can be avoided by riding a bicycle with a drop-frame—*i.e.* a lady's machine.

We cannot indeed imagine a more pathetic situation than that of a cycling vicar who has become a Bishop. 'While I could ride my machine,' he will reflect with bitterness, 'there always was the horrid annoyance of trousers, and the necessity for adopting some plan for preventing them catching in the pedals. Now the trousers have gone, and instead I wear daily an ideal cycling costume. Yet public opinion has forced me to abandon all further thought of cycling, and my beautiful new Beeston-Humber is to be raffled for at the Diocesan Fund Bazaar as "the gift of an anonymous donor to the Palace stall." I only hope it will be won by somebody outside the diocese. It will be the last straw to see a curate riding it over to arrange about a confirmation.'

But is there any real reason for inflicting such torture on the more athletic members of the Bench? We do not believe that there is. On the contrary we hold that the Bishop of —— is setting a most excellent example in thus breaking through an absurd convention, and we hail with delight the thought that we may some day look out of window and see the Venerable the Archdeacon of London threading his way through the London traffic. We confess that we should not like to see an Archbishop with his legs up 'coasting' down a steep hill, but short of that we have not the slightest objection to the whole Bench adopting cycling as a means of exercise, enjoyment, and locomotion.

Cycling is essentially a cheerful exercise, and the Bishops have much to try them. Why, then, should they be precluded from an easy and pleasant way of throwing off their worries ? A Bishop troubled by a rash vicar who is determined to fight his parish to the death over the question of restoring the rood-loft and giant crucifix might find on his bicycle a solution which would never occur to him on foot. It is absurd to say that there is anything so essentially undignified in the bicycle that no man can ride it and maintain the moral elevation required in the dignitaries of the Church. Why should it be more undignified to ride a bicycle than to ride an old grey horse ? We have no anarchical notions about dignity, and do not wish to contend that there are no pastimes or actions which are undignified. For example, we should extremely dislike to see a Bishop on a merry-go-round, and should probably leave the show-field at once, and even though we knew that he was there from the purest motives, and was challenging sea-sickness with the hope of elevating the amusements of the masses, and of proving to them that a man may take even boisterous pleasures innocently and without the factitious aids of strong liquor and profane language. But a bicycle is, we contend, perfectly different from a merry-go-round, and may be ridden by the most exalted person without loss of dignity. It is merely because the bicycle is a new invention that to ride it is looked upon as capable of injuring a man's dignity.

We have no doubt that when the first horses were tamed and ridden primitive society was convulsed by the question whether the priests who polished the fetish-stone ought to be allowed to ride, and whether they would not become ridiculous, and so socially disconsidered, if they did so. One can hear the talk across the ages. ' It would be all right if the horse kept quiet, but suppose somebody was to frighten him and he kicked, and the crowd saw daylight between the priest and his mount and chaffed ? What would then have become of the dignity which ought to attach to the holders of a sacred, &c., &c., &c. ? ' Depend upon it, the Bishops will not be lowered in dignity, even if they adopt the cycle. Their dignity, in truth, depends upon themselves. Dignity in the last resort is based upon moderation, upon calmness of manner, upon good sense and good feeling, and not on the adoption of any special kind of locomotion. If a man is dignified by nature, riding a bicycle in moderation will not deprive him of his dignity. If all cyclists were obliged to ' scorch,' and ' shout ' and ' swear ' at people who did not get out of their way, then no doubt it would be better for Bishops not to ride. But since a man may cycle, and do none of these things, we see no reason why the Bench should not take advantage of their gaiters, and ride a cycle for health, pleasure, convenience, and economy.

EVERY BOY IN HIS HUMOUR

I

THE IDEAL BOY AND THE REAL

THERE is something truly pathetic in the thought of the kind-hearted and scientifically minded naturalist who writes books about country pastimes for boys.

We say pathetic advisedly. It is always pathetic when an ideal creature is compared with the real, to find that the real is either as totally different as the Polar regions from the Tropics, or else looks like a malignant caricature—the distorted and burlesque points of resemblance making the contrast all the more cruel. The writers on boyish pastimes may in their hearts consider the boy as a being occasionally capable of passion and error ; but as a rule he appears in their books as a person 'ever delicately marching' through a whole series of arts and crafts with the utmost moderation and dexterity. He never takes more than one egg out of the nest for fear that the bird will desert. He puts his hand in so neatly, and climbs the tree so skilfully, that not a twig is displaced, and the mother-bird watching from the neighbouring hawthorn, is rather pleased than otherwise by his visit. When he is coming down, he does not peel the lichen and moss off the bark in handfuls by the agonised pressure of his waistcoat against the trunk—a swift and dusty descent ; nor does the band of his breeches catch in a small bough till it breaks with the weight. Instead, he comes down hand over hand, 'always making sure of a firm hold with the leading foot before the foot behind is displaced.' On aquatic expeditions, the boy of the book is no less of a marvel in the sober security of his behaviour. If he wants to cross a stream, he does not trample heavily backwards and forwards three or four times in the muddiest and broadest place. He springs lightly from stone to stone without noise. If he wants to tickle trout, he steals on tip-toe to the bank, and without first heaving in a dozen or so of large stones so as to give the maximum of splash.

Again, the book-boy does not forget to tuck up his sleeves to the elbow. When the book-boy makes a trap for birds it falls when it is wanted to fall, and if he keeps as what are called 'minor pets,' two badgers, an owl, a lark, half a dozen rabbits, and an eel, he tends them with all the method and zeal of the Royal Zoological Society's servants. Their cages are never dirty ; they are never left without water ; they never know what it is to be crammed two days in the week in succession, and starved for the other five ; and they are never teased to make a holiday pass more agreeably. The book-boy is simply incapable of saying to a friend, 'Will you give me your pistol if I let you stir up the old owl with a stick ; you don't know what a wax the old beast 'll get into ?' The book-boy is, in fact, as we have suggested, a mixture of the sympathetic naturalist and the accomplished artisan. He turns from studying the habits of the kestrel or the grayling to the construction of a patent rabbit-hutch or a temporary rat-cage. 'A few simple directions'—directions which read like the integral calculus to the grown man—are nothing in his sight, and with the greatest possible ease he can first draw you a section of a ' rabbit-hole and bolt-hole,' and then proceed to catch the rabbit and teach it to dine out of, and not off, his hand.   Such is the boy as he appears from the books on boyish sports.

Alas, *non sic notus Achilles !* ' The boys we have known have been very different.   They have been anything but kind-hearted naturalists.   Their hearts may have been in the right place, and probably were, but the abstract desire not to disturb the old bird has not prevented them from clutching at the side of the nest in their descent.   They keep minor pets, but it is difficult to know which offers the more appalling prospect for the pet, neglect or attention.   Again, the real boy is anything but a deft mechanic.   As far as we have observed, he is more of a surgeon ; at least, the matter which is subdued to his art is generally the flesh of himself and his companions.   The real boy may set about making a cage for a badger, but he generally desists before even the bars are shaped, because the bandages on fingers and thumbs have made the further manipulation of chisel, axe, saw, and plane difficult— nay, impossible.   In fact, the badger-cage; ' from a few simple hints,' generally ends in an inverted packing-case, on which are piled large stones because of the exceeding strength and ingenuity of badgers in the matter of getting out.   Again the real boy, the boy that we remember thirty years ago, and the boy we see to-day, show little or none of the instincts of the true fisher-

man or gamekeeper.   He shouts and screams and
dances on the bank, he splashes as much as he can, and
he is likely, if he does not pull out the line every three
minutes to see if there is anything on it, to convert the
float into a target and pelt it with stones, content with
the discovery that it does almost as well as a bottle.

The difference between the real boy and the book-
boy is capitally displayed in the frontispiece of a work
on ' Country Pastimes for Boys ' which lately came under
our notice.   We see there a boy in a shapely straw hat,
whose trousers are neatly and thoroughly turned up, and
whose feet are clearly quite dry, walking with firm and
well-directed steps along the stepping stones in the brook.
His pockets are evidently filled with well-selected 'specimens,' and in his arms he holds with a care and precision
that might become the Regius Professor of Zoology in
the University of Oxford a large owl.   The boy carries
him so firmly and yet so gently, that the owl is evidently
quite delighted with his mount.   There is on his face
something which seems to promise the remark of the
old French gentleman at his wife's funeral,— ' Je pense
que cette petite promenade m'a fait beaucoup de bien.'

But even if the owl does not go quite so far as this, and
maintains an attitude of philosophic doubt as to the proceedings by which he has been conveyed from his hollow
in the tree, he is clearly suffering no inconvenience.   The
picture is entitled ' Heavy Laden.'   We feel that just
outside the page and on the opposite bank of the stream
waits a fond parent or kind uncle, who, after tethering
' our feathered friend,' as he will, of course, describe the
owl, with a bit of whip-cord tied in a series of knots as
knowing as those which Ulysses used in the land of the

Phæacians, will run over the specimens in Edmund's pocket and name them out of 'On the Wing,' 'British Insects,' and 'Ponds and Puddles, and their Inhabitants.' 'This,' will say the parent or uncle, ' is the fresh-water crayfish, but why it has only three claws on the right side I am not sure, unless, indeed, the poor creature met with an accident before it came into our possession ; this is the common mussel ; this a somewhat rare form of dragon-fly, right wing slightly damaged ; this is a variety of the vole, and not, as you no doubt supposed, a shrew-mouse. The insects, I think, we had better give at once to our friend the owl, for I promised your dear mother that we would not bring back anything of a crawly nature from our ramble.'

Can any parent or uncle say that this depicts the real case ? Can he put his hand upon his heart and declare that when Jack comes back 'heavy laden' it is in such guise as we have described ? A very different picture rises before our eyes, when the Edmund of the book gives place to the Jack of reality. The brook gleams in the sunlight as before, and as before the water ripples against the moss-covered sides of the stepping-stones. But Jack is not on them. He is splashing through the water intent upon an experiment in hydro-statics—can a man splash water twice as high as his own head ?—and soothed with the delightful sound made by walking in boots completely full of water. Edmund treads with care and precision. Jack does not. He rolls along like a Dutch fishing-boat in a gale of wind, and as he lurches and plunges along the smooth and slippery bottom of the stream, every step looks as if it must be the last. There is something in his pockets in the way of specimens, but specimens of what? His trousers are not tucked up, or rather, one is quite down and the other has half a reef in it, a recollection of an act of legerdemain which he tried to accomplish as he came headlong down the drive two hours ago. In Jack's arms is an owl ; but, oh how changed from the owl we have described above! It is impaled against Jack's waistcoat by his left arm. Originally it was buttoned inside his coat, but it has half-struggled out, and is biting savagely at Jack's fingers whenever they come near. In the book-picture the parent or uncle on the bank awaited with satisfaction the advent of the specimens.

Here no such satisfaction is visible. Instead, the father is gesticulating wildly on the bank. ' I say, look out there, Jack ! Take care what you're doing with the poor bird—don't you see you're killing it ? No, don't drop it, you idiot, or it'll be drowned ; stick to it ! If you're not sharp it'll be smothered. Now you're choking it. That's worse. Oh, do be more careful ! Hurry ! What's the good of trying to tame an owl in mid-stream, and when the poor thing's dead with fright ? Bring it here, I say ! ' When Jack and the owl get to the bank, and the question has been decided whether the poor bird ought not at once to be put out of its misery, Jack begins to get his specimens named. From pockets swollen to the size of panniers he produces a vast collection of wet rubbish. ' Isn't this a very rare stone, father ? ' and then is produced a rock of the size of the chunk of Old Red Sandstone which broke up the Geological Society upon the Stanislaus.

When he has heard an unfavourable verdict, softened

so as to spare his feelings as much as possible, he proceeds to produce 'a splendid crystal, which I should like you to have, because it's the best I ever found.' Alas! it is very wet, very big, very dirty, and has but the very faintest suggestion of crystallisation at one corner. When this geological crown has been put aside, there emerges a dead newt. 'I think it could be revived all right if you would give it some of that stuff you gave the garden-boy when he fell off the roof of the shed. Sal something, wasn't it?' Next come three partially smashed, hard-set blackbird's eggs—a hideous mash of shell and unfledged birds. Then two or three sticklebacks, and a mixed lot of paper, candle-ends, and string, and a peg-top and catapult.. Then there is a pause, followed by, 'Oh, I've forgotten my knife! I must have lost it in the tree. Will you come back and help look? I did as you always told me—that is, to have both hands free when I climbed, and so I opened both blades and held it between my teeth. I think I must have dropped it when the owl hooted at me. I wasn't expecting it just then. I remember I called out something to keep him quiet.' When you say that Jack cannot go back for the knife, or anywhere but home to get dry things, Jack looks like a martyr for two minutes, and then suddenly brightens and says that he believes it's all right after all, and that he left his knife at home. 'But you said you had it in your mouth!' 'Yes, but it must have been your knife; don't you remember I asked you for it just before I went across to the old tree?' So ends a practical day devoted to the country pastimes of boys.

II

JACK'S FRIENDS

IT is needless to say that all Jack's friends are heroes. If you were to get him to note the fact he would, without doubt, accept it as most natural. Of course they are; they would not be his friends if they were not. That is the line Jack would be sure to take, for there is no sort of misgiving in his mind on two points: (1) That people do not count at all if they are not cast in the heroic mould—*i.e.* cannot outshy, outshout, outrun, outswim, and outclimb everyone with whom they can possibly be compared. (2) That all his friends are people who count, and therefore are cast in the heroic mould. The late Master of Balliol is said to have remarked to an enthusiastic undergraduate who discovered men of extraordinary genius in every batch of freshmen, 'I'm afraid, Mr. ——, all your swans are geese;' but no one not an iced wet blanket in human shape could say anything of that sort to Jack while he recounts the 'Iliad' of his friend's doings. But, in truth, there is not the slightest temptation to do so at the moment. Jack's blazing blue eyes and flushed cheeks carry conviction with all his recitals. The hearers catch the infection, and seriously believe while they listen that Robinson or Smith, the garden-boy next door, or whoever may be in question, is, in reality, a monstrous fine fellow.

Of course, disillusionment sometimes comes when the parent meets the hero in the flesh, but that is an accident cheerfully borne. Children of eight have a fine sense of compassion for their elders' induration of spirit, and are not seriously troubled when, and if, they perceive that you do not quite take their friends at their proper value. Your want of appreciation, unless very boldly expressed, is only an example of the usual blindness of grown-up people. You do not regard the thicket as a mighty forest full of wild beasts ; and you are clearly ignorant of the fact that the road swarms with brigands and pirates, for do not you habitually cross it without carrying arms, and without throwing out scouts or sending on a picket to hold the banks while the main body comes up ? How, then, can you be expected to understand all the great qualities of Harry Smith and Bill Dickinson ? The embarrassment of disillusionment, if any, falls entirely on the parents.

One of Jack's heroes is a certain schoolfellow called Jameson minor. By Jack's account he is indeed a lad of mettle—a very devil of a fellow, who fears neither boy nor schoolmistress. Even his admitted faults are superb. ' He's dreadfully cocky, father. He'd cheek the whole school, and not care a button. He doesn't mind an atom about anyone or anything, and even when Rawlins, the head of the school, told him to shut up, he wouldn't.' It was an awful moment when Jack proposed to bring home Jameson minor to lunch. ' Do you think we shall be able to manage him ? ' said Jack's mother, in solemn conclave with Jack's father ; and the latter, after he had rashly consented, had not a few qualms. Suppose Jameson minor was really all that he was painted, might not the result of that luncheon be extremely disastrous not only to the windows of the house, but to the whole moral atmosphere ? If Jameson minor was really capable of cheeking the whole school, he would probably not think twice about cheeking his host. Boys know and care nothing about the canons of hospitality, and to Jameson minor the host would only be Jack's pater. And if Jameson minor were to cheek his host, what was to be done then? It would be clearly useless to tell him to 'shut up,' for had not Rawlins tried that and failed? Imagine the ignominy of trying to steal Rawlins's thunder and failing. But if Jameson minor could not be made to shut up, what would be the effect on the household? It is not always easy as it is to keep Jack in order. Would if not be infinitely harder after he had witnessed a conflict between Jameson minor and his own father, in which his father was discomfited? And then the maids. It would not be pleasant to be worsted in front of them by a boy of eight and a half.

It may be imagined that it was with quaking hearts that the visit of Jameson minor was expected by Jack's parents. As the wheels of the trap were heard on the drive Jack's mother almost gave way. ' I'm afraid they'll be dreadfully excited when they arrive, for the garden-boy is driving them, and Jack and he, even when they are alone, get very obstreperous, and what it will be now I——.' But it is too late for such repinings, and both parents feel that the only possible course is to pull them-selves together and look unconcerned. Jack's mother somewhat hopelessly tries to draw courage from stories about a woman's gentle dignity cowing the rowdiest mobs —' Of course a boy like that is very much worse than a mob of men, but still it might have some effect '—while Jack's father remembers that lions and savages can be controlled by the human eye, and hopes he shall not wink if he is obliged to have recourse to this expedient upon Jameson minor.

And now the 'tub' is at the door, and Jack scrambles out over the shaft—he always says he 'forgets about the door'—while the garden-boy, strangely calm, considering the circumstances, gets out, trying to imitate the behaviour of the groom. At last descends the hero of the hour. Can this really be Jameson minor? Is this he who cheeked the whole school, and would not shut up even at the command of Rawlins? This timid-eyed little boy in an Eton jacket and broad collar 'the cockiest boy you ever saw'! Never was the heart of a swash-buckling, truculent ne'er-do-well hidden by so mild an exterior. Jameson minor, the cockiest boy you ever saw!—why, he is like a mouse in a trap. There is no possibility of trying to quell him with the human eye, for you cannot induce him to look you in the face. As he puts out a frightened little hand he stares at his boots, and his 'How-de-do' sounds thin and weak. The relief is great. The windows are safe, the hens are safe, the baby is safe, and, best of all, the discipline of the house is safe. There is no fear of Jameson minor not shutting up when told to do so. The only fear is that he will shut up all through the afternoon, and embarrass the household by his shyness and his silence.

Strangely enough, Jack seems quite unaware of how the situation has been revolutionised. He does not even seem to notice that Jameson minor is feeling shy. One almost expects him to explain: 'It's all right, father. He'll begin presently. He's only feeling strange just for a minute.' Not a bit of it. No sort of explanation is offered or apparently thought necessary. And, after all,

why should we expect it?   When we have been beating
the wood for pirates, and it has become painfully obvious
that there is not a single one there, Jack never thinks of
explaining away their absence or apologising for the non-
appearance of their buried treasure.   He, God bless him !
never notices the patent discrepancy between his fancies
and the facts.   Why should he behave differently about
Jameson minor ?   Jameson minor is still to him what
he was before, no more and no less.   It is, after all,
only a question of the point of view.   The mistake
arose through acting as if Jack's point of view could be
transferred from him to a grown-up person.   And yet
so strong was the impression obtained from Jack that
the parental mind still retains a feeling that perhaps
after all Jameson minor is not what he seems.   It may
be that 'on his day' he is still the cockiest boy in the
world, and capable of the wildest enormities, and that
it was merely an accident that made things go off so
well.

In regard to some of Jack's friends and heroes one is
more easily disillusioned.   For example, the garden-boy.
You cannot by any means be led to think upon him and
what is glorious together.   Yet there is something very
piquant in contrasting him as seen from your end of the
telescope and from Jack's.   You think of him as an un-
holy urchin, of whom the gardener is perpetually complaining.   The cook is almost sure that it was he who
let the tap run all night and emptied the cisterns.   It
was proved beyond a doubt that he posted the letters in
his pocket instead of in the box in the wall.   The way
in which the cats fly before him has a horrid significance,
and though he has never been *caught* torturing the puppy,

he is justly suspected of having tried to tie a sardine-box to its tail.

In truth, the boy is what old-fashioned people call 'a warmint.' But to Jack he is a hero indeed. He is sixteen next birthday, and 'quite as strong as a man,' and yet admittedly still a boy and not gone over to the enemy—the grown-ups, who like clean hands, who think it nasty to keep a toad in your trousers-pockets, and who do not realise the value of 'rare crystals' detected in very muddy stones. Jack would follow the garden-boy through fire and water, and his tales of that worthy's prowess are innumerable. 'Do you know, father, that William is captain of the Peddlington boys' team, and that they would have beaten the men's this year if they hadn't been very unlucky at the beginning? And father, do listen, his average is thirty if you don't count the four first matches, which is quite fair, as they were in April, and he thinks he'll be a professional and get hundreds of pounds, if his uncle, who's very rich, doesn't take him to mind the shop and go out with the donkey-cart, and he can ride a horse quite well, at least he thinks he could if he tried, and last year he was fourth in the obstacle race at the Oddfellows' fête ; and do you think I could go there this year because there are fireworks, and William could look after me much better than nurse, because he's so much more careful, and doesn't forget things like she does, does he, mother?' Another day Jack will explain how beautifully William can mend various objects of use and ornament, and when you say, ' But he broke my bicycle and the mowing machine, and ruined the scythe,' Jack will reply, quite unconvinced,' Oh, that was when he was trying to make them go better ;

but you should see the catapult he made, and I exchanged for my pigeon and a shilling and one of baby's dolls for his little sister.'

In truth, it is all the point of view. William is quite as genuine an Admirable Crichton to Jack as he is an unwashed rapscallion to the rest of the house. Neither is deceived. Only there remains the wonder of childhood. The poet's alchemy is nothing to that which is to be found in Jack's mind. It makes pure gold where it will, and contrives a new heaven and a new earth in an instant. After fourteen or fifteen it will begin to fade, and by seventeen not a trace of the alchemist faculty will be left. But, meantime, what a gift is Jack's. Fancy, if we could see all our dull friends of the office and club as Jack sees his. Colonel Dicks, an Alexander with the light of conquest on his brows ; Minchley (the bore who wrote the epic), a divine Homer : Heavyside, the M.P., a Solon. Truly the world would then be a much more entertaining place than it seems now. If Jack could catch the drift of this, would not he also say 'Amen,' and add that he had one more proof of the dulness and folly of grown-up people ? A little make-believe and they would be twice as happy, and yet the stupids refuse to take the needful step, and go on, seeing lead where they might see gold. 'They are a lot of duffers.'

III

WICKED BOYS

IT will, we believe, be admitted by those who know anything about the young that in all classes of life there is a certain percentage of boys who, about the age of thirteen—say, from eleven to fifteen—show strong signs of callousness and insensibility in regard to the infliction of cruelty to others.

The boy is something very different from the child. The child, that is, is not merely a weaker, less self-willed, and less active boy, but morally altogether a different creature. Boyhood often. gives perfectly new characteristics to the child. The normal healthy boy— the boy, that is, who has not, either owing to special training or to illness, become more a girl than a boy— is a creature of strong impulses and wild imaginings which are with difficulty checked and kept in order. He has a high code of honour of his own, but it is a somewhat narrow and limited one. He will do anything rather than play the sneak, but there are a large number of people whom he holds that it is quite fair to take in. If you can contrive to put him on his word of honour, he is to be trusted anywhere, like the Crusader who had sworn on the Cross.

If, however, he remains unbound by what he considers a binding form of words he will in many cases stick at nothing. He is chivalrous, and even on occasion gentle, and his feelings every now and then are easily touched, but at the same time his general attitude towards the world is one of war. Like the knight-errant, he is always on the look-out for something to tilt against. It never occurs to him that the boys whose heads he punches in the street, the wayfarers whom he pelts and otherwise insults and injures on the Queen's highway, or again, the farmers whose orchards he robs, or whose cattle he teases into madness, or the maids whom he frightens into hysterics by booby-traps and sheeted ghosts, possess any rights that need be respected. It is almost impossible to get him to see that it is unkind to frighten a timid girl who has to go home on winter evenings through the churchyard. When you say that it is quite as cruel as striking her to arrange blue Bengal lights in such a way that they will flicker along the tops of the graves like corpse-candles, or to improvise a long, low wail from behind the vestry or the porch, he simply regards you as a kill-joy. There are certain laws of nature, like heavy rain and bedtime, which always spoil sport, and your repugnance to let timid girls be frightened or silly whining little boys be tortured, is one of them,—an incomprehensible and disagreeable fact, which can only be left with a shrug of the shoulder.

In a word, the normal boy is the 'noble savage' of Fenimore Cooper and Marryat and Mayne Reid. He is a creature of war and strife, and often as ruthless on his tiny stage as the Redskin of romance, but at the same time as honourable and as capable of generous impulses, high courage, and chivalrous daring. What the boy lacks, and what he gains afterwards, if he becomes, as in most cases he does, a right-minded and wholesome-hearted Englishman, is a sense of kindliness, a respect for the feelings of others, and a touch of gentleness and self-sacrifice. But the lack of these feelings and qualities is in reality nothing but the lack of sensibility —of ability to feel, to comprehend, and to sympathise. Sensibility and sympathy are what the typical boy lacks, and what he gains when he gets out of the Red-Indian epoch and becomes a man and a gentleman.

It is in this lack of sensibility and sympathy, this hardness of feeling, that is to be found, in our opinion, the solution of the mystery of boyish wickedness. All boys show to a certain extent this hardness, but in exceptional boys it reaches to positive petrifaction. The boy's heart seems absolutely turned to stone. Nothing will touch it. The exceptional boys—the boys in whom this hardening of the heart is carried beyond the ordinary limit—are always in danger of doing something which may be positively wicked,—something which may verge upon crime. The history of our public schools affords plenty of examples of boys who have tortured their fellows in a way which would have disgraced a savage. It is to be feared, indeed, that it is accident more than anything else which saves boys of this kind—boys whose feelings have become petrified —from actual crime. They are unable to feel, and their lack of experience of the world makes the fear of punishment but a small deterrent. It is not to be wondered that boys in such a temper of mind may be converted by a series of unlucky chances and opportunities into the thoughtless perpetrators of really grave iniquities.

Fortunately, these boys of petrified feelings do not necessarily grow into bad men. The hardening of their nature as often as not undergoes a complete change with manhood. Their characters grow sensitive again, and the lad of twenty would be utterly incapable of doing things which the boy of fourteen could undertake without the very faintest touch of remorse. We believe that schoolmasters of experience will bear us out in this, and say that they have known plenty of utterly callous boys who later have entirely lost the savage taint, and have turned into normal men. In this dangerous insensibility to which boys are so prone at thirteen and fourteen, the boy is not father to the man. It is difficult to say whence this insensibility comes, and why the child may be full of right feeling, the boy almost callous, and the man again perfectly sensitive to the promptings of the heart and conscience. Though we are not among those who would make the moral nature nothing but an affair of physical well-being, and the soul a matter for clinical treatment, we are inclined to believe that the temporary and partial petrifaction of the feelings and of the moral sense during boyhood, may be due to the great physical changes that are concurrent with it. Those changes affect the boy's whole body, and absorb all his energies.

After all, sensitiveness is a form of energy, and the boy has little or no energy left with which to give his heart its rights. Everyone knows how difficult a thing is a two-o'clock-in-the-morning courage, and how hard it is to feel kind and self-sacrificing when one is half-asleep. Sleepiness or extreme weariness makes one to a certain extent callous and indifferent, and insensible to the fate of others. Well, the boy who is growing up and down and across, all at once, and with a speed which takes one's breath away, is physically as much oppressed as the man who is weary from overwork or loss of sleep. It is true that the exhaustion of rapid development takes a very different form ; but it exists none the less.   No doubt there are boys whose insensibility is deeper, and can only be explained on the same lines as defects of character in the mature.   For the ordinary normal boy, however, whose insensibility is not permanent but temporary, the best explanation is, we believe, that which we have suggested.   The stress of growth, to a certain extent, puts the moral nature under a sort of chloroform.

IV

Children's Manners

THE correspondents of the 'Daily Telegraph' in the autumn of 1896 held a solemn paper conclave on children's manners.   According to most of the writers, children's manners have decreased, are decreasing, and ought to be improved.   They yell, they fight, they hurl stones, they frighten and torture animals, they 'cheek' their elders and betters, and generally they make life intolerable for quiet and peaceable citizens.   Apparently the boys and girls of the past generation never did these things, but with sleek, unrumpled heads, clean pinafores and frocks, and gentle silvery voices, passed through life, if not mincingly, at least with a most pellucid air of sweetness and light.   These virtuous little creatures, if we are to trust the opinions expressed by many persons of fifty and sixty, never slammed doors, or broke windows, never kicked the paint and varnish off cabinets and chairs, never broke the springs of sofas by dancing on them, or ripped up the curtains and blinds.   These acts of wickedness have been, it seems, reserved for the new child. In a word, the child of the present is an untamed savage, while the child of the past was a creature all compounded of duty, tidiness, obedience, and thoughtfulness for others—veritable ministering angels whose only fault was to be over-zealous in good works.

It is, of course, very difficult to controvert this interesting theory of the decay of child manners. The child of the present is here before our eyes to testify to the truth of the picture that is drawn of him. We see him in the flesh, defiance in his eye, a catapult in his hand, and his breeches pockets stuffed with pebbles, marbles, and other munitions of war such as sizeable pieces of old iron, nails, and percussion caps. The child of the past we only know from the recollections of the men and women who were boys and girls in the forties and fifties.

But remembrance is, in such cases, over kindly. Uncle Joseph's memory has, we suspect, though we cannot prove it, a happy knack of forgetting all the diabolic acts performed by him and his brothers, and of recalling only the charities of the hearth as practised by him and his colleagues in pinafores. He remembers the excellent nursery rules against using his own knife instead of the butter knife, against going with unwashed hands 'from morn till dewy eve—a summer's day.' He recalls how shouting on the stairs was not allowed, how sliding down the banisters was prohibited, and how he was always expected to say 'Thank you' and 'Good morning,' and what a strict injunction was laid on against talking noisily and rudely before strangers, making personal remarks, or jumping up suddenly at meals. But while he remembers the rules so vividly, it is to be feared that he has forgotten how often he broke them. He says to his nephews when he finds them plundering the greengage tree, 'Do you know that when I was a boy we should no more have dreamt of taking fruit out of the garden without asking leave than we should of robbing the village shop,' and he no doubt thinks that he was as virtuous as his words imply.

Yet in reality there is lying hidden away in a packet kept in a scented cedar box by an old maiden cousin a letter which, if it could be put into his hand to refresh his memory, as the lawyers say, would give an emphatic negative to the statement that 'When I was a boy we should never have dreamed of taking the fruit without leave.' The letter written by uncle Joseph, aged twelve, to his cousin Nellie, aged fourteen, was something after this fashion.

'DEAR NELL,—We had an awful lark the day after you went. I got up very early, I shouldn't wonder if it wasn't about four, as none of the servants were down, and went and chucked stones at the girls' windows, when Susan poked her head out. I asked her if she'd like to come out. She dressed and got out as I did by the library window. At first I had a lot of fun telling her I should make her come and see a pig killed, and she was awfully cross, and cried and made a baby of herself when I said about the blood and how it squeaked and kicked. There wasn't really any pig, and so we walked about in the long grass and got our feet jolly wet, and then she said we ought to have something to eat as it was very dangerous to be about so long without food, so we went to the kitchen garden and had ten greengages each off that tree which we mightn't touch. There were forty or fifty on the tree, and we meant to leave fifteen, but that old beast, Breecher, came up just then, and said he'd tell "our pa," and that we ought to have a hiding, coming into his kitchen garden like that against orders. And I said it wasn't his garden, and then we ran round the paths and called out to him " I'll tell your pa " until he got in a beastly wax, and then we turned on all the taps, and he had to go and stop them, so we got off. There was a beastly row at breakfast, I can tell you, and mother said it was Susan's fault and father said it was mine, and we had no pudding at dinner and had to stay in all the afternoon, and I had my allowance stopped for three weeks, and if Mr. James hadn't begged Susan off, she wasn't to have had any birthday next month, I believe. We weren't a bit ill, as they said we should be, and I don't believe wet feet matter if only you've plenty of food. So no more from your loving cousin, JOSEPH.

'P.S.—The toad we killed the day you went was alive when we came to look at it in the afternoon, and Miss Mant wanted to punish us for torturing a dumb beast till it hopped at her himself, and then she said it had perhaps be better put out of its misery, so Jack and I did it behind the greenhouse. He had the ash stick and I had one of the big bricks the mason's boy left for us.'

If the fathers, mothers, uncles, and aunts of the present generation could oftener be confronted with such records as these we should, we are convinced, hear much less of the good manners of the past generation, and of the degeneracy of those of the present epoch.

In truth, children's manners are much the same in every generation, and for the very good reason that the nature of children is always the same. Manners are purely artificial things imposed from above. Nobody is born with manners. The most that can be said is that certain people seem born with a faculty for learning the lessons of good manners quickly and easily. That is, some children are more sensitive to teaching than others. This is probably the reason why little girls have better manners than boys. Little girls are, as a rule, quicker and more precocious than boys. Just as they learn to speak and read more easily and quickly than boys, so they learn more readily to have good manners.

But if manners are —as they certainly are—a matter of education, children must have the quality of manners taught them. If they are taught good manners they will have good manners. But taken as a whole, the standard of manners has risen among the grown-up people. The parents, that is, require better manners than they used. Unless, then, the fathers and mothers take less trouble to teach good manners than they used, the children of the present day should be better, not worse, behaved than they were.

And this is, we believe, the truth. The modern boy at a public school is most certainly better disciplined and less a creature of savage impulses than he was. As to the children of the poor, there can be no comparison. Compulsory education has given an excellent daily course in good behaviour to millions of children who previously were never taught how to behave themselves. The Board School training is all on the side of good manners. As far as we can see, there is only one substantial cause for the complaints which are undoubtedly rife as to the decay of children's manners. The nerves of the parents are no doubt far more highly strung than they used to be. For one person who fifty years ago went half crazy over a racket there are now a hundred. We think that our children's manners have declined because we are so much more irritated than we were by petty worries and strident noises. That is, we expect, the fact underlying so many of the wailings poured forth in the 'Daily Telegraph.' Our children don't make more clatter, but we endure it less easily.

V

HOME FOR THE HOLIDAYS [1]

FORTUNATELY, the arrangement of the schoolboys' Summer and Winter exodus is a much easier task than formerly, and there is comparatively little difficulty in managing that those who are bound for a common destination shall travel together. The viatorial vagaries of which a boy travelling alone and given to wool-gathering, or to becoming lost in the blood-curdling exploits of pirate chiefs and their rakish schooners, is capable, are almost incredible. The power of not arriving at his destination which he develops on such occasions is positively portentous. If he has to make a cross journey with just enough time to catch his train nicely he almost certainly misses it, while if he has a good hour to spare the result is much the same, for he is then as likely as not to start off on some external expedition,

[1] A portion of this article appeared as a leader in the 'Standard.'

which brings him back to the station long after the hour at which he ought to have been there. Then, too, he discovers endless possibilities of getting into the wrong portions of trains, of fancying that the slip coach is ' the one next the engine,' and of getting left behind owing to his having become absorbed in the voracious and indiscriminate consumption of mock-turtle soup, buns, hot coffee, chocolate creams, and bottled ale in the refreshment room.

For some reason, however, not easily explained, a party of boys travelling together do not seem nearly so liable to these accidents. Whether it is that a sense of responsibility becomes abnormally developed in the oldest member of the party, and that he checks the errant instincts of the rest of the band, and recalls their minds to the grim necessities of junctions and the ' forward part of the train,' or whether a knot of young gentlemen in round jackets and Eton collars attracts the special notice of the guard, and ensures the supervision of the officials, it is impossible to say with certainty. Whatever is the reason, the fact remains that parties show a tendency to get home, if not always to time, at least before nightfall, while individuals travelling alone very often fare like the Irishman who was wont to complain that, however early he started, he never arrived anywhere at all.

Dickens, in one of his letters, asks how it is that boys home for the holidays contrive to spend the whole day clumping downstairs in apparently at least six pairs of the thickest boots. This curious and interesting problem is at every holiday season presented to the British parent, as well as a thousand other strange and inexplicable habits of his male offspring. It is the charm—or, as a misanthrope would say, the curse—of boyhood never to be able to do anything in the way that it is done by the rest of the world. In this very matter of the stairs, for instance, the unvarying singularity of boys is universally to be noticed. No boy can ever manage to accomplish a simple descent or ascent. His movements, whether going up or going down, are conducted with an earnestness and vigour which it would be quite impossible for any grown-up person to imitate. Putting aside the *glissade* on the banisters, or down the waxed and varnished edges of the treads as belonging more properly to the department of home gymnastics, the most ordinary system, at least for coming down, is that which may best be described as the flying leap—four steps at a time, with an occasional cannon against the wall to vary the monotony of the descent.

If, however, there is sickness in the house a boy of good feeling will abandon this method of precipitating himself as a sort of human avalanche from the top landing to the dining-room floor, and will adopt quite another plan. Probably he has been admonished at some time or other to go down quietly one step at a time, and, making use of this suggestion, he proceeds to carry it out to the letter. Seizing the banisters with both hands, he jumps heavily from the first step, alighting firmly upon his heels on the next, to rebound thence to the one below, and so on till he reaches the bottom. This action, which sounds for all the world like the ghastly antics of some bewitched coffin which has reared itself on end, and resolved to appear at family prayers, is probably that to which the author of ' Pick-wick ' alludes.

At any rate, the system is exceedingly widespread, and is, we firmly believe, considered by many young gentlemen between the ages of eight and fourteen as a specially merciful method of transferring their persons from one story to another. Next to the ability displayed by boys in getting tones undreamt of by ordinary performers out of the front and kitchen stairs is their talent for shaking the whole house by merely walking across an upstairs floor. ' Paterfamilias,' who weighs, perhaps, fourteen stone, when he treads the boards of his dressing-room makes no perceptible vibration. But let Jack, who cannot possibly weigh half that amount, be sent to bring down a book for his father, and anyone in the back drawing-room would imagine that at least a dozen mad elephants had been let loose above. Yet Jack in all probability made no special effort to be noisy, and at most crossed the floor to get to the book case by stepping only on the white squares in the carpet.

No doubt these and plenty of other physical and mental peculiarities of the schoolboy will at first give pleasure rather than the reverse at home. English parents are much too fond of their children not to forget such little annoyances in the pleasure of having their boys home again, and of observing how clever, handsome, or jolly-looking they have grown, and how extraordinarily like they are to their fathers, mothers, grandfathers, or grandmothers, or, indeed, to all their relatives, immediate and remote. For several days the veritable tempests of noise that sweep down the stairs and thunder through the front hall will be pronounced 'quite cheerful,' and there will be a general agreement among the elder members of the family that the house is never a bit like home till the boys come back.

Little by little, however, the charm will wear off, and though the sight of their children will, in reality, be just as much a happiness to their parents as before, a feeling will begin to grow up that there are objections to the sense of perpetual motion which seems somehow to pervade the house. Though the mother of the family would in all probability refuse to admit it, she at last begins to find the banging of doors, without the slightest intermission, a little trying. Then, too, the father of the family, though, theoretically, he may enjoy nothing better than being a boy again among his boys, discovers that it is rather nervous work never to be sure that when he comes round a corner he will not encounter some missile which, although meant 'only for Jack,' is equally capable of 'stinging up' the author of Jack's being.

One of Mr. Bret Harte's characters complains quaintly, but not unreasonably, that 'this dodging of pillows imparts but small ease to the style,' and if Paterfamilias' vocations are of a literary nature the truth of the remark may come home to him with special force during the holidays. To receive a broadside from a bolster battery, meant to hold the maids in check, when one has gone upstairs to look out a quotation in Milton, is almost certain to destroy all suavity of phrase and period. When, again, there is a wet August, and little or no going out is possible, the lot of parents caged up with three or four boys is not exactly a happy one. It is only natural that what ordinary fathers and mothers detest more than anything else in the world is having to decide which of their offspring is in the wrong in a domestic quarrel. But wet days are certain to bring about such home broils, in which it is very difficult for the parent to intervene except by the rough and ready—though often essentially unjust—method of punishing, or at any rate reprimanding, the one who happens to have emerged least hurt from the scuffle.

Though the plan has about it a kind of natural equity—a sort of 'equality of sacrifice,' to borrow a phrase from the regions of finance—which may be supposed to recommend it to the youthful mind, Paterfamilias usually dislikes employing it. In fact, all attempts to administer justice to schoolboys are peculiarly unpleasant, since their code of honour necessarily renders it impossible for either combatant to make known, even in the slightest degree, the rights of the dispute. Add to this that the girls of the family, who were petted by their brothers when they first came home, are, toward the end of the Vacation, in obedience to the universal law that familiarity breeds contempt, mercilessly teased, fagged, and harried. If we take this into account, and remember, too, that the servants, who to begin with thought nothing more amusing than the young gentlemen's apple-pie beds and booby traps, have reached the verge of mutiny by the fifth week, and it is not difficult to realise that the beginning of the next half is greeted with as much joy as was the end of the last.

With boys who go to Day-schools it is quite possible to arrange a *modus vivendi* without making them unduly good and quiet. But the holidays of the boy at the Boarding-school have too much of the nature of a Saturnalia to make them pleasant for parents, at any rate after the first month. When the fourth week is past the coming term is looked forward to with un-disguised delight.

THE SOCIETY BOARDER

IF we are to judge from the advertisements that are constantly appearing in the 'Times' and other newspapers, it is by no means an uncommon thing for 'ladies of title' to take 'young ladies' or 'gentlemen' into their houses as boarders, and to give them, for a consideration generally by no means small, the privileges of an aristocratic home. Take the following example of an advertisement that appeared in an important newspaper, inserted by a lady wanting a society boarder.

'A WOMAN of TITLE, moving in the first Society, will RECEIVE a Young Lady into her house as a FRIEND. Terms, £2,000 per annum. Any introduction of such will be handsomely acknowledged. — " PATRICIAN," 13,720.'

'Patrician' is evidently a person of fine aristocratic feeling. Note the use of the phrase 'a woman of title.' She is quite aware of the way in which 'the best people' talk about themselves, and evidently, to borrow her own somewhat Gampish phraseology, wishes to be known as 'such.' The boarder, it is assumed, will be of a lower social rank. This is marked by the reference to her as 'a young lady.' The 'woman of title' would, no doubt, have advertised for 'a girl out, or just coming out,' had she wanted ' one of us.' She clearly desired to have a person belonging to the wealthy lower orders, and so advertised for 'a young lady.' Experience doubtless teaches that 'young ladies' not only pay much better, but also are much easier to manage than 'girls.' Another typical advertisement runs as follows :—

'THE YOUNG ORPHAN DAUGHTER of a Baronet wishes to RESIDE with a Noble Family, where she will be treated as a friend and find a home. Honoraria given, £1,000 a year.— " DEMOISELLE." '

That these society boarders wanting homes to board in and women of title wanting society boarders are perfectly genuine we have no sort of doubt ; and if we could know all the secrets of Mayfair, Belgravia, and the regions in and around Kensington we should probably discover that we all know a great number of society boarders. For obvious reasons the boarder and the family in which she boards are anxious to conceal the cash *nexus* which binds them together, which makes them sit in the same carriage, occupy the same pew at church, and engage 'next stalls' at the theatre. Hence the outer world hears nothing of the private and 'strictly confidential' arrangement which the 'young American widow' is anxious to make with 'a lady moving in the highest society,' the lady to act as 'her chaperon, &c.,' and hears of the appearance of a new girl at the Joneses' without suspicion.

Ultimately, however, the time will arrive when the thing will have become too common to be concealed any longer, and society will awake with a start to find that the 'cousins' and 'great friends of my eldest girl,' who have been lately so conspicuous, are in reality what the advertisements euphemistically term 'paying guests.' At present, when the Joneses ask Sir George and Lady Brown, Miss Brown, and Miss Cicely Brown to an 'at home,' and when Lady Brown asks to bring as well 'Miss Swartz, a sort of niece of my husband's,' or 'a friend of Cicely's who is staying with us for the winter to see a little of London,' the Joneses think nothing about it, and are, of course, delighted. Ten to one, indeed, Mrs. Jones is quite pleased, for she probably fancies—it is so easy to fancy such things about one's acquaintances—that someone told her that Sir George had some very rich relations with an odd name, and no doubt Miss Swartz is one of them. 'It is all very well for the girls to object to what they call "unknown females" being foisted on us to entertain ; but, considering how foolish Edward is about every girl he sees, it's just as well sometimes to have people to the house who ar'n't utter paupers.' *Omne ignotum pro magnifico ;* and Miss Swartz—'a sort of niece of my husband's'—is sure to be taken for an heiress.

When, however, it is realised that she is 'a paying guest' the desire to entertain her becomes very much less. It is true she may still be, and probably is, an heiress ; but then the suggestion, 'There must be something wrong, or she wouldn't want to pay the Browns 2,000*l.* a year to take her out,' spoils all. Besides, 'Why should the Browns have all that money, and we entertain their boarders ?' is a question which is at once put to themselves by all the Browns' friends. We fear, then, that what the Germans, with their remorseless logic and brutal refusal to use language as a buffer, would call 'the society-boarder industry' is likely to get checked as soon as it becomes common, and so known. Its only chance of being really successful is for it to be secret. It is a plan of earning money which withers the moment it is exposed to the light of day. Indeed, the whole industry, and not merely particular examples of it, may be said to hang by a thread. Suppose some unscrupulous playwright were to put 'the society boarder' into a farce, or that Mr. Anstey were to make on such a subject a sequel to 'The Travelling Companions!' Under such circumstances Othello's occupation would be gone, and many pleasant houses now kept open by means of the boarder's 'honoraria' of 2,000*l.* a year would put up their shutters. Put on the alert by 'Punch' or the Play, we should all be scrutinising each other's houses for society boarders, and the most harmless of nieces and sisters-in-law would be regarded with suspicion. There would be a sort of boarder-hunt in every street, and 'Do you think that Miss Frances Smith is really Mrs. Smith's sister-in-law, or only a boarder of the same name?' would be a constant inquiry.

Let us hope, for the sake of the women and ladies of title—some choose one appellation, some the other — who want to receive a young lady as 'resident, companion, and friend' at 2,000*l.* per annum, that the wicked wit of the farce-monger or the comic essayist will not be practised on them, and that their trade will be spared. After all, it is a very harmless one, and doubtless has kept many a struggling family above water. It is not, perhaps, quite honest, but then, as

Mr. Loudon Dodd explained to Mr. Pinkerton, 'honesty is not as easy as blind-man's-buff,' and she who, under the temptation of pecuniary difficulties, does nothing more dishonest than impose a society boarder on her friends may almost consider she has succeeded in morally holding her own.

It is curious to speculate upon the situation created by the presence of a society boarder paying 2,000*l.* a year in an aristocratic home. For that sum, no doubt, the boarder expects a very well 'run' establishment, carriage, butler, and footman, and everything else in proportion. If she does not get these, and if also she does not get quite as much 'high-toned' society as she expects, does she, we wonder, complain? At Mrs. Todgers's 'the gentlemen' complained very vigorously if they did not have enough gravy, and talked of parting this day week in consequence of the cheese. Do the society boarders, when they do not have enough social gravy, talk of parting this day week? Would, for example, Miss Rancher, the Cattle Queen from Blaineville Co., take Lady Mountargent, of Ballybunion—Irish Viscount's widow, three daughters, and a house in Queen's Gate—aside after breakfast, and remark :

'When I was thinking of coming to you, Lady Mountargent—no, this is a serious matter of business, and till it is settled I really can't call you Aunt Mounty —you told me that you mixed in the highest society, and that I should see at your table the British aristocracy at its brightest and best. As an American citizen, you understand, I don't care a snap about your aristocracy, but I don't intend to go on paying for them without having them.   I have been here a quarter, and one Lord—you said he was an Earl, but I guess I looked him out in the book, and he was only a Baron, and an Irish one at that—has crossed the door.   Now, we Americans are not in the habit of letting ourselves be put on.   Perhaps you are keeping back the best for yourself and the girls, and thinking a lot of common people, Baronets and that trash, is good enough for me. Any way, there's got to be an alteration, and unless I see a little more variety in the way of society I'll have to leave right away.   Now, I haven't seen any of those Dukes with a far-away look in their blue eyes, and a curly moustache, and a regular old-time set of manners ever so haughty and grand, that they write about in the novels, and I am just dying to.   If you can't raise that sort, well, I guess there's others that can, and we'd better part.   No offence, of course, but we Americans like things to go slick, and if they don't we ain't satis-fied till they do.   You've never had such complaints before ?   Maybe.   Well, you've got 'em now, any way. Sorry if I've said anything unpleasant, but just you worry round and get one of those real old-time nobles I was speaking of and you'll find I'm all right.   Get me fixed with a man I can see has had ancestors who've waded through blood, and you won't find me any trouble.   A child could play with me when I'm getting what I think fair.'

Under such circumstances, what does the poor lady of title do, we wonder.   It would sound like a confession of weakness, besides being very humiliating, to point out how scarce Dukes are in England.   At the same time 2,000*l.* a year, paid quarterly, is not to be despised.

And even if the ordinary boarder is not quite so exacting as this, there must be plenty of other possible sources of friction. Suppose the girls draw away the boarders' young men by their superior attractions : what happens then, we wonder ? The situation is evidently full of difficulties, and, on the whole, we do not envy the woman of title. Better cold mutton without a society boarder, than ortolans with. That, however, is evidently not the opinion of many people—witness the number of advertisements daily appearing.

INANE JOCULARITIES

THERE is nothing in the world which produces the sense of mental nausea more completely, or is more certain to turn the intellectual stomach, than the use of certain jocularities of speech with which many persons think fit to adorn their conversation. The people who seem to find it impossible to speak of an unmarried man except as 'a gay bachelor,' with whom the sea is always 'the briny' or the 'herring pond,' and a horse 'a fiery steed,' who eternally talk about 'Sunday go-to-meeting' clothes, and who have such phrases as 'no extra charge,' 'agitate the tintinabulator,' 'the noxious weed,' 'the pipe of peace,' 'forty winks,' and 'braving the elements' for ever on their lips are capable of producing a sense of disgust in those who care to see language kept bright and clean, which is absolutely intolerable. It is difficult to say whether these cant phrases—that is a perfectly proper description of them —are more odious when used consciously or unconsciously ; that is, by people who believe them to be funny, and intend that their hearers should consider them funny, or by those who have merely caught them up and repeat them like parrots, and without any intention, good or bad.

In our own opinion, the use of 'common form'

jocularities is most offensive in those who think of them as wit, though most painful in persons who use them unconsciously and as mere methods of expressing their meaning. We feel that those who try to force a laugh out of such expressions as 'my downy couch' and 'committing matrimony,' who squirm into a smile as they ask if 'there isn't room for a little one,' or who speak of 'japanning their trotter-cases,' might fairly be shot at sight. When some excellent mother of a large and heavily facetious family catches up, and uses almost unconsciously, such phrases as 'getting outside a square meal,' 'the clerk of the weather,' 'she's no chicken,' or 'put on your war paint;' and when even the father mechanically talks of 'performing his ablutions,' the sense of pathos overcomes all other feelings. With such an exhibition before our eyes we can only feel, *sunt lacrymæ rerum,* and pass by with averted heads. As a rule, however, people who take to the use of verbal jocularities combine the mental standpoint of those who try to be funny with the hollow sprightliness of mere imitation. They have a half-hearted belief that they are being funny; but at the same time their chief reason for talking about 'maternal relatives' and 'people of the masculine persuasion' is the fact that they hear those with whom they associate doing the same. They say, 'Why this thusness?' or, 'A fine day for the ducks!' just as they say 'Yes!' or 'No!'

As so many people are jocular without really meaning it, it may be worth while to quote some examples of the turns of speech that they should avoid. In all probability there are thousands of persons of most exemplary behaviour and of excellent moral character in other respects whose speech is inadvertently strewn with the verbal atrocities against which we are protesting, and who are not in any true sense aware of the shocking exhibition they often make of themselves. Let it not be supposed for a moment that it is only the ' minxes' of one sex or the ''Arries' of the other who are steeped to the lips in jocularities. The use of jocularities is by no means exclusively a sin of the vulgar. Plenty of people who would not talk about 'the Marquis' or 'Lord Hamilton' when they meant 'Lord George' may be heard 'recruiting exhausted nature' by a drink from 'the flowing bowl,' and declaring that they are 'full inside,' though they have been very 'peckish.' All sorts and conditions of men and women, boys and girls, are implicated in our charge, and there is no class or set that can be held blameless.

Since, therefore, there are so many unconscious sinners, we propose, as we have said above, to select some specially bad examples of jocularities in order that those in need of conversion may have their consciences awakened, and so be brought to a better way. Those who have never yet realised that they use the most atrocious expressions a hundred times a day will be able to see themselves in a mirror, and to understand what their pet phrases sound like when presented in cold blood. We will begin with what is perhaps the most ghastly example in a vast collection of verbal atrocities placed at our disposal by a champion of what is sound and of good repute in language, thought, and sentiment. We are given to understand that the funny thing, when some one comes near to treading on your feet, is to

exclaim, with the requisite vivacity, 'Ware wheat.'
'Ware wheat,' of course, is equal to 'Look out for corn,'
and so 'Don't tread upon my toes.' Anything more
disagreeably foolish and inanely unpleasant it is difficult
to imagine. There is, of course, no harm in talking
about corns, but this remote and feeble 'jokelet'—to
borrow a phrase loved by the jocular—is positively
ghoulish. After this, such phrases as 'spare my
blushes,' 'to indite an epistle,' 'to be shot' (*i.e.* to be
photographed), 'as the poet hath it,' 'good after tea'
instead of 'good afternoon,' 'playing the giddy garden
goat,' 'the best of everything's good enough for me'
sound almost commendable. They must, however, be
avoided like the plague, for so catching and so insidious
is the habit of using jocularities that a man who begins
with 'spare my blushes' is more than likely to end with
'ware wheat.'

Another very common and very shocking cant
phrase is, 'it doesn't suit my peculiar style of beauty,'
and almost as bad are 'O K,' *i.e.* all right, 'only his
little joke,' 'I like them, but they don't like me,' 'there
isn't a headache in a hogshead,' and 'how goes the
enemy?' There are, in addition, many single words
which, by derivation or association, must rank as
jocularities. We will, however, only cite one. Can
anything be more horrible than the word 'toothsome,'
especially when applied, as we have known it applied, to
liqueur? A glass of 'toothsome Green Chartreuse' is,
perhaps, the most nauseous form of words it is possible
to imagine. It is far worse than that greasy phrase,
'the succulent chop of commerce' which so often passes

for wit in the eating-house when Runting asks Bunter what he is going to have for dinner this ' after-tea.'

It will perhaps be said that we ought not to draw this indictment against a whole set of words and phrases without giving some reason for the disapprobation with which we have regarded them. All people capable of forming a rational opinion will, we may fairly assume, agree that cheap and conventional jocularities of the sort we have given are to be condemned ; but they may still like to have the sources of disgust analysed and investigated. In our opinion, one of the chief reasons why verbal jocularities are so shocking is to be found in the fact that they are blurred and defaced by usage. They were originally made of somewhat soft metal, and they are now blunted and rubbed into shapeless caricatures of their former selves. They are, in fact, like those worn engravings of pictures which one sees in sea-side lodgings. The original picture may have been well enough, but the ten-thousandth impression is a most revolting object. The shadows and lights are all run together, and the total effect is unbearable.

When Diogenes, or whoever it was, asked Aristotle to take ' pot luck ' with him the phrase was bright and clean, meant something, and was sufficiently humorous. Now, however, that it has been used a million times it is as greasy as one of the 50-centime notes that used to pass current in Italy. ' Feeling below par,' again, may have been a tolerable Stock Exchange witticism when Mr. Levison first let it off at the House to an admiring ' runner.' Now it is so sorry a joke that in pity the doctors are making it into a technical expression for a condition of health below normal. The first boy too, who complained of 'a bone in his leg' had, no doubt, a right to be proud of his inventiveness ; but who feels inclined to laugh at it now ? Turns of phrase intended to be comic are all very well, and should not necessarily be discouraged ; but they must be had in, as the shops say, 'fresh-and-fresh.' The moment they are the least bit stale they not merely cease to amuse, but are justly the cause of loathing, and become things as abominable as eggs that have ceased to be fresh. In their case, too, no one has a right to act like the humble curate who replied : ' Fresh enough for me, thank you,' when the green shade in his egg had made the wife of his beneficed brother parson exclaim : ' Dear me, I am afraid your egg isn't quite fresh.' We can keep the unfreshness of our eggs to ourselves, but not so the unfreshness of our jokes.

In addition, also, to those worn-out jokes whose ghosts, like the ghosts in ' Julius Cæsar,' scream and jibber in the public streets, and bear about with them a ghastly mockery of fun, there are jocularities which were never anything but vulgar and disgusting. They are disgusting because they are disgusting, and of him who cannot recognise them we can only say—if we are charitably inclined—as we say of a man who has no sense of smell, that he escapes a great deal. No doubt there remains, when all is said and done, a certain scope for private judgment. The best judges of pictures and music never quite agree in their censures. For example, some would condemn ' A little bird told me ' as a jocularity. To the present writer the phrase is so venerable and so historic that he cannot place it among jocularities. It was under cover of this form of speech that our ancestors passed to each other some dangerous piece of news :—

> Ding-a-ding-ding,
> I heard a bird sing,
> The Parliament soldiers
> Are gone to the King.

That was how the news that Monk was going to bring back Charles spread among the people who had grown tired of the reign of the Saints. To condemn the old phrase may, for all we know, be to condemn primitive man's first attempt at the use of an indirect mode of expressing his meaning. 'The maids who called on Hertha in deep forest glades' doubtless found the phrase invaluable for introducing some woodland *on dit* of their own invention

‘A PERFECT LADY’

VERY few ladies, perfect or the reverse, have gone
through life without constantly encountering the phrase
‘a perfect lady.’   There are plenty of people among the
lower-middle class who have the words continually on
their lips.   Again, among women-servants it is the commonest form of encomium.   It is their highest expression of approval to say of a mistress that she is a ‘perfect
lady.’   The two words when thus used become one, and
take on a different meaning from that conveyed by the
mere substantive ‘lady’ and the adjective ‘perfect’ in
agreement.   To speak of a female person thus is not to
use a vague superlative description, but to place her to
whom the words apply in a category apart—a category
clearly defined and well understood by those who
use the term. ‘Perfect lady’ evidently means something
as distinct as ‘thorough indoor’ or ‘professed cook’—
whatever may be the true and inner meaning of that
strange term.

But though it is quite certain, from the manner in
which the expression ‘a perfect lady’ is habitually employed, that it is a designation, not a mere complimen-
tary phrase, it is by no means easy to say what exactly
is meant thereby.   The classes which use the words
most are, unfortunately, at their weakest in the matter

of definition. Try to get the cook, professed or otherwise, to give you a definition of any household expression with which she is familiar and you will fail miserably. Socrates himself would have failed to elicit from her an intelligible description of the working of the 'dampers' in the kitchener. It would be equally useless to stay the exit of the household after morning prayers and inquire from each member what she meant by 'a perfect lady.' You would certainly stop the house-work for twenty-four hours, and in all probability would get no more than the declaration, 'I'm sure you wouldn't deny, Mum, that a perfect lady is a lady what always acts, and always will, as a perfect lady to all.' A little pressure, and in all likelihood you would be told: 'It's what I've never been accustomed to before, wherever I've lived, to be spoke to like this.' No experienced housekeeper, we will engage, would permit such a question. It could serve no good end, and, if the questioner were a lady, would soon settle the question of perfection irrevocably against her. The only way to find out what is meant by 'a perfect lady,' is to observe how the phrase is applied, and then to proceed by a process of inductive reasoning. There is no lack of instances, and therefore the quest on these lines should not prove wholly abortive.

Those who embark upon the curious speculation we suggest will no doubt at once call to mind one of the late Mr. Keene's most admirable designs. A number of country neighbours are asking the wife of the village butcher what sort of a person is the squire's newly married wife. To these inquiries they receive the oracular but none the less convincing reply: 'A puffect lady—she don't know one joint of meat from another.' Unquestionably this want of knowledge of the crude details of every-day life is 'a constant' in all expressions of 'a perfect lady.' The cynical must not, however, jump to the conclusion that, because of this, 'a perfect lady' means simply anyone who can be taken in at sight. That is a conclusion both hasty and unworthy. Rather it means that this final praise cannot be accorded to those who mix themselves up with the unlovely and harassing trivialities of life. Another application of the words which will be familiar to most of our readers shows this: 'A perfect lady she was; didn't never put her hand to a thing.'

Here we see the phrase applied to a lady who was not always descending from her proper Olympian attitude and fussing about the house doing other people's work—arranging disarranged furniture, tidying up to save the housemaids work, and 'doing it herself' rather than ring the bell and give trouble. This element of a complex problem might, indeed, be reduced to mathematical terms by saying that a lady's perfection varies directly with the amount of trouble she gives. It may at first sight seem strange that this should be the case, but a little reflection will show the reason. If you get to the rock-bottom of the domestic-servant mind you find that what sways cook, housemaid, lady's-maid, butler, footman, and buttons alike is the sense that, in Milton's words, 'man hath his appointed task.' The universal touchstone by which all matters, high or low, are decided, is the question of 'place.' 'Is it my, or his, or her place to do that?' is the first thing which a servant thinks of. Let a servant feel of any other person that he or she is doing what isn't his or her place, or refraining from doing what is, and that person cannot but be in the wrong. To break line in the domestic march, however good the motive, is to do something which must be condemned. But the place of a lady is to lie on the sofa and read a novel, or to entertain company, or at any rate to have nothing to do with the work which others are hired to attend to. A servant would no doubt admit that there was nothing morally wrong in a lady's 'dusting,' or going to the tap to get a jug of hot water in a hurry, to save ringing the bell. She might, indeed, feel actually grateful for the latter act. Her gratitude could not, however, alter the fact that a lady who habitually did little things for herself, though they were somebody else's place, was not 'a perfect lady.' The housemaid would say of her that she was 'a very nice lady,' 'a very pleasant lady,' or 'a kind lady ;' but in view of such conduct as we have described she could not truthfully describe her as 'a perfect lady'—a lady who knows her place and keeps to it.

It must not be supposed, however, that merely lying on the sofa and never offering 'to put her hand to a thing' would win the praise of perfection. That is one essential, but not the only one. No lady who is rude to her servants, who gets into rages and abuses them, will ever win the mysterious and difficult title. Again, no lady who is hail-fellow-well-met with her servants, who chaffs them, or who makes friends with them too obviously can obtain it. That sort of lady may be liked, may be loved indeed, but she will not be called perfect. 'A very pleasant-spoken lady,' 'as good-tempered a lady as ever lived,' or possibly 'a very familiar lady '—a somewhat Malapropian expression in occasional use—but not 'a perfect lady.'   A perfect lady means, then, a lady who keeps to her own place, or what is considered to be her place by those who use the words. She is a lady who lets it clearly be seen that she is incapable of doing anything for herself that a servant can possibly do for her, whether it be putting on coals or tidying a room, who is always somewhat expensively dressed, who keeps perfectly calm and self-possessed whatever accidents happen, who is coldly polite to her inferiors, and yet never rude, and who, in fact, treats her household as if they were made of a different clay. This is the perfect lady. Truly a not very interesting or amiable figure.

But granted that we have got the true definition of 'a perfect lady,' how comes it that this monster is the ideal of the British servant? The question is a difficult one ; but the answer, though hard, is not, we think, beyond all conjecture. It is certainly not because British servants are of a slavish disposition ; for though they show a tendency to snobbishness, they are as a class extremely inclined to assert their independence. We believe that the worship of the perfect lady is due rather to a sense of self-preservation. Servants, like all other people who respect themselves and are in a subordinate position, dread above all things personal humiliation. But personal humiliations arise most easily when there is intimate contact between employer and employed. Hence the servant feels safest and most protected when the master and mistress keep themselves aloof.

The perfect lady is the lady with whom there is least chance of a collision, in which the mistress always starts at an advantage. Hence, though in a particular case a servant may prefer 'a nice lady' in the abstract, what she yearns for is 'a perfect lady,' a lady with whom the chances of words, patronage, or sarcasms are reduced to a minimum. 'A perfect lady' such as we have described is, in fact, the servant's ideal, because it is the type which she feels safest with. Heaven forbid that we should say anything directly in favour of such an unpleasant person! We can, however, easily understand the attractive force to servants of 'a perfect lady.'

WHERE SHALL WE GO?

WHERE shall we go? That is the question that dins itself into the ears of a hundred busy men the moment that the holidays come in sight. There are some methodical and well-ordered men who have the answer perfectly pat: 'I am going this year to the East or West corner,' whichever it may be, 'of this or that district. Last year I did the other half of the county.' 'I am,' continues such a one by way of explanation, 'working through the South of England; and when I have finished I intend to do the Pennine range year by year till I have finished them.' For such a person the holiday question has, of course, no terrors. He knows not only where he is going, but, apparently, what he is going to do when he gets there. The odds are that he will take his reluctant wife and children first through the geology of the district upon which he alights like a locust, then through the archæology, and finally, if there is any time over, he will ' go for ' the parish churches, and copy into a notebook as many of the epitaphs as he can read by wetting his fingers and rubbing the tombstones. For persons not blessed with so mechanical a genius or, perhaps it would be fairer to say, less contented with innocent pleasures, settling 'where we shall go this year' is nothing less than a nightmare. If one were only rich, full of energy, not tired by railway journeys, not sick at sea, contented with grubby lodgings, not annoyed by very hotelly hotel prices, impervious to typhoid fever, and capable of being cheerful under every possible set of circumstances, including the disturbance of every settled habit and the loss of every home comfort, one's holiday would, of course, be a little bit of Paradise.

When, however, one is not endowed with all these advantages, but is simply a plain, middle-class, middle-aged man, with very little snap left in him by eight hours a day at the office since last September, the question 'where to go' comes clad in terrors, many and horrible. Nothing is easier than to face a holiday in the abstract. When a holiday is still a long way off, and when there is no immediate fear of having to put them into practice, it is quite pleasant to make holiday plans. In March one may read in the newspaper of the beauties of Cornwall, South Wales, the Lakes, the Derbyshire Dales, the Broads, the Highlands and the Border without any emotion but pleasure. The brooks that murmur as they run, through the pages of a descriptive magazine article, the stately fanes depicted in the woodcuts, and the delicious country inns, described 'A few practical hints to tourists in Cadwallader's country,' a place where the sheets smell of lavender, and where there is always Devonshire cream, home-made bread, and strawberry jam with whole strawberries in it on the sideboard, please us then.

Alas! for human perversity. When August comes the appetite for such things sickens and dies, and instead of these delights we think only of the 'nastycrechias-crawl-uppias' that inhabit the feather bed in the country inn and of the discomfort of driving six miles in the rain in an open fly, too cross, too wet, and too tired to care whether it is 'Cadwallader's country' or only his maiden aunt's or younger brother's. In the abstract it is delightful to talk about cheap and yet really comfortable seaside places, and be comforted. When they are spoken of in the concrete in the third week in August it is a very different matter. Your wife, not being in business, is, of course, far more methodical, business-like, and logical than you are, and leads off the debate by laying down that what we want 'is a seaside place, not more than three or four hours from London, which shall not be overrun with tourists.'

'The lodging must not be in any horrid terrace or esplanade, but must stand by itself outside the town, and have a garden, if possible ; and there ought to be good sands for the children, and there ought also to be golf-links for you, and cheap riding-horses, for it would be splendid for you to get your exercise in that way. The lodgings in a nice country place such as I mean ought, of course, to be cheap, and there should be nice old-fashioned country shops where you could get everything you wanted. Now, dear, I think I've said all the important things, and I leave it entirely to you to choose the exact place. I shall be quite happy wherever you like to take us, only don't forget that there are some seaside places where there is a horrid little sort of sand-fly that bites one's legs, and would make it absolutely necessary to go away at once—so you won't go there Edward, will you, because I really could not stand it.'

Poor Edward ! where is he to find this favoured spot

of earth ? He fully admits all the conditions laid down by his better half, including even the absence of 'the horrid little sort of sand-fly,' to be reasonable and necessary, but that does not lighten his task. He may talk himself hoarse to the men he meets in the City, or going up in the 'bus, but it is a hundred to one that he will not find any one to tell him of the terrestrial Paradise he is seeking. Brown will no doubt say : 'I know exactly the place for you, only unfortunately it's right in the middle of the town, and the children can't play on the sands in front because of the new drainage works. However, they can go by the old 'bus, if it's running, which I doubt, to Doddering's Cove, where there is a lovely beach. Only, I say, look out for the tide ; its awfully treacherous there, and there are some very nasty quicksands, and the rocks you have to climb down to get to the cove are like iron, and as slippery as butter. Don't forget, too, that every Tuesday, Wednesday, and Saturday the Artillery Volunteers practise there. The shots ought to keep well over your head, but the devil of it is they are apt to be so very careless.'

The same sort of answers are got out of Smith, Robinson, and the rest of Paterfamilias' friends. They all know the exact place, except for a few absolutely fatal objections. In despair, the poor would-be holiday-maker turns to some work intended to settle that question more vexed than even 'the still vexed Bermoothes.' Alas ! no newest edition of the oldest guide-book is new enough to show the 'Eden on sea' for which we all pine. Those who desire perfection will not find it recorded even in the most rose-coloured of guide-books. As the old countrywoman said of life generally, 'there's always a summat,' and in the case of most English watering-places there are a good many ' summats.'

Under these circumstances the man in search of somewhere to go to must do one of two things. He must either resolve to give up the idea of 'perfection and a cheap holiday' altogether, or else he must listen to the still small voice which whispers at holiday-time ' Holidays be d——d ; you'd a deal better stay where you are.' And, after all, why should not the free-born Briton sometimes spend his holiday at home, and, imitating Sir William Harcourt during periods marked by ' irregular jumpings' on the part of the political cat, remain at his own fireside ? After all, there are few places better worth while being at leisure in than one's home. Especially is this true of the city gentleman, who, unless on a Sunday, seldom sees his home, except before breakfast and after dinner. The busy man whose child referred to him as ' the kind gentleman who comes in on Sunday to carve the joint ' would find a month at home most agreeable. The neighbourhood would practically be *terra incognita*, and he might enjoy a delightful time in doing his own district. Even the Londoner might do worse things than devote a month to seeing the things best worth seeing in London.

September is a delightful month in town, and the home holiday-makers, armed with their guide-books, might follow in the wake of the hundreds of Germans and Frenchmen who at that season are always in our midst, ' Baedeker' and ' Guide Diamant ' in hand. Which one of us is there who can lay his hand upon his heart and faithfully declare that he knows his London as well as he knows plenty of Continental capitals? In the abstract he admits that the pictures and sculpture are as good, the buildings as curious and interesting, and the outside excursions as pleasant, and yet he has practically never seen them. Why, then, should not some English couple of moderate means devote their September holiday and their holiday fund to doing London from their home in South Kensington?

ARE OUR MANNERS DEGENERATING?

IT is difficult to feel quite sure as to all the details of the Millennium, but in regard to one point we have no doubt. Though they will, of course, feel generally content, the majority of mankind will, we are certain, declare that the race of old servants has ceased to exist, and that the manners of the young people have deteriorated terribly. Mankind has been saying these two things without intermission since the world began. Palæolithic man, no doubt, complained that it was impossible nowadays to get a slave who could split a flint decently, while the older Lake dwellers certainly grumbled at the younger generation for slamming the trap-doors and swarming up the piles without making the vestige of a salutation or of an apology to their relations or friends engaged in fishing for eels, or sketching mammoths or elks on bone panels. The truth is, the habit of grumbling about the decay of manners has become part of the burden of humanity, and can no more be shaken off than the desire to eat or sleep. As long as man is man, and capable of a syllogism or an emotion, he will hold that 'outwardly at least our manners are changing for the worse.'

This being so, we are not surprised to find even Lord Meath uttering the old conventions and raising the old complaints as he did in the 'Nineteenth Century' for July, 1896. Indeed, we should hardly feel cause for wonder were we ourselves to be caught indulging in like reproaches. There does not, we believe, breathe a man on this planet who is not liable at some time or other to obey the master instinct of the race and protest against the inability of the present generation to open doors for ladies and speak deferentially to the old. We claim no immunity from the influence of a thousand centuries and of millions upon millions of ancestors. We, like the rest, hear the chaunt of ' O tempora, O mores ! ' resounding down the ages, and in our weaker moments have yielded; and may yield again, like Lord Meath, to those silent voices. For the moment, however, we feel calmly indifferent to the tyranny of convention, and can discuss philosophically the momentous problem at issue. Seated for the moment on the airy heights of impartial wisdom, we can say with confidence that there is nothing whatever in Lord Meath's complaint. Nay, we can almost prove that we are right, and that he is wrong.

If manners had really been degenerating steadily ever since the days when Noah noticed with pain that his sons only held out their hands with a grunt to help the ladies of the family across the plank into the Ark, and did not bow, take off their sheepskin hats, and say ' Allow me,' there would clearly be no manners at all left now. Matter may be infinitely divisible, but manners are not, and it is quite clear that if the universal testimony of mankind were true on this point such a thing as a ' Thank you,' or a ' Please,' would be utterly extinct. But we see that this is not so. Therefore the outcry about the decay of manners must in the past have been ill-founded. May we not then assume that it is equally ill-founded in the present?

But, it may be said, it is no good to try to get rid of the problem in this off-hand manner. The fact remains that mankind has always believed its manners to be decaying, and this fact has in some way or other got to be accounted for. Unless there was some reason for it, men in every age and in every place would not have thought the same thought and made the same complaint. When people have been saying the same thing from China to Peru, from India to the Nile, from Norway to Naples, ever since the dawn of history, there must be something in it. The notion of a universal and immemorial, and yet wholly fortuitous and gratuitous, piece of *blague* is absurd. Where, then, is the necessary substantial resting-place for the belief that our manners are disappearing?

We believe that it is to be found in the fact that manners change like the fashions—are, in fact, as much the sport of fashion as bonnets, skirts, mantles, or collars.

But it is notorious that oldish people cannot keep up with the fashions. One of the first signs of that mental induration which comes to almost all men and women some time after forty is that they become unable to see that the new style of collar or way of doing the hair is an improvement. There is no more certain sign that a person is ageing than his or her declarations that the new fashions are hideous and disgusting. But mark, the fact that the declarations that our manners are disappearing never come from the young, but always from persons past forty. The truth is, their minds have become indurated. They have become incapable of following the fashions in manners. But the fashions in manners are not influenced by these expressions of blind indignation. Driven on by that necessity for evolution and change which we cannot ignore, though we cannot explain, our manners—*i.e.* our codes of social behaviour—are in a perpetual state of flux. There is no sudden revolution, of course, but in ten years' time there has been sufficient alteration to make the way we flirt now, or the way we talk to ladies in the drawing-room after dinner, seem strange and outrageously indecorous or absurd to the man who has stood still and not moved with the times.

After all, manners are only conventions—rules as to the pitch of the voice, the turn of the head, the form of words to be used. But it is the nature of conventions to seem good only to those who know them and can appreciate their exact value. An unsympathetic convention is necessarily a monstrosity. If the recognised convention of the generation is for a man who wishes to be polite to a girl at a ball to say ' You might give us a dance,' then there is no real decay of manners in the use of the phrase. It sounds, indeed, to the generation who have developed it and use it the only really polite thing to say, and far better manners, ' in the true sense,' than the ridiculously formal and dancing-mastery ' May I have the honour of a dance ? ' Those who use it are, in fact, not the least conscious of any decay of manners. Men accustomed to the ' May I have the honour ? ' formula are, however, utterly shocked by the ' You might give us a dance ' convention, and the moment when they begin to realise its development they declare that the old courtesy, &c., has died out. It is the same with a hundred other little matters of form. A new fashion in giving an arm or holding open, or even not holding open, a door seems boorish to the older generation, who knew the proper way of doing the thing in 1860, and 'since then have used no other.'

Probably the last resort of those who believe firmly in the decay of manners will be to ask how it is, granted that it is merely a change of manners and not a decay that we are witnessing, that the change is always for the worse—always in the direction of roughness, rudeness, and lack of formality. We recognise the need for an answer to this question. No doubt manners just now appear to be growing rougher and ruder. It is, however, merely a conventional, and not a· real, roughness and rudeness, and the reason for it is plain. The manners of the upper classes in England are putting on a veneer of roughness, are adopting the use of 'rustication,' to employ the architectural phrase, for the same reason that society is always changing, or tending to change, its place of meeting in the Park. That reason is the desire to get away, to keep separate from the herd. The smart people gave up being formally polite and making bows and 'graceful inclinations of assent' when the middle class grew polite and shopboys and shopgirls adopted the etiquette of the old *régime*. When the manners of those below them in the social scale became thoroughly polite the only way of escape was the adoption of a self-conscious roughness. It became the right thing to say, ' May I have a dance ? ' in Mayfair because at middle-class balls a beautiful bow and a formal demand had become the fashion.

Society is only apparently unmannerly because it is

trying to dodge its humbler followers and arrange a set of conventions which will not be pirated. As soon, however, as its retreat is discovered it will have to find a new device. Then, in all probability, we shall see a reaction in favour of formality, and our young men and maidens will bow and simper and pass formal compliments after the manner of the eighteenth century. But, after all, these things are only externals, and really matter very little. The main fact is that our manners in essentials are growing less, not more, rough. If we take the wider view of the social situation we shall see that men are less, not more, disagreeable than they used to be. Let anyone who doubts this compare the way men treat each other when alone to the way in which they acted sixty years ago. The old ideas of what was fair in the way of 'roasting' a fool or a bore or a nervous man have completely changed, and few people now can be found to defend the old-fashioned style of practical joke.

Theodore Hook was not counted a specially rude or discourteous man by his contemporaries. If he tried to practise his form of wit now he would not be tolerated for an hour in the society of well-bred people, and we doubt if even in the stables his ways would be counted possible. Instead of our manners decaying, they are steadily improving. Of course, we English shall never be picturesquely polite ; we are too awkward and self-conscious for that ; but in every other respect our evolution of manners is entirely towards good breeding and courtesy.

BOWER-BIRD HUSBANDS

' Is your husband a bower-bird ? '   That was a question
addressed to a young wife by a social statist anxious to
get his friends well classified under their proper generic
appellations.   As a matter of fact all husbands, if they
only knew it, are either bower-birds or not bower-birds ;
but we admit that the phrase is ·at first sight a little
startling, and requires elucidation.   It will be remembered that the male bower-bird is endowed by nature
with the desire to decorate its home with every conceivable form of ornament.   It is a natural æsthete, and
strives to do for its nest what Messrs. Maple or Shool-
bred do for the villa residence in Wimbledon or
Hampstead.   Nothing comes amiss to it.   With a few
feathers, a shell or two, and some fragments of broken
looking-glass or sparkling mica it will rig up a highly
ornate bower for the alleged delight of its mate.   It is
as if the birds were possessed by the genius of those
good women who write in the ladies' papers under the
heading of ' The Home Beautiful ' or ' Fair Settings for
Fair Faces,' and give ' tips ' to correspondents on the art
of turning a seaside lodging into ' a dream of loveliness '
by the proper disposition of ' a dozen Liberty handkerchiefs, some Japanese paper fans, and a few photographs
of your lady friends in evening or Court dress ; if the

gentlemen are in uniform the effect will be very much improved.'

We cannot discuss here why it is that the bower-bird takes so much trouble to produce what at the best is only a sort of arbour in a tea-garden in miniature—the kind of thing which makes one hot with shame and misery, incoherent in language, and sick at heart for the falsehoods which the tongue must utter, when it is exhibited for our admiration by some amiable rural labourer or retired market gardener. The fact remains that he does so, and that a certain number of men—not the majority, but still a respectable minority—take after him, and display a feverish desire to ornament their homes. Such men when at home hardly ever have a hammer out of their hands, and are usually inarticulate because their mouths are filled with the tin-tacks which they are determined to get in somewhere on the drawing-room wall. In the abstract, women like the notion of the bower-bird man, and they may be heard to declare that ' it is so convenient to have a man in the house who will drive a nail in exactly where and when you want it.' Alas! this is only another instance of woman's pathetic habit of concealing her troubles under a brave exterior. She hides the horrors of her home under a smile—nay, is even known to make domestic capital out of her woes, and to turn them so artistically that they can be used to keep her maiden sisters in their proper place. Of course, it would be immensely convenient to have a man always ready to drive in a nail exactly when and where you wanted it. Unfortunately, however, this is precisely what you do not get in the bower-bird man. He does not want to put in nails on such prosaic principles.   He is bent, as all true house-wives know in their hearts, though wild horses will not drag it from them, upon what can only be described as a crusade of destructive ornamentation.

We know of no more touching scene than that which may be observed almost any summer evening in the house of a human bower-bird.   The man has his coat off—it is, of course, not necessary to take off your coat to drive in a tin-tack, but shirt sleeves is a kind of uniform universally adopted by the villa bower-bird—and he has a hammer in his right hand.   In his left, pressed between the index finger and thumb, is a small carved bracket.   He stands with his weight poised on the left leg, and with the other leg dropping loose.   In his mouth is a reserve of nails.   His head is a little on one side, and he is looking with a half-anxious, half-deter-mined air at the wall.   He is saying, in a voice horribly deliberate in sound, for fear of swallowing the nails, ' I think, Gladys, there is just room for this bracket between the photo of the Imperial Institute and the lithograph of your uncle as Mayor of Danesbury.'   At his side, but a little behind, stands his wife.   Her chin is slightly raised, one hand lightly touches—but here, with apologies to those bold and bad young men, the new English realists, we must drop a style into which we had unintentionally deviated.   The bow has got ' Ulysses and Co.' marked in clear letters on the stock, and we would not presume to bend it, even if we could.   Suffice it to say that the wife is in an agony of indecision.   She would cut off her right hand rather than have her nice drawing-room spoilt by that hideous little common bracket for which a more hideous and even more common little vase will have to be found.

And, even if she did not mind the bracket, she would not want it where it is on the point of going. Her husband says there is just room, and so there is just room ; but brackets which fit in between pictures like a puzzle, and leave not an eighth of an inch of space on either side, cannot be said to improve the look of the drawing-room wall. Still, what is she to do ? If she forbids the tacks her husband is as likely as not to turn nasty, to throw down his hammer, to extract the nails from his mouth as if they were cherry-stones, and, remarking with icy politeness that of course he doesn't the least want to put the thing up, that he was merely doing it to please her, and that if she prefers a carpenter he will be only too glad to send for one, to go off to his dressing-room, there to fix a solitary bracket over his shaving-stand. The wife of the bower-bird is thus doomed to go through a series of doubts and struggles. Which shall she sacrifice—her walls and her drawing-room paper or her husband's temper ?

Many are the expedients employed by desperate wives to save their walls. One of the best and most successful is to turn the energies of the bower-bird from works of ornament to works of utility—to convert the instinct towards decoration into the instinct of mending. Fortunately, the transition is not difficult, and by a little management the bower-bird husband may be changed into that most destructive of God's creatures— the amateur carpenter. It is true that the wife who contrives this transformation jumps out of the frying-pan into the fire ; but what true woman would not readily sacrifice the rest of the house to keep the drawing-room neat and pretty. The best process of conversion is to persuade the bower-bird husband that his real vocation in life is carpentering, and that he is saving pounds and pounds by mending chairs and tables, by rehanging doors, by taking windows out of their frames and by cutting away portions of the fabric of the house so essential that, as the builder subsequently remarks, ' it was fair a miracle that you didn't have the whole place about your ears with that there stay weakened as it was. Why, it looks as if some wild beast had been a-tearing at it ; that it do.'

When once the devil of amateur carpentry has been awakened in a man there is nothing that he will not do in the way of making himself really useful. He ranges through the house with a saw, carried under his arm after the manner in which conscientious Nonconformists are believed to carry their umbrellas, and with a chisel in one hand and a light tool-chest in the other. No place is sacred from his ravages. Even the kitchen gives him prey. As the cook will confess with tears, ' Master's been mending the stove again till he's broke it ; and, please, shall we send for Lion and Higgler or Randsome and Pilledge ? ' The parlour-maid dreads the question, ' Is there any little job that I can do for you, Mary ? ' If she says ' No ' there will be trouble later because she had a man in to see to the taps in the pantry. If she says ' Yes ' the master will spend the half-hour just before dinner, on a night when company is expected, in operations which will flood the basement ankle deep in water and necessitate the stoppage of a purely voluntary leakage caused by the incautious use of a chilled steel centre-bit by means more usually adopted by surgeons than plumbers. But though Mary may know that half a champagne cork, two handkerchiefs, and a strip of an old flannel petticoat are not the orthodox material for stopping the water at the main, they are far better than an inundation.

Happy the woman whose husband tires of plain carpentry, and takes instead to doctoring the clocks. That is a safe employment, or at any rate one in which the liability of misery is limited. It is no doubt a bore to have the dining-room clock dissolved into its elements —to open the door and see the *disjecta membra* of wheels, levers, balances, screws and springs and rods lying on the floor, in the advertisement sheet of the 'Times'—but that is better than having the banisters of the back stairs reduced to what the Americans succinctly describe as 'kindling wood.' Amateur clock-mending is a slow process, and the man who tampers with even the comparatively simple grandfather's clock on the stairs does not arrive at the stage when it is necessary to call in a trained mechanic for three or four days. Your Dent's best pendulum timepiece will last him a week, and a travelling clock even longer. Take it all round, the clocks are the best things to devote to the energies of the bower-bird. He is safest with them. Unfortunately, however, only a limited number of men with the bower-bird instinct will take to clock-wrecking as an amusement. Those who will not must be staved off, as best may be, on broken chairs and tables. The great thing is to protect the fabric of the house. It were better to break a table on purpose to have it mended than to turn the amateur carpenter loose in the space under the roof.

THE BRITISH GENTLEMAN

SOME one—we believe it was the ' Daily Chronicle '—
called the late Mr. Thomson, the African explorer, an
English gentleman.　The remark, if not very original,
was, one would have thought, quite harmless.　It is a
phrase which a writer might use almost without
thinking—at any rate, without any thought of raising
a bitter controversy and impelling a great many worthy
gentlemen on the other side of the Tweed and across
St. George's Channel to ask how long it would be
possible to endure the insolence of England.　Unfortunately, a phrase is like a rocket.　It is a thousand
chances to one, when you let it off, that the stick will
do no one any harm when it falls—will only lodge in a
hedge or lie in a ditch.　Every now and again, however,
a stick comes plump into somebody's back garden, and
either sets fire to the wood stack or gives some bald-
headed old gentleman a knock on the head while he
is serenely taking the air.　An ordinary conventional
phrase has exactly the same peculiarity.　The chance
of it setting fire to somebody or something is so small
as not to be worth considering ; and yet every now and
again it does cause a conflagration.

　　The writer in the ' Daily Chronicle ' who so innocently and light-heartedly let off the conventional

phrase of 'an English gentleman' *à propos* of the late Mr. Thomson experienced the truth of the fact we have just stated. His stick fell north of the Tweed, gave a rap to some fierce Highlander or splenetic Lowlander—we know not which—and produced an instant combustion. It appears that Mr. Thomson was, like Mr. Gladstone, a pure Scotchman. What business, then, had a supercilious and impertinent South British scribbler to call him an English gentleman? Just as if Scotch gentlemen, and, for the matter of that, Irish gentlemen too, were not a great deal better gentlemen than English gentlemen. So the controversy of perverted particularism raged, till at last the heat, the bitterness, and fury generated a new phrase. *Surgit amari aliquid.* Some one suggested the inspiriting form, 'a British gentleman.'

It was a great moment when that phrase emerged. At once the silent watchers at the brink of the newspaper firmament realised that a new planet was sailing into the realms of expression. We felt all that the astronomers feel when they are lucky enough to be present at the birth of a hitherto undiscovered star. 'A British gentleman.' Here was a veritable addition to our language. Here was something to fill a want which, though only dimly perceived before, had been none the less real. We cared not then for the lesser problems—whether the word English could not rightly be applied to all the English-speaking members of the United Kingdom, or how, in any case, so evident an Anglo-Saxon as a Thomson could be hurt by being called an English gentleman. These distinctions and subtleties seemed as nothing when considered in the light of the great discovery—the discovery of a new category under which men can be grouped and described. Till the new discovery we had only the description, 'an English gentleman.' Now we have not only that, but the equally expressive and perfectly distinct phrase, 'a British gentleman.'

Let us endeavour to enter and possess our new domain, to show how ample and splendid it is, and how much our language has gained by our now being able to describe people as British gentlemen. The first thing to be noted about 'the British gentleman,' as compared with 'the English gentleman,' is that the former has much more colour and go about him. We will not say that the British gentleman is florid, but he has a certain air, a dash, a flamboyance of manner which strongly differentiates him. Who has not in his past experience found persons who were distinctly a touch too high in colour to be described as typical English gentlemen? These will be exactly hit off by the admirable new phrase—' A British gentleman.' One sees him stand before one, ' pride in his port, defiance in his eye,' and a fixed determination to do the honourable thing at all hazards, and not take less than 4 per cent. except for Trust investments.

Now, at last, we have got a descriptive phrase that will exactly suit the first-class season-ticket holders on the suburban lines. That admirable class of man has been up till now a terrible difficulty to the conscientious analyst of types and classes. ' How shall you describe them to me, *ces Messieurs* who are now filling the long vast of this station and have all pink newspapers in their hands ? ' (Our readers will remember how the later editions of the 'Globe' make our railway termini blush with a faint carnation, as blush the snows of Monte Rosa in the sunset.) That was a question which, if put a year or two ago by any French inquirer to any English friend bent upon giving the foreigner data for a complete social analysis of the English people, would have been extremely embarrassing. Somehow it would have seemed a little too cold and formal, nay, a little inhuman, to have said, 'These are typical English gentlemen.'

The English gentleman is well enough, but who can deny that there is something in him which partakes a little too much of the knight-errant? He is apt to be a being somewhat too pure and good for the daily 8 o'clock dinner and the 5.17 train. 'Well,' one would have had to say, 'I do not quite know what to call them. I can't exactly tell you that they are examples of the typical English gentleman after what I told you about that type last night.' '*Ah, tiens*, then I enter these seasoners as belonging not to the English gentleman, but to some other category ; and what is that category, *mon ami?*' Here would have been a difficulty indeed. One would have had hurriedly to explain that on no account must they be entered anywhere except as 'English gentlemen, and yet that somehow, &c., &c. But what a hopeless muddle that would have seemed to the clear-eyed analyst of the Latin race! How he would have shrugged his shoulders and talked of the illogical absurdities of the English! Now, however, the situation has been saved. One need not fear such questions as we have described. With a word they are answered. 'No, not typical

English gentlemen, if you wish to be exact, but typical British gentlemen ; it is a more well-marked and highly coloured variety of the type.'

It is almost impossible to exaggerate the usefulness of the expression ' a British gentleman.' When Jones asks one at one's club what sort of a fellow Briggs is how difficult it is to reply! The conscientious man, anxious to be very correct, has sometimes had to eke out an imperfect nomenclature by such roundabout phrases as, ' Well, I wouldn't for a moment say that he wasn't a thorough English gentleman, because he is, in a sense, but if you said that he wasn't, though I shouldn't altogether agree, I should know quite well what you meant.' That is terribly clumsy and roundabout. Now, when Jones asks the question, one will be able to say straight out—' Oh, he is a very good sort of chap— the typical British gentleman.' How convenient, too, the new expression will be for the dramatists and the novelists. A line in the play-bill and we have Mr. Blandford hit off to the life. Again, the fifth chapter will begin :—' Charles Blandford was in every sense of the word a British gentleman,' and the thing will be done. One could write pages upon pages without improving or adding to the description.

For ourselves, we shall make no attempt at a complete analysis of the British gentleman. It is not necessary. One or two points, however, may be noted. One can hardly think of the British gentleman with less than a thousand a year ; whereas the English gentle- man, it is always understood, may conceivably have only a pound a week, or even fifteen shillings. Again, the British gentleman would hardly travel anything less than first-class. Of course, he would always read the 'Times' and give a shilling to the waiter. Lastly, he would have a gold watch, a mourning ring, and drink a glass of sherry after luncheon, standing at the table while the ladies were going out, and crumbling at the same time a piece of plum or seed cake. We are, however, not adequate to the material portrayal of the British gentleman. Our readers who want to see him in his habit as he lives must go to the pages of 'Punch.' The late Mr. Du Maurier has drawn him again and again. In his exquisite designs the British gentleman riots and revels in a hundred scenes. In Sir Pompey Bedell, indeed, he achieves the archetypal form. Who looks for all the British gentleman can be will find him there.

CLERGYMEN'S WIVES

IN much of the controversy that gathers round that insurrection, *en permanence* the revolt of the curates, there is an undertone audible, 'We can stand the vicar, but what we can't and won't stand is the vicar's wife.' To back up this view of the case stories have been told of clergywomen who have dared to give a bit of their mind to the curate, who have criticised his sermons and his dress, and who have even engaged him through an advertisement in a church newspaper.

No doubt there are managing vicars' wives—women who do not scruple to say to the most saintly and eloquent of unbeneficed priests, 'I've arranged with Mr. Jones, the junior curate, that he shall take the evening service next Sunday, as the Smithsons are expecting a niece of the Bishop, and will doubtless bring her with them, and I should like her to be favourably impressed with our church. You will therefore be so kind as to take St. Saviour's [the iron church near the canal]. It will be better for the vicar not to take any duty next Sunday, as I am afraid of his getting his feet wet after his bad cold.' Of course this sort of clergyman's wife is very trying to men who stand 6 ft. 2 in. in their socks, who stroked the College boat, and who, if pressed, will modestly admit that they try, perhaps not altogether unsuccessfully, to combine the piety and learning of Cyprian and the rest of the Fathers with the eloquence of Bossuet and the tact and worldly discretion of the ablest of the great ecclesiastics of Rome.

In spite, however, of such cases, there is another side to the matter. It is very easy to make fun of clergymen's wives, and to represent them as the bustling tyrants of the parish ; but, take them as a whole, we do not believe that there exists a nobler, a more devoted, or a more useful set of women on the face of the earth. No members of the community discharge better the duties which they are called upon to perform, or, acting as soldiers in the army of the State, acquit themselves more bravely and more efficiently. We give little verbal praise or apparent honour to the mother who brings up a body of vigorous sons and daughters, and trains them so that they shall possess the healthy mind in a healthy body. Yet she who performs this task, by no means an easy one, especially on slender means, is, in the truest sense, a patriot. To mould strong, self-reliant, God-fearing men, and to send them out fitted to do their duty to their country, is as important an act of patriotism as to serve the State directly.

Think of the number of governing men in India and the Colonies, of the Generals, Admirals, Judges, and great civil servants who were reared in country vicarages and rectories. The women who made the homes whence such men sprung deserve to be remembered. But if clergymen's wives are, as a class, admirable in their capacity of mothers and trainers of the strong and vigorous men that are needed so greatly by a governing race like the English, they are no less admirable as wives. Their fault, indeed, is that they are too good wives, and often spoil their husbands abominably. If instances of pure unselfishness are wanted, search the vicarages of England. The homes of the clergy are, as a rule, the homes of poor men with large families, but at the same time of men with that high standard of comfort and physical well-being which is taught in the Universities, and which characterises the cultivated class in England.

But in many cases the maintenance of this high standard of comfort means that the clergyman's wife must work as hard as a busy tradesman at managing and contriving for the vicar luxuries which she herself professes not to care for. Of course, there are plenty of instances to the contrary, but in hundreds of clerical households the whole energy of the establishment is concentrated upon making life soft for the man. It is thought nothing but right and natural that the vicar should have the best food, that his clothes should be new and good, that he should be the person to whom a pleasant holiday is an absolute necessity, and that his expensive hobby for books or coins or old oak or what not should be gratified. If the clergymen's wives merely denied themselves to pamper their husbands they might perhaps be pronounced to be more foolish than heroic, but it is the same story with the sons and daughters. The personal sacrifices that are made to send the boys to good schools, to keep them at college, and to give the girls a chance, are untold.

No doubt the clergyman makes sacrifices too, but in nine cases out of ten the real pinch falls upon the wife

It is she who spends the bulk of the family income, and it is therefore she who has to make the economies, and, as a rule, she does it without complaining. The bravery of the clergyman's wife and the way in which she faces her difficulties is often really magnificent. You see her at a garden party with her best bonnet on talking to the wife of Mr. Brown, the retired City man, about the way in which the neighbourhood has degenerated socially, and it seems impossible that she can be bringing up seven children on 400*l.* a year and a house. It is only when you notice the grey hair and the determined ring of her voice that you realise that she is a person whose life is a daily hand-to-hand struggle with domestic worries, small and great. One sometimes wonders that clergymen's wives, at any rate those of the selfish ones, should hold, as they undoubtedly do, a higher rather than a lower view of the priestly office. One knows what the abler courtiers, when they speak the truth, feel as to the more magnificent pretensions of Kings. They may be personally very much attached to their King, but they, most of all men, realise that 'dread sovereign' and 'august majesty' are merely useful forms of words. When you see people in a rage about nothing, or foolishly influenced by the absurd flatteries of a knave or a fool, you are forced to believe that there is a great deal of human nature even in Royalty—for even the best and worthiest of Royalties are liable, like the rest of us, to get occasionally into childish rages, or to make themselves foolish about little things.

In the same way, it must be very trying to hear a man preach with a passionate earnestness of conviction against unselfishness and want of self-control, and extol the duty of patience and gentleness, and next day or the same evening see him in a black ill-temper because his slippers have not been put to warm in front of the fire, or, worse, because the cook has not done the vegetables as he likes them. 'I've asked you, my dear, a hundred times to tell the cook that potatoes done like this are utterly disgusting.' Mrs. Thrale once asked Dr. Johnson whether he ever 'huffed' his wife about the dinner. 'Repeatedly,' he replied, 'until one day she cured me by asking me if I were not ashamed to ask a blessing on food which I was next minute going to declare unfit to eat.' Plenty of other men's wives in all classes have no doubt been inclined to ask that question, but to a clergyman's wife such thoughts must arise not merely in regard to grace before meat, but as to a hundred petty incidents of life. In the abstract, one would think indeed that the position must be intolerable.

It is impossible for a man to be a hero to his wife, and yet a clergyman has to be something more than a hero. Very likely, clergymen are not more selfish and unheroic in little things than other men. Probably, as a class, they are quite as good, if not better ; but then other men have not to set up the same high standard—and remember the standard applies quite as much to little as to big things. The question—'Why don't you practise what you preach ?' does not greatly affect Jones and Robinson, because, as a matter of fact, they do not preach unselfishness, patience, and kindliness, but it comes home with frightful force to the unfortunate clergyman. It really leaves him no room to practise in comfort any of the smaller vices, to be sulky or irritable, rude or lazy, or to indulge even now and again in a 'you may go to the devil for all I care' attitude towards his fellow-men. The impossibility of being a saintly hero to his wife might, indeed, be used as a strong abstract argument against a married clergy. 'If,' it might be said, 'you allow clergymen to marry you will turn their wives into sceptics; they will not be able to bear the contrast between the professions that a priest is bound to make and the sight at close quarters of his necessarily great shortcomings.'

But those who argued thus would know little of human nature. The effect produced on clergymen's wives is not the least that which might be expected. They seem hardly ever to apply with strictness the maxim of principle and practice in the small affairs of life, or to feel disenchanted if the vicar shows himself mortal in such matters as his dinner and his little comforts. As a rule, we should say that there were no more sincere upholders of the notion that the priestly office sanctifies the man and raises him above his fellows than the wives of clergymen. The love of the wife quite neutralises the effects of the contrast between what the clergyman as the expounder of God's word must preach and what as a man he is only too likely to practise in the rough and tumble of life. No argument for a celibate clergy can possibly be founded on the disillusionment of the clergyman's wife.

Clergymen's wives, however, afford on the other hand a very good argument in favour of a married clergy. See what excellent work they do for the Church and for humanity in the districts in which their husbands have their cures. In many cases, nay, in the majority, half the work of social amelioration in the parish is done by the vicar's wife, and it is work that no curate could do—work for which a woman is alone competent, or, again, work which can best be done by a man and woman working together. And in practice this means work that can be done best by husband and wife in co-operation. Thus the marriage of the clergy means the introduction of women into a sphere of work half spiritual and half social, which is peculiarly theirs, but which they could hardly do except as clergymen's wives. The clergymen's wives constitute, in fact, a great body of volunteer workers among the poor.

But though we believe very strongly in the clergy-man's wife, admire her unselfishness and heroism, and recognise the good work she does, we are quite willing to admit that she has her faults, like the rest of us. One of these faults requires special notice. We believe that the vicar's wife is often responsible for the unfortunate way, to use the mildest term, in which, in country districts, the Dissenters are sometimes treated by the clergy. The vicar is perhaps easy-going, and has knowledge enough of the world not to apply too strictly even so cherished a principle as the wickedness of tolerating schism. But his wife, womanlike, is against all compromises. She eggs him on to treat the Non-conformist minister as a heretic, a perverter of the people, and a far greater danger to the parish than the wildest profligate. *Nulla salus extra ecclesiam* is a motto which is to be driven in up to the hilt with all its odious consequences. Her absence of worldliness and her narrow sincerity do not allow her to admit that there is any truth but the one truth.

The most serious defect of the English Church

system in our rural districts is a certain want of urbanity, of kindliness, and of the fostering of a feeling of brotherhood towards the Nonconformist clergy. If only the vicar's wife could be a source of conciliation, instead of the reverse, rural England would be far more united than it is at present. It will, however, be a long time before this happy change is effected. It is to be feared, indeed, that the last persons to think of the Nonconformist clergy as anything but the subjects for that galling virtue, toleration, will be the clergymen's wives.

THE INTERROGATIVE BORE

UNDOUBTEDLY Socrates has much to answer for. The abuse of the Socratic method has shown the world, to borrow and slightly modify a phrase from Dr. South, what a dangerous and dreadful weapon a question may be in the hands of an expert bore. There is no torture greater than that which can be inflicted by a dull and persevering person whose manhood, like that of Uncle Joseph in 'The Wrong Box,' has been early sapped by a thirst for general information. It is possible that when he begins he asks questions with a desire to obtain information, but that phase of the domestic Grand Inquisitor soon wears off, and in the end he probes the knowledge of his friends from pure love of probing. The question is sufficient to itself. The answer is not really material. No subject is too great and none too small for investigations which, strange to say, are both vague and microscopic, and of time and place, appropriateness and inappropriateness, he recks nothing.

The questioning bore will ask you during breakfast (1) What is your opinion of the immortality of the soul ? (2) Who is Mr. Billings 'of whom I hear you talk so much ?'—Billings is a local solicitor who is engaged to your wife's second cousin, and his name was only mentioned once incidentally, but a new name to the true questioner is like the smell of blood to a vulture. —(3) Why did Lord Rosebery fail to get on with Sir William Harcourt? (4) How much are eggs a dozen in your district? (5) Would *radis à cheval* be good French for horse-radish? (6) What were your four great-grandmothers' crests? (7) Do you agree with the atomic theory? (8) What *is* the atomic theory?—To stay a torrent like this what mere human effort can avail? We have seen irony tried, but the effect was nil—nay, less than nothing. When with the appearance of the second batch of toast came the question, ' Is your subsoil a good one?' a young man of a satirical turn and literary gifts most rudely cut in with a few lines from Browning's ' Soliloquy in the Spanish Cloister :'—

> Dare we hope oak galls? I doubt
> What's the Latin name for parsley?
> What's the Greek name for swine's snout?

Did the outraged questioner rise in his wrath and leave the room? Not a bit of it. He listened attentively and then remarked, ' Most interesting. I have myself often wondered what oak galls are, and what they were used for. Perhaps you can tell me. The Latin for parsley I used to know, I'm sure, but the Greek for swine's snout is a very curious point. We must certainly not forget to put it to Dr. Paffingly when he comes to luncheon to-morrow. I suppose there is no doubt the Greeks did have swine. They must, because Ulysses had a swineherd. By the way, what is the price of bacon a score here, and do the poor people often keep pigs, and if so, do they usually kill and cure

them themselves or sell them live to the butchers ? ' &c.,
&c., &c.   And so the talk slides off unconsciously into
another series of questions.

Another way of meeting such questions is to borrow
a device once used by Dr. Johnson.—' Are the average
profits of auctioneers unreasonably high ? '   When such
questions are put to them some people try to intimidate
the interrogator by thundering out, ' I do not know, Sir.
Perhaps no man shall ever know.'   But it is useless.
Probably the remark would merely be a peg for a
regiment of questions directed towards the elucidation
of the true principles for calculating an auctioneer's
profits, as, ' Are not auctioneers paid a percentage on
their sales ?   Could you not calculate the sales ?   Do
they make a return to anyone ?   Would not the Commissioners of Income-tax be able to check their
returns ? ' &c., &c., &c.   But that way madness lies.
The truth is, the best plan is to make no attempt to
check the question bore.   He will only, like Ophelia,
turn your irony or your rudeness ' to favour and to
prettiness,' and found thereon a new mountain of
questions.   From the true bore questioner there is no
escape but flight, silence, or suicide.

There are, of course, attempts at a radical cure.   As
a palliative the following may be tried if the pain is
severe.   Ask the nearest schoolmaster to spend the day
with *you*, but contrive that he shall spend it with
the questioner.   It is ten to one that in the course of
the afternoon the inflammation of mind will be abated.
The cause of the cure is to be found in the fact that
schoolmasters are capable of imparting an indefinite
amount of mixed information without loss of temper.

Long practice on their pupils has shown them that
almost any answer will do to stop the mental leakage of
any question, and that the answerer need never be
perturbed by lack of knowledge. Besides, a schoolmaster, if ever fairly cornered, knows how to apply the
Scotch method of answering one question by another.
For example :—*Q.* ' Have the clergy sufficient incomes
provided for them in Scotland ? '—*A.* ' What is a
sufficient income for a Scotch clergyman ? '

But besides the bore there is another class of persons
in whose hands the question may be ' a dangerous and
dreadful weapon.' Those are they who do not realise
the serious consequences of questions, and fail to understand that asking a question is like drawing a curtain in
a room full of company without having first ascertained
what is behind. It is all very well if there is only a
bookcase. But suppose, instead, there is disclosed a
shelf with a half-empty medicine bottle, a decanter of
sherry, a bottle of hair-oil with a rag stuck in instead
of a cork, an old and rather greasy-looking pair of
slippers, and a broken-down brush and comb. Who
can say that the effect of such a revelation before
company is agreeable ?

It is just the same with questions. It sounds as
innocent to ask a man what was his wife's father's
profession as to draw a red serge curtain, but if the
father in question disappeared about the time of the
Assizes the question may prove a source of acute
misery. Mr. Stevenson makes one of his characters
say that he never asks questions because it partakes too
much of the nature of the day of judgment. He goes
on to point out that asking a question is like setting a

stone rolling down a mountain.   It goes bounding along, gaining force and capacity for evil as it goes, 'till at last some bland old bird is knocked over in his back garden and the family have to change their name.'

That is no exaggeration. We have known an amateur pedigree-hunter worry a whole family with questions about the mothers of their great-grandmothers till he had to be taken aside and told that if he went on much longer he would expose to the admiring eyes of the world the fact that, owing to what people euphemistically call 'a Scotch marriage,' it was doubtful whether the family estates and title ought not to belong to a distant cousin. It is often not a little curious to see the anxiety displayed by middle-aged ladies and gentlemen when some rash and inexperienced younger member of the family is flinging about mixed questions as if the game were the safest in the world. Not otherwise would the head of a dynamite factory look if a set of Zulus had got into the store-room and were ' playing Billy ' with the bricks of explosives. William, who has only just left Oxford, wonders why Aunt Julia snapped him up so when he asked that very innocent question as to how many brothers her husband had. It was absurd, he thinks, for her to act as if such a question were unduly and rudely inquisitive, and to assume an expression of face which said, ' Ask me that again at your peril.' When William has been called to the Bar, and has seen from the papers in chambers a few of the complications of family history, he will sympathise with Aunt Julia's determination that the curtain shall not be drawn aside which hides the disgrace of her husband's youngest brother. If she were to allow the existence of that brother, how can she tell that the next questions would not be, 'What sort of a man was he? Is he alive? Where does he live? Don't you ever see him?' and so on and so on till the whole miserable story must come out? It was once our good fortune to hear of an investigation before an American Commission, the report of which ran something in this way.

Q. 'Did you remove the papers?'—No reply.—*Q.* 'We must insist on your answering this question.'—*Witness.* 'If you press that question I must defend myself.' The report goes on to say that at a sign from the chairman the witness was seized by the attendants and a bowie knife and two revolvers were taken from him. 'Examination resumed. *Q.* "Did you remove the papers?"—"You are taking an unfair advantage of a defenceless man. Under the circumstances I have no option but to tell the truth. I burnt them."'

That is very often the attitude of people worried by careless questions. They show very clearly that if they are pressed they will defend themselves, and if the questioner has not the tact to see and 'sheer off,' it is not unlikely that he will meet with a disagreeable experience, unless, of course, he has the power to disarm the witness. A Talleyrand may be able to turn one question by another, but the ordinary man cannot. All he can do when he sees that the blunderer is going to draw the curtain and expose something he does not want exposed is to hit the offending hand sharply over the knuckles. In truth, questions are dangerous weapons, which ought only to be fired off by careful and experienced people. The young, except on abstract subjects, should no more be encouraged to make use of them than they should be

encouraged to play with firearms.   It is no less dangerous to turn a questioner loose in one's drawing-room
than it is to let a man walk about the house with a
repeating rifle at full cock.   Both rifles and questions
are excellent things in their proper place, but they want
to be kept well under control.

PRINTED BY
SPOTTISWOODE AND CO., NEW-STREET SQUARE
LONDON